TOWER
of the CROW

Also by Dora Polk:

THE LINNET ESTATE

TOWER
of the CROW

DORA POLK

David McKay Company, Inc.

NEW YORK

To Alice Wellman, friend and mentor

The quotations from the poetry of William Butler Yeats at the end
of Chapter 29 are reprinted with permission of Macmillan
Publishing Company. From *Collected Poems* by William Butler
Yeats. Copyright 1924 by Macmillan Publishing Company. ©
Renewed 1952 by Bertha Georgie Yeats.

Library of Congress Cataloging in Publication Data

Polk, Dora.
   Tower of the Crow.

   I. Title.
PZ4.P7677To   [PS3566.0476]   *813'.5'4*   74–25726
ISBN 0–679–50479–6

Manufactured in the United States of America

TOWER
of the CROW

I

It had been gray and overcast all the way down from London. The spasms of fine drizzle against the windows increased as we raced farther west, infuriatingly blocking my view of the British countryside, which I was seeing for the first time. Then, ten minutes out of Fishguard, where the train connected with the boat for Ireland, it started to rain in earnest. Not the best of sailors even on a placid lake in summertime, I began to wish I hadn't come.

On board the ferry, I made a beeline for the lounge and tea bar. Everybody else had had the same idea. The Dutch girl who had been my random traveling companion from London was nowhere in sight. I looked around for adjoining seats for both of us. Only one double was left, two aisle seats in a booth for four.

I asked the middle-aged couple at the window whether the space was free, and if it was, would they mind my joining them. But as they were making polite assenting noises, a young, sandy-haired and bearded fellow came and took the other place. I couldn't justifiably lay claim to it. For all I knew he might already have been sitting there before I came. My Dutch friend would have to look out for herself.

I stowed my denim shoulder bag under the seat, and sat down with a glass of ginger beer. The fellow opposite shuffled his long legs and big feet to yield some under-the-table territory to me.

Even in the shelter of Fishguard Harbour, the sea was choppy enough to rock the boat, threatening a rough crossing. For double insurance, I washed down another pill.

The horsy woman next to me peered down her muzzle at my pillbox, looking as if she suspected me of being a dope fiend. But in a very British accent she said longingly: "Excuse me. Are those for seasickness by any chance?"

"Would you like some?" I said, nodding.

"Oh, could you spare one?" She rushed to help herself. "It was *nice,* you see, when we left Dunstable this morning. Who would have thought . . ."

The florid gray-haired man across from her, whom I took to be her husband, made a braying noise. "Ought to know better. Irish sea."

They each knocked back a couple of pills with the tea they had been sipping. To avoid any appearance of discrimination, I offered the box to the fellow opposite.

He shook his head. "Thanks. Don't need them."

I had met his type before. "I suppose you think seasickness is all in the head," I said, with a slight curl to my voice to undercut the insufferable smugness good sailors always ooze.

He looked abashed. "Oh, that wasn't what I meant. At least, I mean," he stuttered, "it's true I don't suffer with the malady myself. But I don't think it's imaginary when other people have it." He had the slightest touch of an Irish brogue, and a lovely rusty, scratchy timbre to his voice.

The florid man said to him: "Do this trip a lot, eh? Used to it."

"Not an awful lot."

"Irish, though."

"My parents were both born in Eire," the younger man replied. "We went back and forth fairly often when my mother was alive. I still go when I can." Then, the obligations of good manners to his questioner adequately discharged, he returned to me. He said: "I meant that *you* won't need those either," his head motioning toward the pills.

"My word," the woman whinnied, "are *you* an optimist!"

But, with cool good nature, the young man countered: "As we Irish say: 'No need to take your boots off till you reach the river,' is there? Besides, I've been listening to the weather forecasts. A low-pressure area has been moving towards Wales the past few days. This squall may be no more than the southern edge of that."

The older man said hopefully: "You mean you don't think it will come to much?"

"Shouldn't think so. We'll probably pass out of it a few miles out."

Nodding, as though coming over to the young man's view, the older man said: "Could be. June is usually pretty calm."

I told the sandy beard: "I'll believe you when we reach the other side."

He grinned, revealing strong white teeth, engagingly irregular. "The skeptical kind, eh?"

"I don't go much for weather forecasts."

"And I bet your mother told you not to listen to strangers, either."

We all laughed approvingly.

The horsy woman said: "You're from America?"

"Yes."

"Which part?"

"California."

"Ah, splendid. On vacation?"

"More or less," I said, and was saved the usual cross-examination because right then the quay began to leave the ship, and we all craned to see the action.

In the general excitement at being under way, I left the table and went outside to watch the shores of Wales recede. There was not much to see however; the coastline was a ghostly blur with no sight of the inland hills. But the sea smelled good. I unzipped the collar pocket in my anorak and drew the hood over my head. Tucking in the long strands of my hair, which retrogresses into loose curls if exposed to damp, I walked along the deck to a sheltered spot beneath the lifeboats. Some storage cupboards marked "life jackets" helped to cut the wind.

A few minutes later the sandy-bearded fellow came into view. Large, broad-shouldered, six or eight inches taller than my five feet four, and carrying at least sixty pounds over my hundred and five, he strode toward me with powerful grace. "Are you all right?" He seemed sincerely concerned.

"Yes, fine, thanks. Why?"

"The way you dashed outside I thought you might already . . ." He left the sentence dangling.

I laughed. "I just wanted to see *that*," I said, waving aft.

He squinted incredibly blue eyes to peer, like a sailor, into the distance as if to penetrate the opaque veil of the rain. "Pity," he said, shaking his head. "On a good day you can see the Preseli Mountains." Then, getting no response from me after a lengthening pause, he added: "Those are the mountains where the ring of blue stones at Stonehenge came from."

"Really?" I said, my interest piqued not so much by the information itself as by an informant who had such interesting bits of knowledge at his command.

He qualified: "At least that's one hypothesis."

"My luck not to see much."

"Still, *this* weather *is* more typical," he said encouragingly, like a parent boosting the morale of a disappointed child. "It makes you marvel at how those early Celts made it across in their flimsy coracles." Then, as though anticipating my further ignorance and wanting to save face for me, he followed swiftly with: "Those are the little hide-covered boats still used in some parts of Wales and Ireland."

"You must be a historian."

He grinned. "An archeologist."

That figured. I snatched a closer look at him standing tall and strong in well-worn levis and nylon windbreaker. His coarse, curly hair, sprinkled with spray and rain, was a mixture of shades from lion tawniness to honey mink, certain strands bleached selectively by salt and sun to palest gold. His long, weathered face was very good to look at if you liked non-classic features and a rugged outdoor sort of air. His hands were tough and scarred, presumably from working hard in rock and dirt.

"Does that mean you dig most of the time?" I asked.

He shook his head. "During the academic year I earn my bread and butter as a college lecturer. I do field work in the summers."

"I don't suppose it's easy to get financing for year-round excavations."

"There wouldn't be much point in it in any case. You can't do a lot in winter. At least, not in this part of the world, with its short daylight and inclement weather."

"Are you working on a project at the moment?"

"That's where I'm off to now. First to the Valley of the Boyne."

Again he left me room for some reaction. This time I seized the moment to say ruefully: "I'm afraid I'm pretty dumb about things on this side of the ocean. What's in the Valley of the Boyne?"

He looked quite pleased. It was evident he now knew where he stood and it was a place he liked to be—giving information on a pet subject to an eager listener. Dashing the raindrops off his nose, he said: "The north bank of the Boyne River in County Meath is the site of three marvelous ancient burial mounds. Popularly called the Palace of the Boyne or the Burial Place of Kings." He drew a map with his finger on the air. "They stand about a mile apart— Knowth, Dowth and New Grange. A kind of cemetery of passage graves."

"Wow," I said, infected by his enthusiasm. "What date are they?"

"Almost four thousand years old."

"Wow!" I said again. "Who built them? Do you know?"

"There are similar passage graves all over Europe— mounds of stone built over burial chambers. Not only graves, but other megalithic monuments." And when I questioned the word, he translated parenthetically: "From the Greek *mega,* big, and *lithos,* stone. From these big stones we've inferred that a highly mobile and developed civilization fanned out far and wide in the second millennium B.C."

"If I'm in the area, could I see the graves you're working on?"

"Of course. New Grange and Dowth have been excavated and are open to the public. We're still at work on Knowth."

"Are they the only graves like that in Ireland?"
He smiled. "The estimate of sites is up in the thousands."

"Good grief. Where are they?"

"All over Ireland. There's a smashing group in County Sligo that I'm negotiating right now to get a crack at—"

"Sligo! That's where I'm headed."

"Not to excavate!"

"Maybe you could call it that," I said, enjoying my metaphor. "I'm going to do some field work on the Yeats country." And reading his expression as a query, I expanded as he had done for me: "You know—the area associated with William Butler Yeats, the poet."

"I know it quite well as a matter of fact. My father came from that vicinity. What I'm curious about is what your interest is in Yeats."

"My honors thesis is going to be on the influence of the west of Ireland on Yeats's work. Landscape, way of life, mythology and folk beliefs."

"Ah, so you're a student of literature! With a special interest in Irish poetry, I take it." His blue eyes gleamed with approbation, indicating I had risen considerably in his estimation.

The wind's boisterousness had steadily increased since we left port, giving me the world's best facial. My skin felt taut and vital, my eyes must have shone their clearest amber, so I didn't at all mind the new searching way he looked at me. My only fear was with that kind of expression he might become the condescending male and say something awful like: "Not just a pretty face," and ruin everything.

But, ironically, it was I who fell into the stereotype. In a sudden surge of shyness I actually blushed, and was relieved when a wild gust threw tall spray over the ship's rail. Putting a sheltering arm around my shoulders, he said ruefully: "I guess the weather forecaster and I were wrong. We'd better continue this inside."

With two teas from the cafeteria, we went back to our seats. The group of nuns occupying the booths next to us were handling their rosaries as though grimly trying to avert disaster. Across the aisle, two women were valiantly trying to cope with their broods of bawling young ones while their segregated husbands jovially quaffed beer behind thick clouds of smoke.

The middle-aged couple were settled snugly in their corners, napping. As we sat down, the husband cracked a bleary eye and nodded off again.

My new companion said: "My name is Michael Cunningham. What's yours?"

"Jan McDonagh."

"Well!" he said, clearly delighted at the Gaelic patronymic. "We've even got an Irish patriot by that name, I suppose you know."

"He's celebrated in Yeats's poem on the Easter Rising."

"That'll be him. Are you any relation?"

"Ours is M little c," I said, "not M-a-c. Besides, we're Protestants." In a matter of such current sensitivity, it seemed a good way to reveal one's cards without making a big issue out of it. I added lightly: "Though I think my grandfather would have liked it better if we *had* been kin of Thomas MacDonagh."

"Would he, now? Why?"

"He's a professional Irishman at heart. He'd have been proud to have a martyr in his family tree."

"A *professional* Irishman? How does one qualify as that?"

"I suppose by working so hard at an adopted role, you make a profession out of it."

"You mean, your grandfather *pretends* to be an Irishman when he isn't?"

"Of course his family *came* from Ireland, so he's of Irish stock. But that was back in some potato famine in the nineteenth century."

"Does he drink green beer on St. Patrick's Day?"

I made a face. "He's not *that* kind of professional Irishman, thank Heaven. His interests are more—well—scholarly and aesthetic." In case that sounded pompous, I explained: "He teaches literature, you see. At least, that's what he's been doing the past thirty years. He retires next year."

He looked enlightened. "So that's how you got interested in Yeats, I take it."

"I could hardly have avoided it. He's a real Yeats nut."

"Does he live with you?"

"A couple of blocks away. So I was practically raised on Irish fairy tales. Then, when Grandmother died in my early teens, I went by every day to do his housework. That's how I worked my way through school."

His blue eyes had a trick of becoming more brilliant when he was interested or amused—which seemed to be most of the time, in spurts. "So by choosing Yeats to do your thesis on, you managed to finagle a trip to Ireland out of him. Right?"

"Wrong," I said, snubbing my nose at him. "The trip was planned before the thesis had to be decided. The one led to the other. When the time came to announce my thesis topic, I realized my love of Yeats and my upcoming trip combined to give me a ready-made one. A snap."

"So what was the first reason for your coming to Ireland? Just a holiday?"

I ducked that for the moment. "The way it started, it was my grandfather's trip. He asked me to accompany him. Then, at the last minute, he couldn't make it."

His attractive mouth made sympathetic sounds. "What happened?"

"Last week he took a hammer to some stone slabs for the patio he's making. The hammer slipped, hitting his foot." I sighed with residual frustration. "The x-rays showed he'd cracked his metatarsal arch. That's a pretty complicated break. It was out of the question for him to travel in a cast."

"Too bad."

"Still, it's not all that woeful. Next year, when he's retired, he'll be free to come at will."

"Meanwhile, having made arrangements for your thesis, you had to come ahead for that."

I hesitated, wondering if I should leave the matter there. If I should never see Michael Cunningham again, there was no need to go into complicated detail, much less make my grandfather sound like the complete chump that his own children had called him when they'd heard what he had done. But this man was interesting to me, and, I hoped, interested in me. It seemed important to put everything on the line. "Well, actually there's another reason for my coming. I wouldn't want you to think my grandfather a fool or anything . . ." I was already off on the wrong foot, protesting too much. I'd better try another tack. "I don't know how much you know about Yeats. I mean, do you recall that he bought a tower in Gort to use as a summer house?"

He connected instantly: "So your grandfather had the same idea?"

I grinned at his acuity.

He said: "And you two were to spend your summer searching for a tower for yourselves?"

I drew a small sigh. "I only wish that *was* the way he'd gone about it. Instead, several years ago, without telling any of us, he wrote to realtors all over the Gaeltacht to be on the lookout for a tower for him. Then, sight unseen, he put a big chunk of his life savings into this tower near a place called Dunderg. My father and my uncles practically committed him."

Michael Cunningham favored me with his wide, sardonic grin. "An eccentric after my own heart," he said. "More power to him. He wanted it for his retirement, did he?"

The horsy woman in the corner had awakened. Although pretending to be totally absorbed in the gray expanse of sea and sky outside, she was obviously listening intently.

I explained to Michael Cunningham: "He's figuring to use it as a summer headquarters. In time he wants to hold some sort of extra seminar there in conjunction with the Yeats Summer School at Sligo. His pension won't be all that large, especially at the rate things are inflating. So he's hoping to cover expenses for his trip each year by doing something productive and enjoyable like that."

He nodded, rubbing a rough finger along his enticing lower lip. "So you've come ahead to take possession of it, have you? As well as to get your thesis under way."

"I hope to kill two birds with one stone. Stay there while I—"

"You're not going to *live* in it?!" the horsy woman broke in, abruptly abandoning her pose of deaf detachment. Her voice squeaked with disbelief.

"Why not?" I said defensively.

"You can't tell me it's *live*able! I won't believe it."

"That's what the agent wrote," I retorted crisply.

"He did, did he?" she said with patronizing pity.

"At least he claimed that it was habitable enough for summer quarters. A roof over our heads, was how he put it, while we were getting it in shape."

Michael Cunningham smiled encouragement, offsetting the dampening effect the woman's attitude had shed on me. He said placatingly: "In any event, you can start getting it shipshape for next year."

"That's what I thought," I responded gratefully, clutching at any reassurance my waning confidence could salvage. "I'll at least get it cleaned and painted halfway decent—"

"I gather this is your first trip to Ireland," the woman rapped.

"That's right."

"There are ruins all over the country. Thousands of them."

"So?"

Her eyes narrowed with faint derision. "The Irish have a tendency to . . ." She seemed to be trying to choose the words for her blanket indictment with meticulous care. "Well, they seem rather to let things . . . get away from them."

"The realtor would hardly have told us it was habitable if it wasn't," I said irritably.

"Oh, wouldn't he," she said, her voice rough with contempt. "The Irish are well known for their vivid imaginations and smooth tongues. *We* should know, shouldn't we, Daddy? We buy horses from them. They steal you blind if they have half a chance."

The older man looked out from bleared, bloodshot eyes and brayed. "Steal you blind. Tricky lot."

I glanced at Michael and saw the stern set of his handsome mouth. In deadly banter he said: "Turnabout's fair play." It took me a few seconds to realize he must be referring to the centuries-old plunder of the Irish by the English ruling class whom the middle-aged couple exemplified.

The tense moment was aborted by the Dutch girl I had met on the train from London who now loomed into sight. "Loomed" was the right word considering she was almost six feet tall and pretty hefty. But right then a most unhealthy pallor underlay her tan. "I am worried where you are," she said.

"*I* am worried where *you* are," I said, imitating her quaint constructions. "You look terrible."

"I have been up top. I am improved now that the sea is flatter."

It was only then that I noticed that the boat no longer rolled and that the sky was somewhat brighter. I turned to Michael Cunningham. "I believe you're right."

"About what?"

"The weather. It looks like it's clearing." Then, remembering my manners: "Kris, this is Michael Cunningham. Kris Kuyper's from Holland. Michael's an archeologist."

"I am geologist," Kris told him as they acknowledged one another. "I am in love with limestone. Please to excuse me now again." She patted the region of her waist and turned, calling over her shoulder: "I see you when we land, Jan."

As soon as she had gone, I explained to Michael: "Kris is riding with me as far as County Clare."

"Did you bring a car on the ferry with you?"

"No. My grandfather reserved a camper for us at Rosslare. I'm picking it up when we disembark."

"And then?"

"We'll head straight on to the West Coast."

"Tonight?" His tone held disbelief.

"Yes, right away."

He frowned.

"What's wrong with that?" I demanded. "It's light until eleven. That's the marvelous thing about summers this far north."

"You're surely not hoping to make it all the way this evening?"

"It's only a hundred miles or so."

He laughed.

A bit ruffled I said: "What's so funny?"

"You're not a crow."

"I didn't count as the crow flies. I added up the mileage on a road map."

"But the roads aren't motorways. Distances are twice as long in Ireland."

I hooted skeptically.

"You'll see," he said. "Ireland is Never-Never Land. The Enchanted Isle. Where time and space are like nothing you've ever known before."

Right then, the Irish coast came into view, and, as though to lend his claims authority, the sun broke through the clouds and the sea grew smoother than the water in a giant aquarium. We climbed to the boat deck to watch the emerald shores draw closer.

As we followed our progress toward Rosslare Harbour, we each explored deeper into the background of the other, exchanging the salient features of our life dossiers. My ordinary life as an average suburban girl from a modest but comfortable background—my father an executive in a company manufacturing road machinery, my mother a woman of all trades, family housekeeper, chauffeur, chief cook and bottle-washer as well as doer of good works—contrasted rather drably with Michael's life as an archeologist and college lecturer, his summers spent in exotic places like Greece, the Middle East, as well as his beloved Ireland. It all made me want to see a good deal more of him, especially as I'd gathered he was unattached. It wasn't just a physical attraction—though that was undeniable. I was equally fascinated by his excellent mind packed with a wealth of information of a variety and breadth not found too often in our world of specialists.

The boat would soon be docking. The situation called for a head-on approach. I said: "When I've picked up the camper can I give you a ride somewhere?"

"Thanks very much, but I'm going to Dublin. That would be much too much out of your way."

Hoping to hit the right note between eagerness and helpfulness, I said: "I don't have a rigid schedule. In a brand-new country, one route's as good as another. They'll all be new and interesting."

Staring down at the officers and sailors maneuvering the boat toward the car ferry landing apparatus, he appeared to be weighing something up. He said: "I suppose I don't *have* to go to Dublin. I was really only going there to mark time till I reported to my team in Slane."

I waited on tenterhooks, hoping I appeared unconcerned. I meant to keep still until he had thought it through, but he took so long I couldn't resist another nudge. I said: "I've never driven on the left before. I'm a bit worried whether I'll be able to manage it."

That was the clincher. He looked indulgently at me,

fairly radiating the age-old pity of the male for the mechanically inadequate female. It was a look that would have made my women's-lib friends at home see red. But for me at that particular moment it was a major victory. He said: "It just occurs to me that I might as well go and visit my friend in Galway now, as wait until the weekend."

I couldn't have had a better wish come true if I had just then kissed the Blarney Stone.

2

As soon as I picked up the compact van outfitted as a camper, Michael, Kris and I headed north and west out of Rosslare, aiming to get as far as the town of Cashel that evening. Michael took the wheel so that we wouldn't have to lose time while I coped with the manual shifts, the right-hand drive, the winding roads. I could absorb a great deal just by watching him, a good excuse for doing what, in any case, I wanted very much to do. "Besides," Michael said, "your first day here all your attention ought to be devoted to the sights."

The landscape was breathtaking—though "landscape" didn't seem to be exactly the right word. There were none of the dramatic, spacious, sweeping lines of landscape as I knew it—Death Valley, Yosemite, the Grand Canyon and so forth. Here, the countryside was a delicate miniature, like nothing I had ever seen before except in dreams or as an imagined backdrop to a fairy tale; fields and hedges of a spectacularly vibrant green, quaint cottages with yellow thatched roofs comparable only to the primitive adobes of Spanish frontier days back home. Even the townhouses looked like something out of Swift or Goldsmith, with their tall, narrow façades, sharply pitched roofs and puffing chimney pots.

It didn't take me long to realize the truth of Michael's observation about Ireland's unique brands of space and time. A mile was indeed twice as long when it was packed with innumerable things to see and savor—a dozen varieties of significant and sacred piles of stone: ruined towers, abbeys and giant pillars greeting my eyes along the roadside, or enticingly marked just off it on the map.

Before we had covered many miles, I knew that Ireland was a treasury of many eras upon whose huge capital and long-accumulated interest the present richly draws. Another way I saw it was as a parchment or wax tablet upon which each age had made its record after imperfectly erasing what was written there before. It was like a canvas repeatedly repainted, with patches of the earlier creations showing through.

Besides the feeling of taking twice as long to cover the same space, I experienced another strange distortion of my time sense—the sensation that eternity was compressed into each tiny jerk of the second hand. Perhaps it was the light that did it; there was a completely different cast and glow to everything. I got the distinct impression that I was seeing things always through binoculars, through the "right" and "wrong" ends—the enlarging and reducing sides—at one and the same time. Through these complicated lenses of my newfound eyes, every petal, every tendril, stood out in bold relief in a way I had glimpsed before only during the brewing of a storm. My visual sense was so acute I could almost see the sap flow.

I could almost *hear* it, too. For it was the same thing with my ears. In the incredible purr of stillness whenever we stepped out of the car, you could all but hear an ant dislodging a grain of earth, or the anther of a daisy discharging its load of pollen.

And the sky—how can I describe it? The amazing changes of the clouds and the shadows that they cast. Hovering or racing, they produced fantastic moods of shade and gleam, uncertainty and radiance.

And, oh, the colors of the distances—the lavender and heathery-purple of the hills, the dove-gray mists on the horizon to the east, the mother-of-pearl of the western rim like the inside of a cosmic abalone shell.

Kris and Michael kept clamps on me or we would have traveled no more than a mile an hour. They did, however, indulge me in a detour to the cottage in Dunganstown, where President John F. Kennedy's great grandfather was born, and past the nearby forest-park memorial. So it was very late when at last the famous Rock of Cashel, familiar to me through Yeats's poetry, loomed up out of the plain, its jumble of sacred ruins etched against a triumphant scarlet sky.

I said: "Isn't that something!"

Michael took proprietory pleasure in my awe. "It gets more impressive every time you see it."

"It is drama of lovely limestone outcrop humping up," Kris said, clearly less impressed by what the Rock was crowned with than with the Rock itself.

Limp with the day's long journey, and ravenously hungry, we pitched camp in a grove of trees with a fine view of the Rock. The camper came equipped with portable camp stove and utensils, and we had bought a sack of groceries in Rosslare. But before preparing supper, we made arrangements about sleeping. While Kris and Michael unrolled their sleeping bags on ground sheets under the trees, I wrestled to convert the back seat of the camper into the full-size bed it was supposed to make. But the mechanism was like nothing I'd ever tried to work before. It wouldn't yield.

Michael soon came to my rescue. "Here. Let me. You get the camp stove going and brew us some hot chocolate." He thrust an unopened carton into my hands.

The stove was brand-new, stored in its original factory packing. It had clearly never been assembled. It was like no camper stove I'd ever seen before. The instructions made no sense in several different Common Market languages. I wished that Kris, who had gone for water at the brook, would hurry back and save me from disgrace.

I glanced up to see Michael grinning at my helplessness. "Here, let me," he said, gently taking the enigmatic pieces from my hands. "I'll get your bed fixed later. Maybe you could cut the loaf and make the sandwiches?" His intonation said he wasn't sure that I could even wield a knife.

While I hacked hunks of delicious Irish soda bread off the flat round loaf, I luxuriated in the smells and sounds of the longest, most extravagant twilight I had ever known. A whisper of a breeze carried fragrant wafts of mellowing hay over the wall from nearby fields. A fussy excitement of peeps and tweets emanated from our canopy of glossy leaves. As I spread the hunks with creamy primrose butter and topped them off with farmhouse cheese, my pleasure was completed by a cosy sense of camaraderie as Michael pottered at assembling the strange contraption.

At last the stove began to make a shape that might support a teakettle. Michael finally attached the fuel can and set the whole thing on the drywall of rough limestone, backed by a breeze-shield of thick bushes. It was the flattest surface available in the vicinity. He said: "Can you take it from here?"

"Of course," I said defensively, confident I could.

But with the matches in my hand I wasn't so sure. While Michael had his back toward me as he returned to the camper, I puzzled vainly over how to light the thing. In the nick of time, Kris lumbered back, setting down her slopping pail. When she saw me dithering, she came to give directions.

Only hazily understanding the mechanics of the operation, I obeyed commands to light the match, apply it to the proper place, and slowly turn a knob.

The next second, without knowing precisely how or in what order, I was struck off balance, thrown backward, my hands beating wildly; the stove rocked and fell away in the opposite direction; a tongue of flame whooshed out with a great roar, missing my face by inches; my eardrums seemed to split under the pressure of a violent blast.

Picking myself up, I looked, heart in mouth, to see how Kris had fared. She was trying to catch her balance, and seemed, to my relief, all in one piece. Her jaw hung open in inane surprise. The stove was nowhere to be seen.

Michael ran toward us. "Good God. What happened?"

Kris rubbed her eyes. "I not sure. Stove fall and go pouff."

The expression in Michael's eyes matched my own appalled reactions. When he was satisfied we were all right, he said: "How did it fall?"

"Maybe when I pull Jan back, I startle her."

"Why did you grab me, Kris?"

"You lean too far over stove to light her. That not a good idea in case she blow."

"And blow she did," Michael said. "I wonder how."

He approached the wall. Some of the uncemented stones had been dislodged, and one shift in them was still triggering another so the wall looked in danger of collapsing. He stood back waiting for the motion to subside.

Kris said: "Maybe when I startle you, Jan, you knock the stove off balance." She made a rocking gesture with her hand and mimed a plunge over the wall. "Maybe the stove not stable, or the stones move under her."

The sliding stones reached a point of equilibrium and we went cautiously to look over the other side.

The camper stove was a wreck of blackened metal. Whether the unstable wall had caused the accident or not, it was a blessing it had acted as a guard, saving us from harm.

Kris said: "Could the stove falling make so much a bang?"

"If the fuel can was pierced or ruptured in the fall, perhaps," Michael theorized.

I tried to reconstruct the order of events. "I think the flame roared out before it hit the ground."

Michael gingerly scrambled over the crumbled section of the wall. He went and nudged the wreckage with his foot, then stooped to peer more closely at it in the obscuring ferns.

Kris said: "Could the valve have cause her? You make sure she is closed when you attach the fuel can?"

Michael looked up, frowning. "I thought I did. Did you open the valve slowly when you lit the burner, Jan?"

I looked at Kris. Kris said: "She turn it slowly like I tell her. But I don't remember if she turning clockwise."

I twirled my fingers, trying to recall the feel, without success.

Kris said: "So valve *may* have been wide open."

"Still," Michael said, "I'm not sure that would do it."

"Maybe she leak between the, how you call it?" Kris brought thumb and index finger of each hand together suggesting a connection between the fuel can and stove.

Michael nodded thoughtfully. "It could have leaked into the stove box and got trapped there."

"Would she have twist and rip apart, however?"

"In such a confined space, a large enough accumulation might act like that."

Shaken by the whole affair, I quavered: "I thought these

things were foolproof nowadays. Aren't there pretty rigorous tests and standards they have to meet?"

Michael shrugged: "I suppose you can never entirely rule out human error."

Kris was obviously still puzzled. "Perhaps a combination of defective valve leak and fuel can bursting when she fall?"

"Perhaps," Michael said. "But whatever the cause, the important thing is nobody was injured. A stove can be replaced a lot easier than a face or eyes."

3

After a rather cheerless supper with cold water for a beverage, we all turned in. But when I settled into my down sleeping bag on the camper bed, I couldn't sleep. Too many exciting and disturbing things had happened in a single day, culminating in the near-miss, which could have proved so terribly disastrous. It was just a fluke that Kris and I had gotten off scot free. What if it had blown up in our faces? It made me ill just to think about the possibility.

I steered my thoughts deliberately away from such unnerving might-have-beens by concentrating on the spectral aura of the floodlit ruins through my camper window. But as I stared, my imagination called up the cold spirits Yeats had conjured there, filling me with another kind of fear. The night was eerie, full of mystery, the wind rustling in the trees, nightbirds calling, mists rising all around like wraiths, so that not even sight of Michael's sleeping form could give me reassurance. I had not known I was so impressionable. Imaginative, yes, but I had always thought there was a good bedrock of practicality in my personality. Now I found myself wondering if Yeats's occultism was not rooted deep in fact—something assimilated through one's very skin, out of the air, the light, the sky, of this timeless country.

Before I knew it, the Rock had drawn me like a magnet to explore its ghostly ruins. Without quite knowing how, I found myself in Cormac's ruined tower, my hair streaming about me, my body spinning like the dead dancer's in Yeats's poem. As I whirled, birds reeled above me, dipping and screeching. If I didn't get out of there fast I'd lose my eyes.

Somebody was calling me to safety. "Rise and shine," a voice was saying, and Michael Cunningham came into focus, his face wreathed in a teasing grin. Above, a cacophony of caws and squawks shattered the peaceful morning, merging dream into reality.

"Good grief," I said. "What's that?"

"Daws," he said.

"Daws?"

"Jackdaws. Members of the crow family."

I craned to see. Fifty or more birds, some almost the size of parrots, glossy black with touches of gray about their round, fat heads, were performing extraordinary aerial acrobatics above us, and voicing their displeasure at our invasion of their private territory.

"They must have caused my dream," I said, relieved. "When you woke me, the birds of Knocknarea were about to peck my eyes out."

Over a breakfast of bread and instant coffee heated on the stove that Michael had gone into town to buy while I still slept, I told them of my nightmares.

Kris said: "You have what my grandmother call cheese dreams."

We laughed, and I said: "It's a good thing I'm with scientists. You're so comfortingly rational. My first night on Irish soil, and me with one hundred percent Irish blood in my veins and all, I thought I must be developing second sight."

But the levity didn't exorcise my uneasiness. Everything that day should have been marvelous. Here, swaddled in crystal air, psychically nourished by the intense beauty of the sky and the emerald land, accompanied by two exceptional intellects, one a strong, good-looking male whom I increasingly admired as the day wore on, I should have been in the highest sphere of bliss. But the undercurrent of disquiet persisted.

Perhaps it was composed of other things besides the disconcerting dream—fears derived from intuition, or from things peripherally perceived, one of which was even then working its way into awareness. After we had passed the umpteenth ruined tower, I said: "That woman was right."

"Which woman?" Michael asked.

"The woman I sat next to on the boat."

"What was she right about?"

"The condition of the towers. I haven't seen a whole one yet."

"Ah, well," Michael soothed, "they're more picturesque as ruins. Just think, in the eighteenth century they used to *build* ruins to make a place romantic."

I said acidly: "But just to *look* at, not to *live* in them."

Michael cast a sidelong glance in my direction. "So that's what's eating you."

"*Eating* me!" I said, nettled by the criticism his words seemed to imply.

He was silent for a moment. "You'd gone very quiet. That's all I meant."

Kris said: "Why so many towers anyway?" Her matter-of-factness, her intellectual curiosity and scientific detachment at once defused the tension, and Michael treated us to another of the capsule lectures he dispensed so brilliantly.

The round towers, almost as tall and narrow as smokestacks, were defenses against Viking raiders during the Dark Ages. The wider, squatter round towers were remnants of ponderous Norman castles erected in the Anglo-Norman occupation of the twelfth century. But by far the commonest towers were the square "fortified houses" built by the English from the fifteenth to the seventeenth centuries to subdue the Irish. To this group belonged Yeats's tower, Thoor Ballylee. The English Crown's offer of a £10 subsidy for these tower houses had stimulated quite a building boom.

"How many towers are there altogether in Ireland?"

Michael shrugged. "Of the tall round towers alone, more than a hundred still survive—and they're the scarcest. Altogether they run well into the thousands."

"That is lot of towers for country of only four million people," Kris remarked.

"Which explains why they're neglected," I said dolefully. "People don't prize what they have a lot of."

In the fatherly tone he used on me to keep my spirits up, Michael said: "Cheer up. You're just about to see a beauty."

Reaching Gort in the late afternoon, we dropped Kris off lower down the stream which ran past Yeats's tower. I had read her a stanza from one of the poems describing the stream's disappearance underground, and its reappearance at the estate called Coole Demesne several miles distant. The geology, if not the poetry, had fascinated her.

Michael and I arrived at Thoor Ballylee when the shadow of the tower was longer than the tower itself. The scene that met my eyes authenticated in every detail the scene that Yeats's poetry had conjured up for me a half a world away. I stood on the ancient bridge staring down through braided crystal to the pebbled stream bed, listening with the poet's ears for the wind in the old thorns, the splash of a rat, a stilted water hen, or a sliding otter—noises heard with imagination's ear as I read his poems. Now there was only the music of water lapping the foundations.

Inside the tower, snatches of Yeats's poetry continued to bombard me, echoing off the cold stones like aural ghosts a half a century old. They whispered all around me as I climbed the winding stair up to the blue-walled living room, the bedroom, and higher yet, to the Stranger's Room—that chamber arched with stone with its gray stone fireplace, where, by mysterious candlelight, the mystic poet had worked and dreamed. Places and objects in the poems leapt into being before my eyes as though called out of the vast repository of images of the racial memory in which Yeats had believed.

Michael followed close behind me. "Well?"

"I'm spinning." Was it possible—I didn't dare utter it—that our own tower might bear some resemblance to this fabulous place?

We emerged onto the crumbling ancient battlement roofed on that beautiful evening with a mosaic of darkening blue sky and variegated cumulus. From the top of that storm-beaten watchtower we saw a flock of the ubiquitous daws mill around Yeats's ragged elms, cavorting on the wind, free falling like daredevil parachutists, opening their wings in the nick of time to zoom up and off into the sky.

The poet's presence was so strong now that I saw with his eyes and thought with his words as I viewed the surrounding countryside over to Gregory's wood and the one bare hill which cut the force of the Atlantic storms against the tower. I was permeated with the poet's "excited reverie," feeling the emblematic force that the tower with its "winding, gyring, spiring treadmill of a stair" had had for him.

The sun's rays slanting from the west cast a golden aura around every natural object from the dark stretch of Coole woods to the Sliabh Aughty hills. As I stood there touching the stones of the parapet where Yeats had leaned, I felt as close as I'd ever been to a mystical experience. Standing beside me, Michael was a vital, integral part of the rightness of the moment—I couldn't conceive of having had the experience without him. When I turned to share my minor ecstasy, I found him looking at me in the strangest way. His eyes held an expression that I couldn't quite translate.

To conceal the nakedness of my emotions, I fumbled for my pocket camera. The second I pulled it out, a great plummeting rush of raucous wings swooped like a strafing dive bomber, and a beak like a stiletto pecked a red hole in my hand. Even as I cried out at the pain, the black flurry had become a streamlined projectile shooting away beyond the battlements back to the trees.

Michael snatched the camera from me and swiftly tucked it in his pocket before attending to my wound. It bled profusely and he staunched the flow by compressing it with wadded tissue. Visited by an absolute welter of emotions—shock, pain, and even nervous pleasure at Michael's gentle, tender ministrations—I trembled like an aspen leaf.

"What do you suppose that was all about?" I said when I got hold of myself. "I mean, why would a bird take after me like that?"

"Your camera may have done it. That's why I shoved it out of sight."

"Good grief, what do you mean?"

"They are known to attack people holding something black."

"Why would they do that?"

"Perhaps it looks to them as if one of their colony is captured."

"That's incredible."

"Daws are fascinating, enigmatic creatures. We've got a lot to learn about them."

With shaking fingers I rubbed my other hand over my face. "I'm glad it wasn't personal."

"Still, they've probably marked you as an enemy, so you'd better watch your step. You're liable to have a treeful of them after you the next time. They'll have passed the word."

I wished that he was really kidding, but I knew he wasn't. The speed with which he rushed me to the camper, and the rattling, scolding chorus that followed us down the lane put teeth into his jest.

4

The bird's attack stayed with me a long time afterward, not just the discomfort of the wound, which was fairly deep, but the implications of the episode. First, it had interrupted a moment that was full of promise when I had thought Michael had been sharing some of my own thoughts and feelings. Second, it was unnerving to think one might be the target of such creatures. It was bad enough to find out they were a threat hitherto never considered. It was terrifying to learn that they possessed some sort of sinister intelligence enabling them to hold a grudge.

My inner turmoil was dispelled a little by Kris's high spirits when we picked her up. She was garrulous with marvels, and nothing would satisfy her but a trip to Coole to examine the mysterious lake fed and drained by the subterranean stream she had explored along its course. Her own interest saved my having to propose the plan myself. Coole Demesne was the country estate of Lady Gregory, Yeats's long-time friend and patroness.

The light was already thickening when we drove up its tree-tunneled drive. The trim gardens once neatly hedged with box were now a wilderness. Of the house where Lady

Gregory played host to many poets and artists of the Celtic Renaissance little remained—a few red floor tiles, splinters of blue slate, the rubble of red brick and old gray stone, among stands of sycamore, lime and chestnut trees. Standing in the ruins of that noble house, I recalled Yeats's premonitory poem of a time, now come, when those passages and rooms would all be gone, nettles and saplings rooting among the broken stones.

But there were still the Seven Woods through which to walk in Yeats's own footsteps, to see, at last, how the brimming water of the lake mirrored a still sky, with the thunder of the mounting swans filling my mind's ear.

By the time we returned to the camper, twilight had fallen, so we camped near old buildings that must have served as stables in the heyday of the house. We dined off canned sausages and beans heated on our new camper stove. It was all very convivial, but always out there under the dark trees the mist curled and wove, leaves whispered, branches creaked.

As we sat around the stove heating milk for cocoa, Kris said suddenly: "I think about that stove last night."

"What about it?" Michael asked.

"I still wonder why she have behave so. Could make so fierce a bang a little can of gas like this one here?"

I said sharply: "What else?"

"Is it possible she could be, how you say it, booby trap?"

Her words rasped across my nerves like emery boards. I said: "But that's ridiculous. Why? For what?"

"I don't know why for what. I am just considering the way she have explode."

"But it was a brand-new piece of equipment," I protested. "Straight from the factory. Never been out of the carton. Who could have tampered with it? It was stapled closed."

Kris shrugged. "Maybe it sabotage by workers. This *is* Ireland."

I reminded her: "Eire, not Ulster." And realizing the weakness of that argument: "Besides, when Michael put it together, he'd have noticed if it had been fixed or messed with."

Kris held thumb and forefinger an eighth of an inch apart. "These days this much explosive in a letter bomb have kill a man."

I looked at Michael, who looked apologetic at having to say something I didn't want to hear. "With the sophisticated new explosives, a plug so small you mightn't notice it could do the job. Especially in conjunction with ignited gas."

Kris said hesitantly: "Maybe she should have been reported to police?"

"I did," Michael said. "I went by the Garda station on my way to town this morning. To offer payment for the damage to the wall. I dare say they'll investigate."

The milk billowed up the saucepan, almost boiling over. Kris turned the flame out just in time.

Pouring milk into our mugs, I said: "You're just alarmists. You like to blow things out of all proportion." When they said nothing, I said scornfully: "It used to be ghost stories we told around camp fires to put the wind up people. I guess this is an updated version."

Kris said mildly: "I don't know why you get so hot about it, Jan. I only wonder. That is all."

I lay on my camper bed long after Kris and Michael had bedded down under the trees. Feeling strangely vulnerable, I cowered in my sleeping bag as rigid as a stick, rehashing the theories of the stove's explosion, reliving the bird's hostility to me that afternoon.

As if it wasn't enough to feel threatened by the violence of unknown man and beast, I had to stupidly go and flash on this claim Yeats once made about how he'd haunt the woods of Coole long after he was dead. I had already been feeling apprehensive about facing another troubled night. The prospect of spending it in those eerie, spirit-ridden woods was unendurable.

The last straw was an odd tapping on the roof, scaring me half out of my wits. At the moment I called Michael's name, he sprang up, swearing, and raced toward the camper calling Kris to follow suit, a reaction out of all proportion to my timid call. It was then I realized that rain was falling in huge, heavy drops. A second more and it was coming down to beat the flood in Genesis. I threw open the camper door and they piled inside, their bedrolls already surface wet.

"Good job you heard it start," Michael shouted over the loud drumming on the roof. "We'd have been soaked in another half a minute. The road's already running like a river."

"You must be the light sleeper, Jan," Kris said with wonder, since she slept like a heavy log herself. In order to return to that blissful state, she was already arranging her sleeping bag head to toe with mine, leaving Michael a foot or two of lateral room the other side of me. I was in danger of being crushed to death, sardined between those two powerful six-footers, but it was infinitely preferable to that isolated terror I had just been suffering.

Since chance had so conveniently intervened on my behalf to conceal my nursery fears, I saw no reason to confess my weakness. To Kris's comment, I responded lightly: "Let's just say I'm lucky."

"Or psychic," Michael said.

5

I slept well, waking refreshed to the thrum of dripping trees and the green scent of fresh-washed woods, and was in fine spirits until I remembered this was the day I must relinquish my two traveling companions. Michael's friend lived in a village on the north shores of Galway Bay, not many miles distant. We would drop Kris first on the south shore of the bay at the little town of Kinvara. Her destination had been one of those small-world coincidences that she and I had discovered in our conversation on the train from London. The fact that my research plans called for a visit to Duras, near Kinvara, had lead us to join forces. It was at an old country house in Duras that Yeats and Lady Gregory had first talked of stimulating the Irish intellectual movement culminating in the establishment of the Abbey Theatre.

Kris was interested in the area because that part of County Clare and Southern Galway provided spectacular examples of limestone geology. She planned to spend several weeks combing the Burren, an area of limestone hills and pavements whose sparse soil nonetheless supported a remarkable and varied flora. She was also going spelunking in the complex cave system of subterranean streams around

Lisdoonvarna. If I had had a more leisurely schedule, I might have been tempted to join her for a couple of days.

The journey across the Realm of Stone from Coole to Duras couldn't have been more gloomy. The land was poor, like a starved animal, all skin and bones. Hardworking peasants had cleared the impoverished earth of millions of stones over the centuries, jigsawing them into a network of low walls to mark off fields and small holdings. The weather didn't help any. The sky was woolly gray, as overcast as my mood. The wind blew across the almost treeless landscape, buffeting the camper and sometimes pelting it with rain so hard it had the sound of hail.

Neither Michael nor I found much to say, but the unsquelchable Kris regaled us with her various enthusiasms. Now she waxed double-dutchly eloquent about turloughs—disappearing lakes in limestone. Now she had us get out of the car to see hart's tongue and maidenhair ferns and wild orchids growing in limestone clefts. But neither her gaiety nor her interesting tidbits could dispel the ache of approaching separation.

Kris had arranged to put up at the Kinvara Youth Hostel. And where was that? Nowhere else than in the famous old house where the Abbey Theatre had been conceived. But after the warden had shown us the house and gardens, and I had momentarily abandoned myself to the vibrations of the place, my gloom returned. I said good-bye to Kris as if she were a lifelong friend, making her promise to head north to see me in a week or so.

For the first time since I had hired the camper, I climbed in the driver's seat and took the wheel. Having watched Michael closely, I needed little coaching, and he seemed comfortable enough to have me drive across those coastal flats still teeming with gray stones and dry walls, the gleaming roads reflecting the steel sky. For a while we were both as uncommunicative as earlier. Perhaps he thought I needed quiet to concentrate on driving, but the reason for my silence was my fast-eroding optimism. Nor did it help my mood at all to see yet another ruined tower come into view.

When I sighed he asked: "Something bothering you?" I shook my head. But I felt his eyes remain on me.

After a few seconds he said: "You're not upset at me? It isn't anything I've done?"

"Of course not."

"Then what? You might as well share it."

I sighed again. "It's nothing and everything. I'm feeling like I wish I hadn't come."

"I don't get it. We had a marvelous day yesterday. At least I did."

I stole a quick look at him. Half turned toward me, he was smiling persuasively as if to snap me out of my glum mood. But his efforts had the opposite effect. I could only think of how this afternoon, tomorrow, would feel without him. Yet I could hardly tell him so. I said instead: "Look at that mess over there," nodding toward the crumbling tower a little off the road. "That's how my grandfather's will look."

To his credit, he didn't try soft-soaping me into thinking otherwise. He confined his comfort to remarking: "If the worst comes to the worst, you can unload it while you're over here."

I laughed, without mirth.

He said wryly: "Well, you can *try*."

"That wasn't why I laughed," I said. "However derelict it was, Grandfather wouldn't dream of getting rid of it."

"Why not, if you made him realize he'd bought a pig in a poke?"

"You don't know him. He's an irrational Celt. As unrealistic as they come, and stubborn as a mule to boot."

"If you wrote explaining—"

"If I as much as *hinted* I had any doubts, he'd feel betrayed. He's convinced himself that he and I are the only members of our family with any guts and imagination. He'd think I'd let him down."

Because it seemed to be Michael's way always to try to put the best construction on events, I thought he'd wind it up by having something encouraging to say, like not to count my unhatched chickens. But surprisingly he said: "When you get there, if there's any problem, promise me you'll leave it for your grandfather to solve next year."

Startled, I said: "Why do you say that?"

I felt him shrug. "No reason in particular."

"Is it because of what Kris said last night?"

I could sense him choosing his words carefully. "It doesn't cost anything to be careful."

I was perplexed. "But even if Kris's theory were true, sabotage is such a random affair. The chances it would hit twice in the same place are practically nil." Then the nickel dropping with a clonk: "Good grief. You don't . . . you can't think the stove blowing up had anything to do with me! You're not saying I'm *personally* in danger?"

"I'm not saying anything."

"That's ridiculous. No one knew I was coming."

"How did your grandfather reserve the camper?"

"How does one *usually* reserve a camper," I said impatiently. "Through an auto-rental agency undoubtedly." And when he made no comment, I said: "And even if, in its impersonal way, that *does* mean someone knew we'd be here, who could possibly care?"

He sighed elaborately, as if he were sorry he'd brought the matter up. "It was just a thought, a friendly caution to tread gently. In case."

"You've got the Irish jitters. Or been reading too many spy thrillers lately."

He laughed perfunctorily. "You'll probably be concentrating on your thesis anyway. Off different places in your camper doing research." That thought seemed to ease his mind. "Your twenty-eight-day charter doesn't allow you any too much time to get it done."

His fussing ended with our entry into a small village, neater and better kept than many we had driven through along the width of Ireland. Michael said the residents competed annually for the national award for prettiest village, and he thought they had a good chance of winning it this year. The window-boxed geraniums and the fresh coats of pastel paint backed up his view.

In the middle of the tiny shopping section of the single street, Michael had me stop outside a whitewashed cottage with a storefront window. "O'Reardon, Gifts, Refreshments," the painted board above it read. A display of folk crafts glimpsed beneath looked enormously inviting, and when Michael got out of the car, I followed him.

As he reached the door it was opened by a beaming middle-aged woman, who threw her arms around him. When she released him, Michael introduced me as a "new friend," and she welcomed me with warm words, though her eyes were curious.

Michael said: "Where's Cathy?"

"Gone to take Father Conley's books back. She'll be disappointed that she wasn't here when you arrived. She's been so looking forward to seeing you."

I felt a twinge of shock followed by dismay. The friend was a *girl*—and *waiting* for him, yet. The possibility had never crossed my mind.

I am no masochist. I said: "I've got to be on my way. Good to meet you—"

"Good heavens, no, not yet," Mrs. O'Reardon said, clasping my hand. "At least have a cup of tea with us."

"You can't go without meeting Cathy," Michael put in

disappointedly. "And you've simply got to see the beautiful things she makes."

That much I couldn't quarrel with. We went inside. The shop was divided into two parts up front. The overcrowded stock on one side, the small refreshment area on the other, with workrooms at the back. Cathy created all kinds of jewelry, working primarily in silver-mounted Connemara marble—a locally quarried serpentine transmuted out of common limestone into magic patterns of mottled green and white. Her additional talent for ceramics was amply demonstrated on the shelves by beautiful fat seagulls, sleek badgers and seals, and a russet fox.

I must have examined every object that was on display: exquisite brooches in Celtic shapes, designs, and symbols; black plaques and crosses of compressed peat; and a variety of handwoven and hand-knitted garments made locally.

I bought what all the tourists buy: a knobbly blackthorn shillelagh, so-called after its venerable ancestors grown in the great forest of Shillelagh in County Wicklow; and one of the heavy natural wool sweaters knitted by the Aran Islanders in personal, unique designs to identify their menfolk drowned at sea. For casual gifts, I bought variegated woollen belts called *crios* that would tuck into letters to my friends.

When I had finished my selections, tea and cakes were waiting on a round oak table in the window. There was still no sign of Cathy. As we sat down Mrs. O'Reardon said: "I would have offered you coffee. But Americans don't seem to like the way I make it."

Having already been the victim of a gruesome brew made with boiled milk, I asked her if that was how she made it.

"I do," she said emphatically, as if I had accused her of neglect.

"There's your mistake."

Her mouth fell open. "How else should I do it?"

Balking at trying to impart the mysteries of good perked coffee in one easy lesson, I advised her to serve instant coffee as she did tea, with cold milk and sugar on the side.

She looked dubious, her eyes wondering if I was being serious.

But just then the store bell tinkled. I turned a shade too fast for manners, to see a girl with shining black hair, creamy skin, and eyes the color of the shamrock marble in which she worked. She stood tall and poised and slender in the doorway, and I wanted to dislike her instantly.

In a second, Michael Cunningham was on his feet and at the door. In another second, Cathy O'Reardon was in his arms.

A wave of realization swept over me, leaving jealousy and disappointment in its wash. As I struggled to keep myself from foundering, I became very interested in the design around my plate. It featured the phoniest four-leaf clovers I had ever seen.

6

I stayed only long enough to nibble a currant bun and swallow a few sips of tea. It was a painful five minutes, full of lulls and awkward glances, as Cathy probed me with her vivid eyes as though trying to make out how I came to be there, and whether I posed any threat.

When I insisted I must be on my way, she and Michael took me out and saw me into the camper. We exchanged the usual polite phrases, glad so-and-so, sorry-not-more-time, see-again-soon, so on, so forth. I did a grade-A job of concealing how I felt behind a kind of I-couldn't-care-less super cool. The last I saw of them in my rearview mirror, they were standing very close together.

But the minute I was out of sight, my whole arrogant façade collapsed. I felt sick and bitter at the cruelty of a fate that could deal me such a rotten hand. Here was a man who had everything I wanted, who, in a couple of days of being comrade-close, had bowled me completely over. Yet I had nothing to blame but my own naïveté. He had said nothing—even remotely—to suggest he had no woman in his life. Where had my common sense been? One didn't need a lot of it to entertain the merest notion that such a man might already have a girl friend. I could at least have given it even odds that the friend he would be visiting in Galway Bay was feminine. But no, the possibility had never entered my stupid head, much less the prospect of his being amorously involved with her. What made it all the worse was the knowledge that it was I who had taken the initiative in getting him to ride with me, practically corralling him by the outrageous strategy of female weakness. My friends at home who thought the wiles of the conniving female a sellout of their sex would figure I'd gotten no more than I deserved.

By now the sky had cleared substantially. The winds off the Atlantic had chased away the last tatters of gloomy gray, leaving mounds of sudsy clouds in the laundered air. As I drove farther north along what Michael had advised me was the most scenic route, the sky sparkled like a Waterford cut-crystal goblet that would ring the truest note if you tapped it with a silver spoon. When ruffled, the boughs and lakes looked like chased sterling, and, in calmer moods, like freshly polished mirrors reflecting every tree and bank and mossy boulder, thus doubling the beauty that was everywhere. So dark in contrast was my mood, it seemed for all the world as if nature were laughing in my face.

The better weather permitted me to make good time, and I drove hard toward the Sligo border with only a few slowdowns, once for a flock of sheep, another time for a couple of wagon families who hogged the road for several miles, spilling dogs and children right and left so that it was impossible to overtake.

It was late afternoon when I completed the main leg north and came to a point where I needed more precise directions to my final goal. I guessed from my road map that I would have to take a tertiary road toward Dunderg. It was time to dig out the envelope of instructions my grandfather had given me when I left the States. I stopped off at a small café on the farther outskirts of a town and, while I sipped a lemonade, rummaged in the bottom of my denim bag.

The envelope was sealed. When I tore it open I pulled out a detailed list of places I must visit to get firsthand information on the life of Yeats, all annotated from the poems and the *Autobiography* in my grandfather's neat script. It would be a marvelous aid for my research, but right then it helped me not at all in getting where I had to go. What I needed was the tower's exact address and the kind of street map that you draw when you invite friends home for the first time. I had assumed the realtor had sent my grandfather these essential facts, and that those were what I had been handed at the airport when I left.

Another item in the envelope was no more helpful than the other pages, merely containing a list of "things to bring back," such as one-inch and two-and-a-half-inch Ordnance Survey maps, a fisherman's cap "like the one worn by Yeats's fisherman," and various books and photographs. Those two items were the lot. Nothing else was in the envelope. My dear old impractical grandfather had done it again. If it hadn't been so frustrating, it would have been laughable.

Well, no good crying over the salmon that leaps out of the net, as he would have said in a similar predicament. What did I remember? Not much. I knew the tower's name—Tur Beag. I knew it stood in the vicinity of Dunderg. I knew roughly where Dunderg lay. And though it wasn't on my large-scale road map, I could buy one of those Ordnance Survey maps my grandfather requested and work from that.

A corner store next door to the café luckily supplied me with a decent area map. I spread it out and, after several suspenseful minutes, found a little village called Dunderg. A couple of towers and a castle were marked in gothic script along that stretch of road, though nothing precisely in the area where I surmised our tower should be. Perhaps my impressions were mistaken. I had collected from my dream-and-cloud–brained grandfather only the vaguest notions of the tower's whereabouts, which, since I took after him, need not have been his fault. Moreover, when the purchase was transacted, I'd been younger, less aware, and worried about school. Having never expected to come alone, I'd had no reason for precise instructions—until the last minute, when I'd depended on his writing them all down.

Sighing resignedly, I deformed the map against its natural folds to turn the section that concerned me outermost. There couldn't be all that many towers in the area. The thing to do now was to case the territory itself, go to the spot where my memory said the tower must stand, and see if it was really there.

This was the first time I had traveled along a lesser road. Michael had kept to main and secondary arteries all the way, and I had taken a through route north. The road that I turned onto now was actually not much more than a dirt track, and obviously not popular with cars and trucks.

The whitewashed cottages, with their black stacks of bricks of peat, were few and far between. On one side of the road, great bald mountains towered in the distance, range upon range; on the other, the land dropped off to a rocky shoreline and the sea. A sense of isolation and remoteness enshrouded me like fog as the lonely road went on and on for miles and miles. I wished Michael were with me. Or even Kris. I wished today was yesterday and today had never been.

My whole experience in Ireland had been like one big seesaw. For three days I had teeter-tottered over a wide range of emotions on the ups of pleasure and the downs of gloom. It was therefore not extraordinary that the minute before I saw the tower I should feel that everything was hopeless, my trip there a dead loss, while the next minute, when I laid eyes on it, I should feel exactly the reverse. Driving around a curve in the vicinity where I had a hunch the tower ought to be, I saw it straight ahead. I could not believe my eyes.

Think of a tiny lake, brilliantly white, set prettily among hills enameled to a vivid emerald green. Think of the foil of a dark wood of oak and beech and holly, covering the slopes, and thickets of lush hazel, and a dense fringe of willow and rushes at the water's edge. Sketch purple and brown-orange masses of mountains in the distance against an azure and soap-bubble sky. And there beside the lake, backed by a sheer drop of rock perhaps thirty feet high, place a fairy-tale tower of gray stones. Put it all together and you have a miracle.

I cried out to the humming motor: "It can't be." And I firmly drove on past.

Continuing for several miles more along the road I had been traveling, I reached a tiny village that turned out to be Dunderg. According to my hazy recollections, this meant that I had overshot the mark. My heart pumping in my ears, I turned the car around and retraced my tire tracks.

The second view from the other direction was, if anything, more breathtaking. Right then it didn't matter what sort of shape the tower might be in, inside. From the outside it looked so utterly beautiful, the price was worth the scene alone. A tower on its own, it possessed no adjacent cottages such as Yeats had integrated into his home at Gort. But the tower was neither fat, circular and dumpy, nor tall and skinny like the round towers. It was a solid, four-square fortified tower-house as near as made no difference to Thoor Ballylee.

Still, I was not about to take anything for granted, ever again, after the blow I had received that day from Michael and his girl friend. I would take my time, tread warily, find out if this tower was indeed Tur Beag. There was no call for hurry, no justification for jumping to conclusions. Before I started congratulating myself, let alone writing my grandfather, I'd make darn sure that this gem belonged to us.

A small farm consisting of a long cottage and some cowhouses lay on a heather-covered slope maybe a thousand yards from where I'd stopped to stare. If anybody knew about the tower, its name, who owned it, it should be these neighbors.

As I approached the farmhouse I saw a woman in a blue calico dress and a shapeless knitted cardigan ambling across the front yard. She was clucking the chickens and throwing grain to them out of the apron she held bunched up in one hand to form a temporary receptacle. She was gaunt and stooped and perhaps a little deaf, perhaps preoccupied, because I had drawn up at the gate and turned off the ignition before she became aware of me.

As she looked my way in mild surprise, I saw a face as withered as last season's apple haloed with straggling wisps the color of trodden snow.

I got out of the car. "Good afternoon," I said.

She cupped a bony hand around her ear, and shuffled toward me on shabby carpet slippers molded over swollen joints. "Eh?" she said.

In a loud voice, articulating carefully and pointing to the tower I said: "I wonder if you could tell me what that tower is called?"

She squinted out of age-pale, sunken eyes, first at me, then at the tower, then back again, as all the time she chewed her lips with toothless gums.

I figured that I hadn't reached her. Perhaps my idiom, perhaps my accent . . . "That tower," I shouted, pointing. "What is its name?"

"Name?" She frowned and shrugged her humped, bony shoulders.

For objective corroboration, I had hoped to get the answer without having to suggest it. But impatience got the better of me. "Is it Tur Beag?"

"Tur Beag?" she said, cocking her head as though listening. She pronounced the "t" with a slight aspirate, so the word sounded close to "thoor."

"That's right," I said, encouragingly. "Thoor Beag."

She repeated: "Thoor Beag," then shrugged again.

My hopes began to sag. "That *isn't* what it's called?" I said, forgetting to speak up.

But she wasn't deaf, only leery of the stranger at her door, apparently. "Maybe there was a time they called it that."

What did that mean? I said, "What do they call it now?"

"Not anything, I doubt," she said, continuing the shrugs.

"You mean it doesn't *have* a name?" I asked, incredulous.

"None I know of."

"Who does it belong to? Who owns it?"

"It wouldn't belong to anyone, I shouldn't think."

"Why not?"

"It's just a ruin."

"It must belong to *some*one," I insisted.

She appeared to be tired of this fatuous exchange, ready to terminate it now by agreeing to anything I wanted. "You may be right."

"But you don't know who."

She scratched a little snowstorm from the scalp above her forehead. "The O'Hara's owned it maybe, long ago."

"How long ago?"

"Long ago," she said. "Before penal times. Maybe it was the O'Garas, though."

I muffled my sigh and racked my brain where to go from there.

She said: "You are from school to study the history, is it?"

There seemed no point in establishing otherwise. I simply smiled. "Is there anybody else around here who'll know more about the tower?"

"My son, perhaps."

"Your son? Where can I find him? Where does he live?"

"Here," she said, as if my question was absurd.

"Is he around now?"

"He's after calling home the cattle."

"When will he be back?"

"It'll be a bit yet."

"Can I go and look for him?"

She squinted far over the fields and up the slope toward the foothills, then shook her head. "I don't know where he'd be."

I said: "Mind if I wait, then?"

She made a gesture with her hands indicating it was all right with her. Then she resumed, in slow motion, her feeding of the hens, who scurried about, high-stepping, sticking out pompous dirty white or gingery-copper breasts, and tipping their tail ends in the air. Hen droppings blotched the stony dirt and weeds of the ill-kempt yard. The whitewash of the cottage was grayed and flaking under a scruffy thatch.

It occurred to me that I was indulging in the same disdainful self-righteous thoughts as those skin-deep puritan countrymen of mine who went around Europe, their bags full of tissues and aerosol cans, holding their noses and watching their step. Criticism came easy, but perhaps these people barely scratched a living from the thin flesh of soil stretched taut over the limestone skeleton; perhaps the sheer grind of subsistence took so much out of them, they had no time or energy left over for tidying things up.

I followed her around the far end of the house, where a wire-netting run of adolescent chicks, half fluff, half feather, scrambled over each other in a greedy flurry to reach the corn she strewed into the run.

A chain clanked inside a barrel lying on its side in the corner of the walled yard. A dun dog, flat-haired to almost hairless, grossly muscled, grotesquely shaped by his strange mixture of breeds, rushed out of it. What shocked me most about him as he danced around, straining at choking tension on his long chain, was the fact that he was muzzled with a tin can still covered with a salmon label. The beast's frustration must have been enormous, more than likely aggravating his natural fierceness to the point of violence. I wouldn't want to be around if he were unleashed.

When I followed the woman back around to the front door, she said: "You can come in, if you want to," and I went inside.

This was the first Irish cottage I had entered. Like many I'd seen along the way, it was long and narrow, for the reason—so Michael had informed me—that it was considered unlucky to enlarge a house by widening it. Extra rooms were simply tacked on, as the family expanded, at each end of the original single room.

This cottage had a half-door at both front and back, perhaps for ventilation. As I stepped inside, I noticed the low lintel and the thick stone walls into which the frame was set. In the center of the back wall of the living room a primitive open hearth held a mediocre turf fire. Wisps of pungent smoke curled over the high mantel deepening the sooty black stains on the ceiling. From the rafters hung clumps of dusty dried herbs, a piece of smoke-brown country bacon, and an ornament of woven reeds that I later learned was Brigid's Cross. A silver medallion of a cleric, possibly the Pope, mounted in a plaque of Connemara marble, sat on the mantelpiece between two tarnished candlesticks and a pair of china cats.

The old lady gestured me into a wooden armchair pulled

up to the stone slab of the hearth. She added lumps of turf to the white-ash fire to heat the kettle suspended from an iron bar. Unhooking three brown and yellow cups from an old kitchen dresser, that my mother, an antique collector, would have coveted, she set them on a soiled checked table cloth half covering the unscrubbed table of rough deal. Everything was dusty, shabby, grubby. The floor, part uneven flagstone, part worn linoleum, boasted a length of frayed coconut matting for a heathrug.

When steam jiggled the lid of the teakettle, the old lady spooned tea from a brass cannister into a teapot of brown earthenware.

After she had "wet" the tea and sat down to pour it, I tried to ingratiate myself with proper conversation: "These are handsome cups."

"Blue china makes the tea look thin," she said.

After a little silence, she asked: "Where do you come from?"

"The United States."

She sipped and set her cup down. "Knobby O'Brien came back from there a couple of years ago."

"Did he come home to retire?"

"He came looking for a bride to take back with him."

"Did he find one?"

"His dead wife's second cousin's daughter, Annie Pyle."

"Kept it in the family," I said. "Very smart."

She pressed the knitted cosy more securely around the teapot. "Have you come looking for a husband?"

I laughed. But it had been no joke. She didn't crack a smile. So I said facetiously: "Do you have someone in mind?"

Just then the latch rattled and the back door dragged open, grating on the flagstones. I turned to see a chunky man come tromping in. In its rough way, his face might have been attractive if it hadn't been for the slack sensuality of his mouth and the puffiness under his eyes, suggesting, dissipation.

Taking off his cloth cap, he flopped it on a nail behind the door. He did not, however, take off his rubber boots, thick with barnyard muck, which he blithely tracked across the kitchen floor.

As he approached the hearth he eyed me with a look halfway between a frown and a leer. Obviously surprised and puzzled, he said, almost questioningly: "Good day to you."

"And a good day to you," I said, expecting his mother to explain my presence, initiating an exchange of names.

She said nothing, however, only added water to the teapot from the purring kettle, and poured tea into the third cup set out on the table.

The man pulled out a kitchen chair. One of the chair's legs caught in a tear in the linoleum, and his rough jerk enlarged the hole. He sat down, his knees and brawny thighs spread wide, the elbow of one thick, muscled arm propped on the table. He smelled pretty gamy, and I turned casually aside to draw a breath.

His mouth and eyes now frankly leered at me. "It is looking like more rain," he said.

"I hope not," I said, in genuine dismay.

He slurped his tea, and set down the cup with a nerve-jangling rattle. "You are here on holiday?"

"Summer vacation."

"From America?"

"I am," I answered, Irish-fashion.

"Knobby O'Brien went over there. Came back a couple of years ago."

"So your mother told me," I said evenly. "But I'm not here on the same mission."

"A shame it is, seeing I'm a bachelor." His expression grew more suggestive. I avoided it by trying to figure out the pin in his lapel. It looked like a sprig of mistletoe.

I said: "The reason I stopped by was to ask the name of the tower across the lake. Your mother invited me in to wait for you."

The grin left his face to be replaced by an almost animal look of curiosity and wariness. "Why are you after wanting to know that?"

A buzzer sounded in my marrow, a sort of private alarm system apparently built into me. I had experienced it on occasion before in my life, warning me to be on guard. Against what I wasn't sure this time, but I knew I should at least be noncommittal. "Just wondered," I answered nonchalantly.

"You're interested in old buildings, are you?"

"I am," I said, which was no lie. "Would you know the name of this particular tower?"

He made a grimace, conveying doubt. "Around here we call it just the Tower," he said. He pronounced "tower" like the French "tour," with the merest suspicion of a tongue thrust on the "t."

I had no option but to suggest the name to him. "Could it be Tur Beag, by any chance?"

The wary look returned. "Where did you hear it called that?"

"I thought I saw it on some map along the way."

He shrugged. "That could have been its name when it *had* a name. Who knows?"

His lackadaisical attitude grated on me. "Isn't there anyone around here who'd know for sure?"

His suspicious look was back. "What difference does it make? One tower is like another. There are plenty of them hereabouts."

I swallowed my last sip of tea. "I don't suppose you know who it belongs to, either?"

"Belongs to!" he said, his tone mocking me for such a silly question. "It's on the mountain."

What did he mean by that? That it was on public or common land, and thus not open to private ownership? "You mean nobody owns it, and couldn't if they wanted to?"

"If it's to go and see it that you want, you don't need leave. I'll take you by there."

His offer was tempting but his slack, wet mouth and lascivious eye warned me against accepting it. The time to see the tower would be after I established its identity.

While we'd talked, the tiny windows had grown darker and the room had fallen into heavy shadow, relieved only by the fire's glow and a candle burning in a glass case in the rafters. Since it was early evening, I figured that the dimming of the daylight was caused by storm clouds. It gave me a good out. "Thanks all the same. But the weather doesn't look very promising."

He grunted, sounding mildly thwarted. But he no longer looked suspicious of my strange inquiry—I obviously wasn't very interested or I'd have taken up his offer.

As I got up to leave, he peered at me closely in the gloom. "You staying hereabouts?"

"Dunderg," I said, inventing answers as I went.

"Who with?"

"A bed-and-breakfast in the village."

He frowned. "Bed-and-breakfast in Dunderg? Who is that?"

"I forget the name."

"Who would that be, Mother?"

The old lady ruminated, mumbling her lips between her gums. "I don't know, Padraic. Could it be Mrs. Rory the Post Office?"

I was saved from having to say yes or no by a lash of giant droplets like a fistful of gravel against the window pane. "I'd better go, and fast," I said. "I don't like driving in the rain." I hurried to the door, boots and coats cluttering its sides, and pulled it open. I called to the old lady: "Thanks very much for your hospitality."

"Drop by tomorrow," her son said, winking knowingly, "and I'll walk you yonder to the tower."

7

I sped out of the rutted driveway, anxious to escape. Back on the dirt road again, and feeling safer, I slowed down to thirty. The tower lay to my left like a breath-taking photograph in the *National Geographic*, yet, to my amazement, I caught myself feeling relieved that the tower was probably not ours, hoping that ours was somewhere else. Though it was even more beautiful now with its backdrop of bruised purple hills and lowering, roiling rainclouds, still the implications of the farmer and his mother had tarnished my original delight. I couldn't pin down precisely what I'd found repellent. There were, of course, the substandard, slummy aspects of the farm and the vegetable stupidity of the old lady, which had somewhat put me off. Then there were the son's leers and his innuendo that I might serve him as a bride. But it wasn't only that I didn't relish the prospect of having them for neighbors. There was something negative, almost threatening, in the situation, that I couldn't place or name.

The rain held off after the first few spits and sprinkles, but the sky had grown so heavy it seemed as though dusk had fallen hours before its time. I was going to experience another of those long, scary evenings when an eerie light fills the last hours of the day with a green gloom, inculcating fears of the supernatural in even the most practical of people. Never before, except in troubled dreams, had I known anything remotely like the Celtic twilight and the weird moods it can inspire.

In the few miles that I traveled to Dunderg, I grew so unnerved by dread of a repetition of the terrors of the two previous nights that I abandoned my intention of seeking a campsite by the road or near the beach. At the outskirts of the village, I stopped to check the bed-and-breakfast listings in the Irish Tourist Board booklet I had acquired on the boat, but there were no entries for Dunderg.

So, hopeful of turning the white lie I had told at the farmhouse into the truth, I decided to look for Dunderg Post Office. In the single street, the largest building, a two-story house of stone, had OIFIG AN PHOIST above the plate-glass window. The blinds were drawn, the front door closed, so I went around the side, and barely made it under the glass porch before the rain came down in torrents.

A short, gray-haired man with a neat moustache answered my ring. He wore a comfortable bulky pullover, baggy slacks and tartan slippers. "Oh, my word," he said, his head nodding at me and then at the rain, "it's a tipping down, isn't it. Come in. Come in."

I entered a long passage where threadbare oriental runners covered worn but polished tile. I said: "I'm looking for bed and breakfast. Could you put me up?"

"Oh, my word," he said again. "The wife isn't here right now. As a matter of fact, even if she was . . . Well, what I mean is, what with her rheumatics, she hasn't been doing much of it of late, taking people in, I mean."

"Oh, dear," I said, discouraged. "Do you know anybody else who does it? There's nothing listed in my Tourist book."

He scratched his cheek, then slowly shook his head. "Ennis will be the nearest for you to find anything. I can't think of anybody between here and there."

"That's a long drive in the rain."

"Well," he said doubtfully, "you can come in and sit down until the wife comes home. I mean we wouldn't want to see you stuck without a place."

"How long will she be?"

"She shouldn't be much longer. Her Dadda's laid up with the gout. She goes back and forth to look after him."

"Then she won't feel much like coping with an overnight guest."

"She wouldn't see you suffer, neither."

I said shamefacedly: "I'm really not that desperate. I mean I have a camper parked out front. I've been sleeping in it the last several nights. But I had company then." I added lamely: "It's not too cosy when its raining. Besides, the windows leak."

"And we're in for quite a blow the next day or two, we are indeed. Oh, yes, indeed we are." He clucked his tongue. "The wife's rheumatism is a good barometer."

I followed him into a room where a bright peat fire glowed in a black iron grate adorned with foxglove tiles in a mahogany chimneypiece. More worn orientals graced simulated wood linoleum, and comfortable upholstered chairs and sofa sported slipcovers of colorful chintz. Crisp curtains, and wallpaper as fresh as the spring flowers in its design, completed the room's welcome.

"Sit down and make yourself at home," he said. "If we can't come up with a better solution, you can at least drive your van behind the house here."

That sounded comforting. "It's very good of you to be concerned about a stranger." Nor was that hollow chatter. The difference between the atmosphere of this place and the farm was the difference between cream and creosote.

"You're no stranger," he said smiling. "You're almost an old friend already. Let me introduce myself. Dan Rory." He stuck out his hand.

"Mine's Jan McDonagh," I said, shaking hands with him.

"Jan McDonagh, is it?" he said delightedly. "Then you'll be from here originally."

"My great-grandfather came from County Donegal."

"Is that a fact now? Then it is on your way you are to see who you can find that's left of them up there."

I eyed the kindly face with its bright hazel eyes peeking shortsightedly under gray tweed brows, and saw no reason to prevaricate. "Not right away," I said. "Maybe later. At the moment, I'm looking for Tur Beag." This time I pronounced the "tur" as "thoor."

"Tur Beag?" He looked at me intently as if to find the answer on my face. "And where would that be now?"

"That's what I'm trying to find out. All I know is it's supposed to be within a few miles of here—if I've got the right Dunderg."

"Is it actually *called* Tur Beag?" he asked. "You're not speaking of some 'little tower' in general descriptive terms?"

Intrigued, I said: "*Beag* means 'little,' does it?" And when he nodded, I answered: "Tur Beag is supposed to be its proper name."

He pulled at his moustache. "It's not an address I recognize. And being postmaster, I thought I knew them all." He added thoughtfully: "If address it *is*, of course, and not a pile of stones."

He crossed the room to a glass-cased secretary, and pulled down the writing flap. From one of many well-filled pigeonholes inside, he pulled out a map, spreading it upon the chenille-clothed table. It was a large-scaled contoured Ordnance Survey map with much more detail than my own.

After a brief search along lines representing the "main"

road, he went back to the desk for a magnifying glass. Continuing to scan the section, I could make out the letters "CAS" in old English script printed at roughly the spot where I had seen the tower that afternoon.

"Look at this, Mr. Rory," I said as he returned. "See where it says 'CAS.' Do you know its name?"

He peered through the glass. "They've got it wrong," he said. "It's a tower, not a castle. I know it well. But I don't recall ever having heard it *called* anything."

"No one ever lived in it? No mail goes there?"

He shook his head. "I doubt it's even habitable. Another ruin." He tapped the map east of the "CAS." "The Herlihys live here. This is their farm. They'd be the only ones to know."

"An old woman with a son called Padraic?"

"That's right," he said.

"I've already called on them."

He eyed me sharply. "You did, eh? What did they say?"

"They didn't recognize the name Tur Beag. Like you, they didn't think their tower had one."

He tossed his head, a gesture I could not interpret. "And why are you so concerned to find Tur Beag?"

Again I looked him in the eye and liked what I connected with. "My grandfather bought it a little while back for a summer place."

"Ah, did he now! So if we can locate it, we shall be having you for neighbor, is it? A very pleasant prospect, I must say."

"*If* we locate it," I said skeptically. "I'm beginning to wonder if it wasn't a big swindle. If the name isn't a figment of some con artist's imagination."

He looked perturbed. "Oh, don't say that. Who sold it to your grandfather?"

"A realtor in Sligo."

"Sligo town or Sligo county?"

"I have no idea."

"You don't have any papers?"

"My grandfather has the correspondence and the deed, of course. At least I *hope* he does. He was supposed to have written down all the particulars in this envelope. When I opened it down the road a way, the information wasn't in it." I added apologetically: "He's rather absent-minded."

"An estate agent in Sligo," Mr. Rory said. "And you don't recall the name?"

"If I knew it, I've forgotten."

"Well, if it *was* an estate agent, I don't doubt that it's all properly signed and sealed, and that the tower exists all right."

"If it does, it ought to be in this vicinity. I can't be too far wrong on that."

"Let me see," he said, gazing at the ceiling, his brow furrowed. "I have a book somewhere." He looked at me with a self-deprecating smile. "I have a lot of books. But I don't always remember what they are or where they went. I used to be a schoolmaster."

"What particular book are you thinking about now?"

"Something on ancient monuments. It's upstairs more than likely. I'll get my wife to fetch it when she comes." He tapped his chest. "The stairs have been forbidden to me the past twelve-month. My wife, poor soul, does all the running." He sighed. "And her with her rheumatics."

That moment, a great draught blew along the hall, pushing in the door of the room and sucking the smoke out of the chimney. "There she is now," Mr. Rory said, grabbing a newspaper from a neat pile near the fireplace and rushing out with it into the passage. I could hear his wife stomping, presumably on the newspaper, as she rustled and puffed out of her wet top clothes.

She came into the room with her head swathed in a huge fluffy towel. The rain apparently had caught her unprotected. While Mr. Rory continued bustling in the passage, she briskly rubbed her hair, standing just inside the door.

At last she dropped the towel around her shoulders, and bent over to pull down her stockings. At that moment she caught sight of me. With a frightened squeak she straightened, smoothing her skirt.

"Don't mind me," I said. "Go right ahead. Take them off before you catch cold."

"Blessed saints," she said, ducking behind a high-backed chair to finish removing the sopping hose. "I had no idea anyone was in here."

I said, "I'm Jan McDonagh. I came looking for a place to stay, and Mr. Rory kindly asked me in out of the downpour."

Her husband joined us, bringing his wife's slippers. "In all the scrabble, Mother, I forgot to tell you. This young lady doesn't have a bed tonight. I couldn't bear to turn her away in such wicked weather."

Mrs. Rory said reluctantly: "I expect Mr. Rory told you I don't take in visitors anymore. What with stiff joints and my father up and down, it's too much for me."

"If you have a room," I said, "I'll gladly look after myself. I won't be any trouble. Just for a day or two."

Mr. Rory said: "Otherwise she'll have to sleep out in the van. It's too far to Ennis on a night like this."

Alertness replaced fatigue in Mrs. Rory's face. "Van? What van?"

"It's parked out front," I said.

"Yours?"

"For a month. It's rented."

"Blessed saints," she said. "And isn't there a purpose in your coming here at all? Fair exchange is no robbery. One good turn deserves another. With my knees so bad, I can't cycle anymore. And four miles is a long walk twice a day."

I understood immediately. Apparently, neither of them

drove a car. "You need a ride to your father's place, do you, Mrs. Rory? I'd love to do it."

"*Would* you?" she said with grateful eyes. "Only to run me over in the mornings and fetch me in the evenings. It would be such a help while the weather's bad."

Mr. Rory beamed. "Give-gave make good friends, heh, Mother? Jan may as well be using one of the upstairs bedrooms, as them go empty all the time."

After a swift calculation of a ridiculously low rate for bed and board, Mrs. Rory sent me upstairs to reconnoiter on my own and settle myself in while she made a "sup of tea." A distinct feeling of festivity was in the air, as though they looked forward to my company.

Mrs. Rory said: "Both beds are aired and made up ready, dear. Take your pick. Then come down for a bite."

"While you're up there, Jan, girl," Mr. Rory said, "look for that book on ancient monuments. There's a good chance it's in the bookcase on the landing. If I recollect, it had a leather binding—reddish, worn."

The two upstairs bedrooms, modestly furnished with pieces which back home would rank as fine antiques, were as welcoming and immaculate as the rooms below. On the floor was the ubiquitous cheap linoleum, every inch of it agleam with polish, despite fadedness and wear. Everywhere I went in Ireland, I saw the pinch of poverty, so that even in this comparatively comfortable middle-class household, there was clearly no margin for extravagance. But the difference between this home and the Herlihys' seedy farmstead was pride and self-respect, a kind of loving stewardship of however little that one owned.

One room looked out toward the ocean, obscured now by dark slanting rain whirled into a maelstrom every now and then by boisterous buffets of the wind. The other room overlooked the "main" street of the village, a string of poky cottages and a few shops, one with a single antique gas pump. At the end of the street rose a plain, fairly modern church beside an ivied ruin—perhaps of a medieval monastery, such as the many I had seen across the breadth of Ireland. I chose the latter room to sleep in. Less exposed to the storm outside, it did, indeed, as Mrs. Rory had suggested, seem more snug and "comfy."

In the bookcase on the stairtop hallway, called "the landing," I found quite a library on Ireland's history, archeology and literature. Many books bore nineteenth-century publication dates. The more recent vintage of the others testified to a genuine and continuing interest in the subjects. A large, heavy tome of wine-colored calf, titled *Book of Ancient Monuments*, must be the book Mr. Rory had referred to. It looked enormously authoritative. But when I checked the copious index, I found no listing for Tur Beag.

Disappointed, I carried the book downstairs and had Mr. Rory double-check me. But he got the same result. He quickly reassured me, however, that the book could certainly not be considered the last word. It was too old; so many new bits of information were being dug up by scholars and researchers every day that no work could ever be regarded as definitive. "The most sensible thing to do," he advised me, "is to write your grandfather for exact particulars and go from there."

A mouth-watering aroma emerged with Mrs. Rory from the kitchen to change the subject. I had not had a decent meal all day, so the serving dish of steaming "patties" engaged my full attention. These proved to be delicious concoctions of minced meat and onions fried in nut-brown batter. For a side dish she served canned baked beans out of the belief that they were as much a staple of American diets as potatoes of the Irish.

The meal well under way, Mr. Rory addressed his wife with the wishful title that had—I gathered from stray information—stuck to her ever since their one and only child arrived stillborn: "Mother," he said, "Jan is looking for a tower in this neighborhood, called Tur Beag. Have you heard of it by any chance?"

"Tur Beag?" she said, a forkful of patty arrested in midair. "Can't say I have."

After a while he said to her: "You know that tower near the Herlihys?"

In case she might have trouble identifying which we meant, I supplied: "About four or five miles east of here, Mrs. Rory. Back off the road maybe a quarter of a mile, across a little lake."

She looked at Mr. Rory. "The one a mile or so past Dadda's?"

"That's it."

"I *should* know it! I've seen it all my life. As kids we had to pass right by it on our way to Leprechaun Ravine."

She stopped to offer a spicy pickled condiment she called chutney. The pause increased the burden of suspense.

I said: "What do you know about it?"

"Not much. We used to give it the widest berth we could without falling in the bog."

A pulse ticked in my neck. "Give it a wide berth?" I said.

She thought I hadn't understood the idiom. "We'd steer clear of it. Not get too close."

"Why not?"

"Its reputation."

"What kind of reputation?"

Her eyes blinked nervously. "A fearsome place. To be avoided at all costs."

"Good grief, why?"

"A haunt of the *Bean Sídhe*," she said, as if forced to state the unpleasant obvious.

"A haunt of *what?*"

She looked uncertainly at me, perhaps wondering whether I was kidding her. But Mr. Rory understood my problem and spelled it out for me. Then he translated from the Gaelic: "The lady of the little folk, the fairy woman."

"I get it!" I said. "The banshee." Mrs. Rory's Gaelic pronunciation had differed slightly from the popular version. "The supernatural woman who wails at wakes."

Mrs. Rory said: "She appears as a white apparition walking the battlements at night. Wailing and weeping. Luring men into the bog. Some call her *Bean Fhionn*."

"The white lady to you," Mr. Rory said, and spelled out the Gaelic name.

I was having difficulty swallowing the baked beans, which courtesy required me to finish, since she had served them for my sake. It was becoming more important by the minute that that "jewel" of a tower that I had seen that day *not* be the one my grandfather had bought.

Mrs. Rory was continuing: "I've also heard her called *Maighdean-mhara*, the Lady of the Lake. She has been seen sometimes combing her hair beside the water. She lives at the bottom in a house of glass, though an aunt of mine once saw her riding a snow-white horse out of the rath."

Always eager to elucidate, Mr. Rory put in: "Mother means the hill behind the tower. Its commonly believed to be a fairy dwelling. The little folk live either under water or in the bowels of the earth."

Many of these supernormal characteristics of the *sidhe* had been reported by my doting grandfather during my impressionable preschool years, so they sounded neither silly nor far-fetched in folklore terms. What bothered me was the fact that I, who had taken these fairy tales, and all other supernatural claims, with a good shrewd pinch of skepticism since my elevation to the Age of Reason, was now retrogressing to a state of trembling uncertainty. As during the two previous nights, I astonished myself with these self-discoveries. The rational segment of my brain, which broke down this wailing woman into mist, wind, tricks of the moon and imaginative fear, no longer held its own, and it was fortunate the tower where she walked was nameless, so it could not possibly be ours.

But *was* it nameless? True, Mrs. Rory had no knowledge of a tower called Tur Beag. But she hadn't said that she didn't know what the tower near the Herlihys was called. If she could name it, it would cinch forever that the eerie place, encumbered by such unsavory neighbors and unnerving legends, did *not* belong to us.

A little hoarse, I said: "Living so close to it all your life, you must have learned its name."

"Of course," she said, stacking the empty dinner plates to clear the table for dessert.

Mr. Rory prompted: "What did you call the tower, Mother?"

"Tur Bron," she said.

Relief poured through me as when irrigation waters flooded parched orange groves back home.

That the tower had a name at all intrigued Mr. Rory. "Well, fancy that. But you're sure Tur Bron isn't just a name you kiddies put on it? I mean in keeping with the dire stories that you heard about the place?"

"I shouldn't think so," Mrs. Rory said, preoccupied with serving fruit and clotted cream.

If I felt a few residual pangs that such a picture-postcard beauty spot had gotten away from me, they were effectively dispelled by Mr. Rory's footnote that "Tur Bron" meant "Tower of Sorrow."

8

With Tur Bron disposed of as a possibility, I would have spent a restful night had the weather been kinder. The wind howled continually and the rain assaulted the windows with the sound of riddling shot. Though nested comfortably in a feather mattress on a great iron bedstead with black rails and brass knobs—a bed that would have brought a fortune in Los Angeles—I slept only fitfully. There was no electric light on the second story, so when I came too wide awake, I had only a dip candle to keep me company. Even then, after my fumbling to light it, instead of dissipating my night fears, its feeble flame called shadows from the corners. The shadows fluttered like giant birds behind the cage-bars of the bedstead, until my feverish imagination demanded that I blow the candle out again. Moreover, in the sleepless stretches, a sense of loss oppressed me; last night there had been Michael, now not even the hope of him.

Eventually the long night passed, and another new day wheeled round, though weatherwise no more promising than the last. When I went downstairs, a pleasant hum of chatter seeped from the living room. The parish priest, a Father Flanagan, had come from Mass with Mrs. Rory, and we all breakfasted together on scrambled eggs and rashers of back bacon as lean as ham. The Rorys brought Father Flanagan up to date on who I was and why I'd come and did he know a tower called Tur Beag.

The priest had a face with the ancient boyish features of a leprechaun, his nose and chin almost scissoring together as he munched. He gave me a knowing, Arthur Godfrey kind of grin, and said puckishly: "I don't know about a Tur Beag"—he pronounced it "beg"—"but I know a *Big* Tower, if that's any use to you." He quite obviously volunteered the information solely for the charge of punning on big and beg, but oddly enough the fatuous little witticism stirred something in the subsoil of my mind. I said: "Where *is* this *Big* Tower?"

He looked surprised that I'd be interested. "Several miles west of here, towards Knock Áine."

My inchoate thought angled toward the light. I said: "If there's a *Big* Tower, it's possible there's also a *Little* Tower, isn't it?"

"I don't know if that follows," Father Flanagan said, laughing to take the sting out of his criticism.

"Still, it could be," Mr. Rory said, "the tendency people have to identify things by differentiation. Do you remember, Father, if there's a tower anywhere to the west of Big Tower that might be the contrasting Little Tower?"

"There's a tower near Ennis," the priest said. "But I don't know what it's called."

I could hardly wait to check it out and generally explore the area. So I was glad Mrs. Rory didn't ask me in to meet her father when I dropped her at the cottage about a mile short of Tur Bron.

The best part of the morning went in ferreting out ruins along a twelve-mile stretch of road that formed the backbone of innumerable branching lanes and criss-crossing dirt side roads adding up to many, many miles. It was a hard

job peering through a steamed-up windshield that teemed
with a steady drizzle falling out of a sky as dark as dusklight.
But a slow, thorough search of these byways netted varying
piles of tumbled stones from a holy well to a four-square
eighteenth-century mansion—a "Protestant" house, according to the neighboring cottagers, that had been so long in
litigation, it had gone to rack and ruin before the law had
settled the dispute. I also found a half a dozen weird groups
of prehistoric standing stones called dolmens—to be further
examined when I had more leisure—and another ruined
abbey. But the only tower I came across stood about a mile
beyond the generous limits I had set myself, six miles or so
beyond Dunderg the other way.

When I saw the tower in the distance, my heart
accelerated. Here was more than a mere possibility. But
immediate investigation only corroborated what the map
revealed—if I had heeded it—that the tower stood upon a
promontory overlooking the sea. If my grandfather's tower
had had such a vantage point, I would have certainly
remembered it. As it was, as I drew close I realized the
tower was nothing like the picture I had built in my
imagination when my grandfather had first spelled out the
details. For example, there had been mention of a lake—but
definitely—small, but big enough for fishing, a passion of
my grandfather.

This tower that stood before me now, although in sad
repair, must have, in its heyday, been considerably larger
than the tower Mrs. Rory called Tur Bron. No cottage was
at hand for me to ask its name. The only sign of life was a
beaten-up old camper parked on the tower's seaward side.

As I drove closer to it, the camper opened and a lanky,
shag-haired fellow stuck out his head. When I turned off the
ignition, I heard him call: "Would you have a light by any
chance?"

I held up my box of wooden matches, and he dashed

across the cropped grass with a groundsheet tented protectively over his head.

Thirty-year-oldish, with a twang reminding me very much of the Beatles, he said he was from Liverpool, a commercial artist who painted watercolor scenes weekends and holidays. He worked even in the rain, but today he thought he'd have to pack it in. Did I want a cup of coffee that my match would make it possible to brew?

I followed him to his cluttered, messy quarters. Tubes of paint nested in the teabag box, wet brushes lay cheek by jowl with unwashed spoons. He had to clear the seats of rags and palette before we could sit down.

I admired his work in progress, a very skillful, though rather conventionally representative rendering of the castle in front of us, and he pulled out a couple more, one of the ruined abbey I had seen that morning, and another of a tower I didn't recognize.

He said: "That's Grogan's tower, thirty-odd miles from here."

The exciting implications of this windfall meeting suddenly struck home. I said: "You must know all the towers in this vicinity."

"I should. I've painted most of them."

"Do you know their names and histories?"

"Well, I've picked up a fair bit of information here and there."

"What's this tower here called?" I motioned at the one outside.

He slid open the window a few inches to throw scraps to hovering seagulls as he cleared the decks. "Its popular name's Big Tower."

I should have guessed from Father Flanagan's account. "Does it have another name?"

"I dare say it must have in the old days. The MacSweeneys—or was it the O'Downds—had it as a family seat at one time, I remember reading somewhere."

"Have you ever heard of a tower called Tur Beag?"

He mulled this briefly as he poured boiling water on the instant coffee. Then he shook his head.

"I'm told 'beag' means 'little,' " I prompted.

He shook his head again. "Doesn't ring any bell."

He wanted to know why I was interested, so I filled him in with a few economic brushstrokes and resumed my questioning. "Doesn't it sound reasonable that if this is called Big Tower, there'd be a little one to correspond?"

My logic didn't seem to impress him. "It's just bigger than all the others in the area, is all. Or must have been before it started falling down."

"Which others? Can you name them?"

He ran down a list of six he'd painted, describing their locations, all fairly wide afield. Nothing clicked.

But there must be more. "You've left out at least one that's pretty near here. Tur Bron."

"Tur Bron?" he said, looking puzzled. "Where's that supposed to be?"

"Four or five miles the other side of Dunderg." When he still couldn't place it, I continued: "Below a cliff, beside a lake. You've missed something if you've never painted that."

His face relaxed in recognition. "Of course! You mean Bran Tower. You bet I've painted it. It's my best seller. A real beaut."

Bran. Bron. Such shades of change, due to mistakes in spelling or pronunciation, were what kept scholars busy tracing names and folk tales to a common source. It was fascinating to experience the process actually happening.

The Liverpudlian was saying: "Come to think of it, the chappies who owned this place last"—he gestured to the tower before us—"owned Bran Tower as well. This was the family seat, if I recall. The other place was for the eldest son."

This casual bit of information induced such a disproportionate surge of Alpha waves, it was as though someone had flipped on a switch inside my skull. "Where did you learn that?" I said. If his source had been a reference book, it might have a lot to tell me.

"Oh, I don't know. You pick up a bit here, a bit there. I shouldn't depend on anything I say, if I were you. I don't read up on these things for accuracy—just for atmosphere and curiosity."

But the merest hint of a connection between Big Tower and Tur Bron was enough to turn me round again. I said a swift good-bye, promising to hold him to his offer to make a picture of our tower if I should ever find it.

I drove back to what my Liverpudlian referred to as my "digs" with as much speed as I could muster—which admittedly wasn't a great deal. My visibility was cut not only by the inside fogging of the windshield but by a new cascade outside. My wipers swished and sprayed as they described their noisy arcs on the swimming glass.

But all the while that the surface of my mind was trying to cope with the arduous job of driving, the deeper layers were worrying the implications of this latest bit of information. If the Big Tower was the family seat of the MacSweeneys or whoever, then might not the second tower, the lesser seat, if reserved for the firstborn or the heir apparent, have been designated, at least informally, the "little tower"? Whether I liked the implications of this line of reasoning or not, it certainly put Tur Bron or Bran Tower back into the running in my quest for Tur Beag. It at least called for another, closer, look at Mr. Rory's *Book of Ancient Monuments*.

Mr. Rory must have seen me drive up, for when I

entered the passage he emerged from the connecting door between the post office and the living quarters. "Here's a letter for you, Jan."

A quick glance at the neat script told me it was from my grandfather. As we'd arranged, he had sent the letter in care of General Delivery, Dunderg. I said excitedly: "Maybe Grandfather woke up. Let's hope he's sending on the information he forgot to give me at the airport."

"No luck along the coast, then, Jan?"

"Nh-nh. Not yet."

The bell tinkled in the post office, and Mr. Rory excused himself.

I tore open the envelope and read the letter. Undoubtedly, by this time, my grandfather had written, I had seen our tower. He couldn't wait to hear from me. His foot was doing nicely, but he was restless, wishing he were with me. Among other questions the letter posed about our property was this: "What is the fishing like on our own Lough Bran?"

The sight of the name was like a charge of electricity. I either hadn't heard before—or hadn't registered—what the lake was called. Wasn't it more than feasible, I reasoned grudgingly, that the lake had shared its name at some time with the tower that stood upon its banks?

With trembling hands I reached down Mr. Rory's *Book of Ancient Monuments* from the corner of the bookcase by his chair. The text had every appearance of a sound, authoritative work. So how could it be silent on such a crucial subject? You couldn't tell me a tower of such exceptional distinction and preservation had not deserved at least a mention. The answer surely must be that it had. But where? And how?

Once more I searched the index for Tur Beag, without results. Next I tried Big Tower, Tur Bron, Bran Tower. Nothing. This was a fruitless avenue.

But as I was about to put the book away, I noticed that the entries were by county. I rapidly thumbed through a number of pages until I found the name Dunderg. More diligent scanning and the word "Bran" leapt before my eyes.

Caisleán Bran.

The grid, the parish, the distance from Dunderg, all joined to place it where I'd seen the tower near the Herlihys' farmstead.

My eyes seized more: "The present edifice was erected in the sixteenth century on the site of a much older castle, the stones of which were used in the building of the present tower. This fine example of a modest fortified house follows the standard plan of the £10 castles designed as defenses for the Pale counties—the statute of 1429, in the 8th year of the reign of Henry VI, having provided a subsidy therefore. This tower is sometimes referred to in the records as Caisleán Beag, Little Castle, to differentiate it from Caisleán Mór, Big Castle, the latter being the principal family seat of the MacSweeney clan nearer Knock Áine."

That clinched it. The only reason that the index hadn't yielded up the information was that the older designation "caisleán" had survived the fortress's rebuilding as a "tur."

Despite the fact that the possibility had been fermenting, albeit tightly capped, for several hours, the realization that Tur Bran was ours gave me an unpleasant jolt. Not even the vivid flashes on my inner eye of lichened stones, green woods, blue ruffled lake and purple hills could make me easy, much less happy, at the news. All the stories Mrs. Rory had told the night before about fairies, banshees and phantom ladies—stories that had produced relief when I'd concluded that Tur Bron could not be ours—now returned to bother me. And if it wasn't the White Lady's shadow which cast a pall over that flashing scene, it was the gross, leering image of Padraic Herlihy.

But there was no way to refuse the facts, short of blind obstinacy, of which I liked to think I was incapable. The tower my grandfather had bought could be none other than the Tower of Sorrow.

The book, however, like the Liverpudlian, had called it Bran, not Bron. Opportunely, Mr. Rory re-entered the living quarters just then, and I lost no time in asking him if there was a separate word spelled "bran," and if so, what it meant.

"There is," he said, scrutinizing me as if to ask what tangent I was off on now. But the schoolmaster took precedence. "Bran was a giant god-hero in ancient Celtic myth. You can read about him in both old Irish and Welsh manuscripts. Stories about his voyage to the Otherworld. The resurrection of his severed head. Why do you want to know?"

"That's better," I said, genuinely relieved. And to answer him directly: "That tower near the Herlihys looks as if it *is* ours, after all. And *if* it is, I'd much prefer it to be named after a mythic god than called the Tower of Sorrow."

I filled him in on what I had learned from the Liverpudlian. Then, round-eyed and whistling softly, he read the entry in the *Book of Ancient Monuments*. Closing the book he said: "However, if I were you, I'd want a good bit more to go on to be satisfied."

When I showed him the letter from my grandfather with the reference to Lough Bran, his expression grew graver. "Even so," he said, "don't act on this till you've confirmed it with him." His tone seemed to hold an extra shade of warning over and above a paternal admonition to use ordinary prudence.

The post office bell summoned him again, and he left once more through the adjoining door. But in a second he had poked his head back around to say: "Incidentally, I meant to tell you, 'bran' has another meaning. It's an older word for crow, or daw."

A panic of black wings swooped through my head. The round scab on my hand throbbed as though punctured that moment by the angry beak.

I had thought the name "Tower of Sorrow" bad enough. "Tower of the Crow" was ominous.

9

Well, it was no good sitting there stewing. I'd better haul my heart out of my rope-soled shoes and go and look the tower over. If it really was too ruined for a residence, that would wrap it up. A simple matter of accurate reporting, and my grandfather would forgive me in due course for "giving in."

If I talked to Mr. Rory, he might try to coax me out of my intentions, so I simply honked the horn to let him know I'd left the house.

In the day's rubbed-charcoal weather, the tower and its setting looked even more incredibly beautiful than in the changing moods of yesterday. The scene was muted now, modulating from pearl white through ash and slate to scumbled black wherever it was not a succulent green. But the beauty of the place and the prospect of renovating it held no seduction for me now. Given all the negative vibrations, I placed all my hopes on its being a white elephant.

If only to avoid having Padraic as a self-appointed escort, I felt it wiser to keep the Herlihys ignorant of my activities, especially since my built-in buzzer continued sounding an alarm. Until the situation was resolved one way or another, the less they knew about my business the better. The sensible thing to do was to approach the tower on the opposite side from where the farm lay, keeping as low as possible.

Using a hayrick as a blind, I carefully surveyed the area. If I calculated correctly, taking the back road from the cottage of Mrs. Rory's father would bring me out somewhere behind and on the "off" side of the tower. From there I could reach it through the cover of trees and examine it in peace.

But the muddy lane soon became a rutted track. One yard more and the camper would sink into the ditch up to its axles. Only one form of locomotion would work in such conditions. I parked the camper and got out.

I clomped farther along the lane, my shoes gathering mud and getting heavier by the minute. On both sides lay marshy meadows patched with hazelnut and bramble. The bushes close to me hung with myriads of droplets, the more distant receded into mist and drizzle. Everywhere the vegetation grew luxuriantly, thanks to the obviously perpetual supply of water from the skies. That itself was a minor miracle. Back home, by now, the sprinklers would be working overtime.

At a turning in the lane I glimpsed the tower's hazy outline through the trees. Gray, solemn, ancient—and, to all appearances, intact. I had only to cross a bush-strewn area and I'd be there.

My heart beat fast—with apprehension, not anticipation. The area bristled with reeds and rushes. At my first step into the field the turf felt slimy underfoot. Patches of pale green and sage among darker grasses suggested spongy moss. Although raised on deserts and arid foothills, where clouds of dust more often than of mist and rain characterized my true habitat, I knew by instinct that such areas were treacherous.

Did I dare proceed?

As if my need could conjure its own answers out of the air, a bicycle appeared in the lane from around the curving hedge. The rider wore a slick black raincoat and sou'wester hat. The milk pail balanced on the cross bar explained his mission.

What little of his face peered out between the deep, floppy brim and turned-up collar registered alarm at sight of me. Braking hard, he had to drag a foot to save himself from skidding at the same time as he steadied the wobbling pail. When he had stopped, I said: "Gee, I'm sorry if I took you by surprise. I'm trying to reach that tower. Can I get to it from here?"

Through pitifully styed lids, he eyed me warily and wordlessly. Then he raised his hand to point toward the meadow and make a sweeping arc in a roundabout direction. I craned to figure out the detour. When I turned back to ask for further details, he had already taken off.

Ah, well. I guessed he knew the area and wouldn't steer me wrong.

I started gingerly across the field. Every couple of steps I slithered on wet turf into waterlogged depressions the size of hooves. Sometimes I'd light by chance upon a solid tuft. I should have brought the blackthorn that I had bought from Cathy's shop, to test the ground. That knobby, crooked walking-stick-cum-cudgel was clearly indispensable to that terrain.

I didn't exactly know where I was going. Underbrush made an obstacle course out of the swampy land, and the teeming rain and mist blanked out all but the few surrounding feet. Trying to identify the toughest clumps for stepping stones, I pushed ahead.

The next minute I froze, one foot extended over the rim of a deep brown pit which yawned suddenly out of a heavy patch of mist. I grabbed for the nearest bush to save myself. It happened to be a thorn bush, and for a moment I warmed the air with oaths.

Sucking the punctures in my palm and fingers, I gazed appalled into the pit. The texture of its shiny black sides suggested small bricks laid in herringbone pattern. It dawned on me these must be the marks made by the slane, the special spade for cutting peat. From the top layer of its growing surface, bound with sphagnum moss, down to its lower levels of dense brown sod compressed for eons almost to a state of lignite or brown coal, the cutting was deeper than the deep end of a swimming pool. The bottom of the trench was filled with coffee-colored water filmed with an oily sheen over which hovered a squadron of leggy crane flies. Heaven knew how much deeper the trench might go below the water level. That dumb cyclist should have warned me—he must have known that it was there. If I'd fallen over the edge, I not only could have hurt myself, I might have drowned.

Were there more hazards up ahead? Should I go on? I had every reason not to. I was shaken by the unsuspected hole. I was a miserable mess, my levis splashed and soaked, my anorak smeared and dripping. Above all, I was chilled to the bone, my face pinched. It was as cold as any midwinter day I'd ever known in California.

Besides, the area beyond the hole looked very questionable. It was bumpy and uneven, covered with heath, low brush like cranberry. The stems of yellow-flowered plants with juicy leaves resembled drinking straws. Even in my inexperience, it struck me as the flora of a virgin bog. If it was, how dangerous was the stuff?

My mind flashed on bog-butter, stored centuries ago in

the cool, airless bog to keep it fresh, and sunk from sight till discovered by some recent turf-cutter. I flashed next on the bog-people preserved a thousand or so years in the body-pickling chemicals of peat, the skin of their squashed faces as tanned and tough as saddle bags, their hair still tied in swabian knots. I'd be an idiot to go on.

But there, on the other hand, behind the veil of rain and trees, lay the tower, beckoning. Like some handsome but amoral person, its attraction blinded you to danger. You couldn't care less what harm it boded as long as you got close.

Mustering courage, I made a sidetrack to try advancing from another angle. The bouncy cover squelched and quivered but held my weight. I began to feel more optimistic.

The next second I was bemired up to my ankles.

Oh, Lord. What did I do now?

Through swirls of low-lying mist I glimpsed reeds and other signs of wetter ground. It would be the height of folly to continue.

When I tried to pull one foot out of the sticky, noisy suck, I felt my deck shoe pull away. The foot came free without the shoe. Going down again in the struggle for balance, it sank even farther into the ooze, up to my calf.

"Cool it," I told myself. "Keep your finger off the panic button and you'll be all right."

Casting around for something to hold on to, I grabbed a root protruding from the saturated soil. But pulling myself out of the morass, I went down even deeper in another spot.

That second, a baby rabbit darted out of the underbrush. Its natural instincts must have been scrambled by terror of whatever was pursuing it, for it streaked into the treacherous bog and was trapped instantly like a fly in molasses. Abetted by the tiny creature's floundering frenzy, the bog closed around it like an anemone around a water snail. Before my horror-fascinated eyes, the furry head sank out of sight.

Now I was really frightened. Only a few steps farther back lay firmer ground. But I was terrified to try returning. One false move and I'd be in out of my depth.

I just stood there, petrified, sick with myself for not having exercised a modicum of common sense. I shouldn't have been so silly as to pass up Padraic Herlihy's offer to escort me. I shouldn't have been so trusting of that passing cyclist. I should have been more patient and waited for a better day. I should have gone back for my shillelagh. I was a stupid, reckless fool.

In the middle of this inner tirade, I heard a nasty grating sound like a . . . like an animal's snarl. Alarm pyramiding on alarm, I peered in the direction from which the snarl had come, suddenly, pricklingly afraid that it could only have issued from the creature that had chased the rabbit to its doom.

There, between the bushes, without chain, muzzle or master, crouched the hairless hound.

IO

He apparently spotted me at the same time I spotted him. For he broke into frenzied yapping, his body tensely bunched as though ready to spring.

I was caught between the devil and a flaming pit. The ugly, muscled body quivered only a few feet away, yet I didn't dare move lest I go deeper in the mire.

But the dog took no more than a few slinking steps toward me and stopped dead. Though still in the clutches of a vicious rage, he apparently knew the perils of the bog. It saved me from his bared fangs for the moment.

We stood glaring at each other, neither of us daring to make a move. But he had only the bog to fear. I was cornered, back against the wall.

There were other complications. My feet felt frozen, especially the foot without its shoe. If by some fluke I found a way to make a dash for it, my feet might be too numb to carry me. Yet make a dash for it was what I'd very shortly have to do. The level of the bog had risen at least an inch against my calf since I first ploughed into it. I was slowly sinking. But if I did manage to flounder my way out, I faced an imminent mauling. My only hope was that the dog would tire and give up. I was almost desperate enough to wish another poor helpless rabbit would pop out of its hole and entice him after it.

But the dog just lay there, tense and watchful, intent on outlasting me, absolute master of my fate.

It must have been several anxiety-racked minutes later that I heard a whistle. I didn't dare hope it was anything but the call of a bird. But when it was repeated, the dog's ears pricked. He shimmied back a length and got up on all fours.

I called: "Help. Whoever's there, please come."

A man's voice came back: "Where are you?"

"Here. Here. Stuck in the bog."

I guessed who it would be before he loomed in view. His stocky form appeared around the misty edge of drizzled bushes, his lecherous face split with a sadistic grin.

"Well, well," Herlihy said, tipping back his cloth cap in a gesture of derisive comment. "What do we have here?"

"I'd appreciate it," I said, "if you'd save the comedy and come and help me."

It was plain he savored my predicament. He made no attempt to get me out, but just stood there, his thumbs hooked in the pockets of his baggy pants. "What do you think you're doing out there in that muck?"

It was such a stupid question, I had to bite back a sarcastic answer. I was dependent on his good graces for a helping hand. "With your dog sitting there snarling, I was afraid to move."

"How did you get there in the first place?"

I said defiantly: "I was trying to reach the tower."

The grin faded, but his eyes remained narrowed, not in derision but suspicion now. "Why didn't you come and let me take you like I offered to?"

He made me angry, making no move toward me, scolding and cross-examining me as if I was a trespasser and in no need of aid. I said: "There's no law says I can't go on my own, is there?"

He didn't respond, but just continued standing where he was, squinting at me through slitted eyes, his mouth working as though he was eating the inside of his cheeks.

I said hoarsely: "Look, are you going to help me out, or aren't you?"

"What's so important about yon tower?"

"At least throw me a stick. I can prod my own way out."

He began to rip a branch off a nearby bush. "Here, Buller," he told the bristling dog squatting beside him, "take this to the lady, boy."

"No, please," I begged. "Keep that beast away from me."

He gave a deep wobbling belly laugh, and threw down the broken branch with a triumphant extravagance of force. Having made me cry uncle, he was willing now to come and help me. He ploughed toward me in his gum boots, striding through the thick mud with the casualness of one well-accustomed to its nature. His boldness clued me that there was less danger in the bog than I had feared, and I started scrambling out under my own steam. But he shouted harshly: "Stand still, or you'll be in over your neck."

Terrified, I froze until he got to me. When he reached my side he grabbed me roughly by the arm and almost lifted me onto what proved to be a limestone outcrop several feet away. I cried out at the pain of bruised flesh, and shook myself free while he balanced beside me laughing contemptuous gusts of breath that smelled of decaying teeth and puffy gums.

I longed to say something cutting, but belated good sense warned me to tread warily with him. So I said instead: "All the same, I'm glad you happened by."

"It's just luck I did," he said. "I wouldn't have been within a mile of here, except I'm off to fetch the bull."

"The bull," I said, recording one more menace to my health and safety. The hairless dog sat quivering a dozen yards away, baring teeth which looked as yellow as its owner's.

He chuckled, making a coarse gesture. "To put it to my cows."

I turned abruptly toward the higher ground. Since the mud had claimed one of my shoes, I must get back to the camper and head for base as soon as possible. And in such filthy weather, if I had any sense, I'd stay put once I got there.

Behind me I heard the dog growl. Then I heard Herlihy say: "If you still want to go by the tower, I'll take you there right now."

I hesitated. My curiosity had actually been sharpened by the setbacks. Half turning, I said cautiously: "How do you get over there?"

"If you want to keep your feet dry, you'll come over yonder across my field and take the path."

"Do you mean that that's the only safe way in?"

"It is."

I pulled a reed, silently weighing this disclosure. It didn't make sense that there was no easy access to the tower. Splitting the green tube, I scraped out the inside with my thumb nail. When I let it go, the compressed pith sprang, intact, into a long, rubbery white worm. I asked: "How far does your land extend?"

He pointed to the left, away from the tower toward his farm. "You see those trees over yonder?"

"Not that way. I mean this way."

He chewed his cheek, then flicked his head toward the tower and to the other side of it. "My cattle graze as far as Lowry's fence and over to the road."

"Some of the land must go with the tower."

He stared queerly at me. "I already told you. It's on the mountain."

"I'm not sure what that means."

His brows bunched with irritation. "The mountain's free for all. It's land that doesn't belong to anybody."

Trapped by exasperation at his obtuseness into going further than intended, I said: "Some of it must."

He jumped on me with arrogant impatience. "Why must it?"

In a sudden reflex of retaliation, I let the warning that my built-in buzzer had been sounding go unheeded. "Some of it happens to be ours."

He looked as if I had clobbered him with a two-by-four. "What do you mean?"

It was too late to regret my impulse. I justified it by telling myself that sooner or later he'd have to know it anyway. "My grandfather bought the tower."

His face was a study in incredulity. "Bought the tower?!" he said.

"That's right."

His upper lip twitched. "But that's ridiculous. It's all common land."

"Not according to the deed my grandfather possesses."

He looked in the direction of the tower, then back at me, then at the tower again. His mouth hung open, catching rain. "Why would anybody want to buy it? What good is it?"

"He plans to use it as a summer residence."

He made a sound of harsh contempt. "A summer residence! It's just a ruin."

"That's what I'm interested in finding out."

"If that was why you wanted to go and see it, you could have saved yourself this trouble."

"What do you mean?"

"You can't get in it. It's boarded up."

"Boarded up? Why?"

"Because it's dangerous."

"Who says?"

"No one has lived in it for centuries. It's only fit for cattle."

An hour or so ago that was precisely the condition I had prayed for it to be in. Now, perversely, I felt sharp disappointment. "Still," I said, keeping a mild manner so as not to seem to doubt his word, "I'd like to judge what it would take to put it back into commission."

"It would take a fortune."

"Maybe. But maybe not."

"In any case, whatever it would cost, there wouldn't hardly be much point," he said. "It's sitting in a bog."

I had nothing useful to respond to this.

He said: "There isn't any way to reach it except across my land."

I said: "It's got to have it's own way in."

"Why does it?"

"People *did* build castles to *live* in them. Which means they were bound to have had some way to get in and out."

He laughed mockingly.

"What's so funny?" I said angrily.

"The last people who lived in this castle owned all the land as far as eye can see. They could come and go at will. But that was hundreds of years ago. When I bought my last strip, it cut off the ruin entirely."

"Nobody would sell a place that didn't have an access," I said with more scorn than I actually felt. "It at least must have a right-of-way across adjacent land."

"Well, it'll not be across my fields, I'll warrant you," he rapped, calling the dog to heel with a sharp jerk of his hand. The beast came like a well-programmed robot. But there was nothing robotlike about the tight coil of quivering muscles under the rain-gleaming skin.

With as much crispness as I could muster from my rapidly dwindling confidence, I said: "We'll have to see about that."

Softly sinister, he said: "We will indeed."

II

There was absolutely nothing more to say, so I limped off on my one shod foot toward the camper, painfully aware of what a ridiculous spectacle I must be putting on for Herlihy. I was relieved when the dense crush of undergrowth and reduced visibility soon screened me from his sight.

As I hobbled along, I kept turning over in my mind the implications of this new turn in events. If Padraic Herlihy was to be believed, the tower was a dead loss on two counts—it was inaccessible as well as derelict. My father and my uncles had been right: my grandfather *had* wasted a good hunk of his life savings on a clutch of addled eggs. How better to describe a ruin, charming as it was, stuck in the center of an impassable bog?

But as I turned into the lane, the hedge thick with dripping white clusters of yarrow and cow parsnip, it came to me that perhaps all was not lost. The realtor could be forced to give us back our money for having misrepresented Tur Bran Beag as livable, and if that didn't work, there surely was a principle in law allowing the buyer the right to void a contract where it turned out there was no entry to the property. With these two solid grounds to claim a refund, no one need ever know I had personally been turned off the tower by Mrs. Rory's spooky tales and a repulsive character at a neighboring farm.

Back in the relative warmth and comfort of the camper, with more of my psychic stamina returned, I began having second thoughts. Perhaps I had been too ready to believe what Herlihy had told me. As I changed into a pair of dry shoes which I kept handy in the camper, I felt less ready to condemn the unknown realtor on such flimsy hearsay evidence. As far as access went, the smallest little pathway of reasonably solid ground would be enough to get one in, if only one knew where to tread. Why should I take Herlihy's word that there was no passage through the bog? And even if there weren't, mightn't a right-of-way exist across his land that he didn't know about? Maybe, indeed, he *knew* about one and his bullying tactics were designed to stop me finding out!

That, I thought, as I started the car and pulled out into the lane, raised another interesting question. Why was Herlihy so hostile? Why had there been such a sharp deterioration in his attitude? Yesterday he had been making insinuations about "hanging up his hat" with me. If he was the aggressive bachelor he had wanted to make out he was, and if I was the good American catch he had implied, why wouldn't he have welcomed me as a potential neighbor with open arms? I wasn't being immodest about my charms, but simply trying to psych out why such a rapid alienation had occurred. Only mildly curious at first of my interest in the tower, he had become increasingly suspicious, and, finally, when I claimed ownership, had turned nasty to the point of driving me away.

Still, a pity I hadn't kept my mouth shut a bit longer. I really hadn't played my cards very well. I should have accepted his offer to take me to the tower before I showed my hand. I could have somehow taken a peek inside the boarding to satisfy myself it really was a gutted shell. If it turned out to be beyond repair, the matter would have closed right there, no decisions, no self-recriminations. Me and my impulsive tongue. We'd really blown it, hadn't we. Just for the stupid satisfaction of knocking some of the spots off him.

By this time I had reached the village. A few seconds more and I pulled up at the side door of the Rorys, looking forward to a soothing tub. But before I could indulge my yearning, I would have to find out how to light the complicated water heater in the bathroom.

I went around to the front door of the post office to ask Mr. Rory for a briefing. It was the first time I had been in the business section of the house. It turned out to be less post office than general store, the government office occupying only one corner of the premises. The shop offered just about everything from apples to zippers, with the major emphasis on groceries. In a large striped apron made from a tough fabric like old-fashioned mattress ticking, Mr. Rory presided in front of shelves crammed with canned goods of many sizes and varieties. Between us lay a counter loaded with candies, biscuits and loaves of bread. In the small space between displays kept free for service, Mr. Rory was putting up an order in a wicker basket. The store was empty of customers right then. As I went in he was softly whistling "Danny Boy."

His face lit up to see me. "Hello, Jan girl. You look a trifle damp. Have you been exploring?"

"Those are both understatements," I said wryly, and filled him in with a few brief sentences.

As I described my final unpleasant exchange with Padraic Herlihy, Mr. Rory rubbed a hand over his frowning face: "I'm sorry about that," he said. "Padraic is not known for being very sociable."

"You can say that again."

"It is not safe to put his back up. He is not a stable man."

"There was no way to avoid it."

"If you had only let me know where you were going, I'd have warned you to keep clear of him."

"Ah, well," I said. "Sooner or later he had to know the tower is ours. Better sooner. What if I hadn't told him? Think how mad he'd be when he found out. It would've looked mighty fishy if I'd kept it dark."

"You may be right," Mr. Rory said, meticulously folding down a paper bag and tucking in the ends. "If you hadn't come out and told him right away, he might have thought you were afraid of him. A lot of people are."

Mr. Rory went into a side room, emerging with two greaseproof packages of cheese and butter for the basket. He checked them off a list penciled on an envelope.

I said: "Why is he so hostile?"

"They're that kind of people. It's in their blood. His father was the same."

"It's more than that," I said. "He was friendly enough until I mentioned we owned the tower. Then he turned meaner than that awful dog of his."

Mr. Rory handed me a crisp Marie biscuit from a large tin box into which he dipped to fill a paper sack. "Padraic has probably been making free with the land around the tower these many years. He'd not relish having to pull in his horns."

"There's not much land about it," I said, nibbling the cookie. "It's mostly bog."

"Even bogs have value when you only have a thirty- or forty-acre farm to work. In good weather they dry out a bit and make good grazing."

"Now there's a thought. If the sun would just come out and dry it up, I could reach the tower without having to depend on him."

He looked ruefully out of the rain-distorted panes. "I am

fancying that won't be very soon," he said. "And even when the weather clears, you can't depend on the sun shining long enough to do much drying out over an extensive area."

A bright idea flashed through my mind. If I had learned nothing else from my competitive father, I had learned to turn defects to advantages. If there was not enough dry land to cross, there was plenty of the other stuff. "Hey. Why couldn't I row a boat across the lake?"

His mouth smiled, but his eyes looked troubled. "Herlihy wouldn't take that too kindly, would he? I mean wouldn't it look as if you were deliberately defying him?"

"Why should I let him tyrannize me? It's our property. We paid for it."

He hunted up the sleeve of his white shirt and fished out a handkerchief to mop his brow. "Look, love," he said. "Go warily. He could be dangerous. To give it to you straight, it is gossiped that he makes potheen."

"Potheen?" I repeated, puzzled.

"Poteen," he said, as if the subtle difference in pronunciation would clear it up for me.

"What's that?"

"You never heard of it? Illicit spirits. They make it in a poit'in or a pot still, hence its name."

"Ah," I said, the dime dropping. "Moonshine. You think maybe he makes it in the tower?"

"I'm not thinking anything. I'm just telling you the rumors that go round this neighborhood. They say that's where to go to get a drop."

"So that's his little game," I said. It would certainly account for why he'd tried so hard to put me off the place.

"Don't go jumping to conclusions, or you'll make me sorry I mentioned it."

"Oh, I'm not jumping to conclusions, Mr. Rory. But if

Herlihy *does* have a still set up in our tower, he'll have to move it out of there."

Mr. Rory looked alarmed. But the door was opening upon a customer and he could do no more than murmur: "Go easy, girlie. We don't want to see you come to any harm."

12

I suppose I have enough of the Irish in me to be called headstrong, though I prefer to think of myself as "tenacious." When I get an idea in my head I am like hounds after a fox. I have to chase the thing to earth.

It was like that with my notion of rowing a boat across the lake to reach the tower. I had to get inside the place like now. Not that I was totally heedless of Mr. Rory's warnings: I conceded to myself that I should wait perhaps until twilight to take the trip across. In the meantime I had to locate a suitable vessel to get me there.

After I figured out how to run the ingenious Rube Goldberg monster called a "geyser," I had a quick bath, and changed into dry slacks and sweater. Then, after a very late lunch of homemade bread, sweet red tomatoes and strong cheese, I headed to the cove below the village.

In view of Mr. Rory's quite obvious apprehension, it seemed wisest not to ask him for directions, but to scout out the situation for myself. What I needed was a rentable small boat with some way to transport it to the scene. That didn't seem to be too tall an order in a coastal village.

But down on a beach not much larger than a tennis court,

there was only one craft in sight, a fishing boat that was much too long and cumbersome to consider rowing it across the lake alone, much less hauling it by road behind my camper—even if I could find a trailer to accommodate it, the remotest of this sequence of unlikely possibilities.

There was one other person on the rain-shrouded beach, a boy of eight or nine to judge from his physique, but several years older when you looked into his eyes. Shrugged into a threadbare jacket much too large for him, he had a runt-of-the-litter look about him. Between the short, shabby pants, held up by suspenders, and the large, worn, sockless boots, spindly knock-kneed legs appeared. He was leading a small, bedraggled donkey from whose sway back hung traditional basket-woven side-creels loaded with wrack, a tangled mass of seaweed washed in by the high waves. From time to time the boy stooped to pick up a stick of flotsam, and threw it for a mangy-looking terrier to chase.

"Hey," I called. "Would you happen to know where I could find a boat?"

He hesitated several seconds. Then leaving the donkey standing, he dropped the leading rope and came halfway to meet me. His eyes were of such watery blue they seemed to liquefy before my very glance. Pale lashes sticking straight out from red-rimmed eyes in a pale face gave him an albino look, but a heavy seasoning of freckles on nose and cheeks nullified that diagnosis. His gaze was straight, his face expressionless—a deadpan poker face, as though he were accustomed to concealing what he felt. His hair was very red.

I said again as I drew close: "Do you know where I can find a boat?"

He nodded in the direction of the fishing smack I had just passed.

"Too big," I said. "I need something I can manage on my own."

The dog had now approached, perhaps to see why his game had stopped. With his wiry terrier's coat plastered close to him by rain and foam, he was all skin and bones, as stunted and undernourished as his master. But he barked cockily and wagged his lavish unmutilated tail, shedding a shower of brine and sand on me.

"Cute pooch," I told the boy, bending down to scratch the terrier's head. The rough hair of his coat was matted with wet sand.

"You could look in the next cove," he said, pointing east beyond a headland.

"Are there boats there?"

"I saw a rowboat once."

"Do you know who it belongs to?"

He shook his head.

It looked a good mile down the sands to the jutting rocks. But since the next cove had to be closer to the tower than was Dunderg's, I'd be better off if I could find a rental there. I told the boy: "I guess I'll take a walk around there and find out. Thanks for the information."

His puckish face did not return my smile. But the eyes grew brighter, like a sun glade momentarily appearing on water.

When I had gone twenty or so feet beyond him, he called out after me in a piping voice: "If it isn't on the sands, look in the holes."

The rain still slanted down in a gentle drizzle. The sea was roily, shooting long, racing scallops of lather up the narrow beaches toward low cliffs green-capped to the very edges. Meeting no one, I walked across the honey-beige sands and iridescent rocks of that wild stretch of Atlantic coastline, filled again with the ambivalence I'd felt ever since I set eyes on the tower. If only all the ifs were ironed out, what a marvelous vacation spot this place could be, with beach and ocean as well as lake and mountains on our doorstep.

Pushing against the squalling wind I rounded the small headland. The second cove was also empty of both people and boats. But back in the cliffs beyond the sand and shingle were several large black holes. Perhaps a boat was stashed inside of one of them.

A group of black-headed gulls flapped up out of rocky crannies as I stooped to enter the closest of the holes. Then a voice rang out. Startled by the imperious shout and the scrabble of scared wings, I stopped dead under the arch of rock.

"Don't go in there," the voice shouted. "Stay out."

Striding toward me from the opposite direction from which I had come was a tall, powerful man with the good looks of a classic Irish face. The cut of his putty-colored pants and jacket gave him a military aura, enhanced by his athletic bearing and the note of authority in his voice. Although it was not the uniform of a Garda, an Irish policeman, he very well might be some other kind of official.

As he came closer, his stern look melted into an engaging grin. "Sorry if I startled you."

"What's the problem? Why can't I go in there?"

"Those caves are dangerous."

"Dangerous? Why?"

"They've been undermined by the pounding of the ocean."

I looked at the gaping holes lying far back from the water's edge. "The ocean doesn't reach them, does it?"

"It's low tide now," he said. "At high tide, especially spring tide, the water runs right in there. That's how they were formed."

"Ah, yes. I see."

"The roofs are ready to fall in at any minute. The merest vibration could set them off."

"Thanks for warning me. But what would I have done if there was nobody around?"

With four well-cared-for fingers he combed his hair behind his ear. "It's well known around these parts to steer clear of this stretch of coast."

"That's okay if you're local. But how about strangers? Don't you think they ought to put up warning notices for people like me?"

His dark-fringed, smoky eyes were taking careful stock of me, though as unpointedly as possible. "I don't suppose anybody ever thought about it. We don't have many tourists along here, you see."

"I'm really not a tourist," I said crisply, peeved by this customary display of Irish insularity.

"With that accent you can't tell me you're from anywhere *this* side of the Atlantic."

"That doesn't stop a person coming to reside here."

"Reside here?" he said sharply. "I know practically everybody in a twenty or thirty mile radius. You're not from *these* parts, that's for sure."

"I am now."

His curiosity intensified the smoky luster of his eyes. "Did you marry somebody?"

I laughed at his male chauvinism. "Women don't have to get *married* these days to move around. After all, this *is* the late twentieth century. I'm free and single."

"You've come to work here? Teach perhaps?"

"We've bought a place here for a summer home."

The wind kicked up a little squall and he squinted his eyes protectively. He said mildly: "Have you now. Where at?"

Since he had claimed to know the neighborhood, he

might corroborate the name. "Do you know Tur Beag?"

"Tur Beag?" he repeated, frowning. "And where is that?"

"Doesn't the name ring a bell?"

He shook his head. "I've never heard of it."

"How about the name Tur Bran?"

A small flicker of his eyes told me he'd connected. "What about it?"

"That's apparently Tur Beag."

He rubbed a large brown hand slowly down hip and thigh. "Let me get this straight. You're supposed to have bought that tower for a summer place? Is that what you implied?"

"That's right."

He laughed, showing strong, even teeth. "Someone saw you coming."

I joined him in ironic chorus when he added: "It's just a ruin."

I said dryly: "Ruin or not, it's ours."

"Who's *we* and *ours*? You mean your parents?"

"My grandfather."

He shrugged his strong, broad shoulders. "It's not even on private land, I didn't think."

"We have a deed to say it is."

"Probably not worth the paper it's written on."

"We'll have to see about that."

There was a long pause during which he occupied himself brushing rain out of his curly, well-cut hair. He said casually: "I suppose you've seen inside it?"

"Actually I haven't. That's what I'm working on."

"Ah, yes. If I remember, they blocked it up."

"Who's they?"

"The local health authorities, I should imagine."

"Well, they'll have to *un*block it, won't they?"

He said: "Last time I saw inside, it was full of water rats."

I suppressed a shudder and said coolly: "So poison bait will lick them."

"There were bats, too," he said. "They get tangled in your hair."

"Bats don't like to live where people live. They'll leave when we take over."

"You can't exterminate the ghosts, however," he said, smiling enigmatically. "They like having people around to haunt."

I dashed the rain out of my face exasperatedly. "Why is everyone so anxious to put me off the place?"

He cocked his head as though hearing a strange noise. "Who's everyone?"

"Like the Herlihys," I said.

"Which Herlihy is that?"

"Padraic Herlihy, the farmer near the tower."

He lifted his dark brows in recognition. "It's not a question with me of trying to put you off," he said. "I am after telling you the truth. What you do with the information is none of my affair."

"It's just I like to judge things for myself," I said, femininely contrite so that he didn't read my independence as an affront to his male ego. "I *would* like to look it over."

"Padraic Herlihy will take you by. He'd be only too delighted." He grinned his wide, attractive grin, full of teasing innuendo.

"Thank you very much, but I'd rather go alone. As a matter of fact, I'm trying to find a boat to rent—"

"A boat?" he said, surprised.

"That's what I was looking for when you warned me off those holes."

His heavy brows were almost touching. "Why would you be looking for one here?"

"Some little kid told me he had seen one over in this cove."

"What little kid is that?"

"Just someone I met casually in the cove below Dunderg. I don't know who he is."

"He's dreaming. No one would even think to run a boat from here."

"Why not?"

"There's a nasty riptide off that headland. It's death to small craft."

"How do you know?"

"I run a boat up and down these waters. There's not a current I don't know. Besides, my cousin lives here. That's his house up there. His fields run right down to the edge. I know this spot like the back of my hand."

"You have a boat," I said excitedly. "Where is it berthed?"

"Back at the harbor."

"Would you rent it out to me?"

"What do you want it for?"

"To row across Lake Bran to see the tower."

He laughed so hard, he could say nothing for a minute. Irritated, I said: "What's so funny?"

Wiping his eyes, he said: "She's a forty-foot seagoing boat. For deliveries along the coast. Our family business is farm equipment and supplies."

Not the least deflated, I motioned up the cliff: "Does your cousin have a rowboat?"

"Not he," he said. Then, as a joking afterthought: "Unless you count the curragh in his cowshed."

"A curragh?" I said, imitating the sound without knowing what the word would look like, much less mean.

He nodded. "His father-in-law brought it from the Aran Islands when he came ashore to live with them."

"Will it still float?"

His fine eyes crinkled. "I don't know why it wouldn't."

"Would he rent it to me, do you think?"

His eyes still danced. "He'd be honored to have you borrow it, I'm sure."

"I wish you'd take me seriously."

At least he straightened out his mouth. "Well, it won't hurt to ask him, will it? Let's go and see."

13

Across the beach, we headed up a narrow track along a sort of a gully in the cliff. Tall grasses and thick bushes gleamed with a million crystal seeds of water which burst on touch, soaking us wetter than we already were. As we climbed I looked around. Down below, the violent waters surged and receded over rocky ledges which rose in giant steps, carrying the eye to a small protuberance nestled in a cleft. Resembling a beehive, its stones matched the gray rocks surrounding it, but were obviously laid and mortared by human hands. The beehive, surmounted by a cross, must be a holy place, perhaps a holy well.

On the clifftop, a lone cottage stood. We let ourselves through a twig and wicker gate hinged on wire hoops and approached the door. A woman, toothless though still on the younger side of thirty-five, answered our knock. A brood of dark-haired children gathered around her, the smallest tugging at her flowered apron. Clearly surprised, she said: "Why, Sean, what are you doing here today? I thought—"

But what she thought remained untold when she caught sight of me. She said: "Come in out of the rain, the both of you. And make yourselves at home."

I followed Sean across the threshold where he patted heads, squeezed tiny shoulders and chattered with the children. Then he told his cousin-in-law: "This lady's looking for a boat to rent. I thought upon your Dadda's curragh. Do you think it could still be seaworthy?"

She looked from me to Sean and back to me again, as though seeking an explanation for the strange request. "The big one is long gone. Would it be the little river curragh you are wanting?" And when I nodded enthusiastically, she said: "If you wait a minute, we'll go over to the byre to look at it."

Crossing to the fireplace, she stooped to lift the lid of an iron kettle suspended from a pothook on an iron crane to nest among the smoldering turf. A delicious smell of onions, carrots and cabbage wafted through the shabby room before she closed the pot again. Telling the children to behave themselves while she was gone, she donned an overcoat and a man's soft hat from a peg behind the door.

"Himself is over in the other meadow," she informed Sean as she led us across the muddy yard where a couple of bedraggled geese were pecking worms.

"No need to bother him just yet," Sean said. "The curragh may not serve at all."

The small oval boat was propped diagonally across the far wall of the byre, which at that moment housed no cows. It looked a nice manageable size for me to row across a lake, and my spirits soared.

But walking closer, I could see beneath the layer of thick dust that it was a very primitive affair made of tarred canvas stretched taut like skin over a wooden frame. I was reminded of Michael's talk of coracles, and recognized the affinity of curraghs both in kind and name.

In the dim light from the door left open for that purpose, I scrutinized it closely. The canvas skin looked cracked and brittle. "What do you think?" I asked.

Sean made a gesture with his hands indicating perhaps yes but perhaps no. "You'll have to try it out and see."

The woman said: "What do you want it for?"

Sean said: "To row across Lough Bran."

The woman looked stunned. "Why would you be wanting to do that?"

"To reach the tower," I said.

"Why can't you go to her by land?"

"There's a marsh all around it."

"The lake is very deep," she said, and appeared to be on the point of saying something else. But instead she shot her cousin-in-law a queer look. Then her eyes went past him to the door. A man stood there, so tall and wide that he blocked the gusts of rain blowing through the opening, and darkened the inside of the byre. He had obviously heard all for he said: "She's quite watertight."

When he came and slapped the curragh's side as though to show how stout it was, I asked him: "What about these cracks?"

"They're nothing. Just surface drying. She's a good snug boat."

14

I would have welcomed an offer from the attractive, competent Sean to come with me to launch the river curragh. But he was already late for an appointment even before he lent a hand to load and rope the light shell on my camper roof. The moment it was done he had to hurry off, but not before he thoughtfully arranged to have his cousin's eldest son accompany me.

The gangly adolescent followed on his bicycle. With very little help from me, he lifted the light curragh off the camper and slid it down the muddy bank. As soon as it was nestled in the reeds, he touched his forelock, mumbled something about having to get back to finish mucking out the barn, and pedaled off.

Although it had been all my own idea, it was a bit unnerving to be left alone facing the prospect of rowing an unfamiliar boat across a body of untried water. Still, I would not have wanted the boy along. I remained none too confident the boat could safely hold me, much less the combination of our weights. Moreover, there was no question that investigation of the tower was a job to be handled on my own.

I surveyed the situation from the muddy bank. A misty drizzle all but obscured the far shore of the lough. The tower appeared as a blurred, ghostly outline through the fuzzy swirl. Should I attempt a crossing now, or wait for the rain to ease a little? But I might have to wait indefinitely. Hadn't Mr. Rory warned me that the bad weather might go on for days?

Despite the rain, the surface of the water seemed smooth enough. And the drizzle was really an advantage, concealing me from the hostile notice of Padraic Herlihy. Besides, austere and beautiful behind its tantalizing veil, the tower waited. I was consumed with curiosity.

I slithered down the bank. Sticky goo coated my feet, hands, legs and seat. Bobbing like Moses' little ark among the bullrushes, the boat seemed flimsy and unstable. But I managed to climb aboard without upsetting it.

When I poled out of the reeds, something flew up out of the dense growth of water plants, startling me enough to rock the boat. It wobbled uncertainly for several minutes, but steadied down as I distributed my weight.

As the shore receded and I hit a rhythmic stroke, I congratulated myself on making a good start. The boat handled well, and I began looking forward to my visit to the tower. Ever since I'd seen it, it had kept stringing me between desire and revulsion. Right now the accumulation of frustrated efforts to get close to its mysterious beauty almost made me feel I wanted to possess it.

But as I oared toward the middle of the lough, it began raining harder. In another minute it turned into a heavy downpour, pocking the surface of the lake and needling my face. In short order the rainstorm turned into a nasty squall, tossing the curragh like a paper boat. The wind came mostly from ahead, blowing into my face so that I made very little headway. Perhaps it would be smarter to turn back—except I was no longer sure which way "back" might be. The boat kept turning, almost as though it rode the outer limits of a whirlpool which might soon exert an irreversible pull on it.

So little could I see through the slanting rain, I was like the newly blind. Making matters worse, the rain began collecting in the bottom of the boat. Why hadn't I had the foresight to bring along a can or bucket as a bail? What an idiot—always going off half-cocked, never sufficiently prepared, failing to think the consequences through.

But this was no time for self-reproach. The boat was filling very fast. Faster than seemed logical even for a storm. Dear God. It couldn't be the rain alone that was responsible for such a volume. The curragh must be taking on water. I should have trusted my own intuition that it wasn't seaworthy.

Without even looking, my eyes had caught the spot where it was leaking. A crack in the canvas was opening beside one of the ribs. In fascinated horror, I watched it widening perceptibly. The lake poured in at such a rate that even if I'd thought to bring a pail, it would have been no use.

A riot of disconnected thoughts raced through my mind. Among them, my recollection of the woman saying that the lough was very deep. Her husband should have had more sense than to let me loose on it in such a ramshackle affair. He hadn't even known if I could swim. Though what good would knowing how to swim be if there really was a whirlpool or some kind of rip of conflicting currents in the middle of the lake? Well, I'd know soon enough. The little craft was swamping fast. In a moment it must sink.

Groaning a prayer, I plunged into the lake.

The ice-cold water shocked the breath out of my body. Gasping, I sucked in water, and coughed and floundered, totally disoriented, barely managing to keep afloat.

But the panic-quelling mechanisms that had been drilled

into me from early childhood by parents, teachers and camp leaders, came to my aid. I made myself relax, and almost immediately recovered my breath and found my stroke. Not having the least idea which way I was headed, I sliced through the water, praying I wasn't headed toward some guzzling vortex. The water's temperature was crippling, but I continued swimming, sheer doggedness eking out my waning strength.

After an age, I saw the fringy edges of the lake loom out of the rain and mist. Tremendously relieved, I reached out and grabbed a handful of the reeds and hauled myself ashore.

But my feet did not meet terra firma. There was more of that awful sludge to navigate. Like a recurring nightmare, my feet again sank into it up to my ankles. But this time the mud was not even the consistency to hold my legs erect. As I slid down in it, I scrabbled to hang on to the rushes, but they came out by the roots in handfuls under the strain.

I cried out, not for help, not even purposefully, but in a fury of frustration. Miraculously, however, my cry brought an answering call. Out of the swirl above me materialized a scarecrow with a puny face. As fast as it appeared, it disappeared again behind the curtain of the rain, leaving me groping like a wasp in jelly, powerless to extricate myself.

But in another moment a rope flew through the air toward me, whipped expertly almost right into my hands. When I had caught the end, the rope grew taut. With a glutinous plop my feet wrenched free. A few more yards of heavy ploughing through viscous glue and I at last touched firmer ground. I leaned exhaustedly but thankfully against the wet trunk of a tree.

There, a few feet away, stood my rescuer. It was the child I had met that morning in the cove. He was coiling up the rope, the other end of which was tied around the neck of his poor, mangy donkey. Together this half-starved, patient little pair had pulled me free.

15

What would I have done if those guardian angels hadn't happened by? Through absurdly chattering teeth I tried to tell the boy how much I valued the help he'd given me. But, as I gathered from his twitching face and the way he ducked his head, I only ended by embarrassing him. He did, however, let me shake his small, thin hand, and I gave the donkey several caressing pats before he led her off in the opposite direction from where I had to go to get the camper.

All the way back to the village, shivering as I drove, I reviewed the day's activities, especially my aborted efforts to reach the tower. If I had been superstitious, I could have believed some kind of jinx was operating to stop me reaching it.

But there was something in my nature so perverse that the greater the obstacles appeared, the more determined I became to overcome them. Nothing, however, would persuade me to try crossing the lough again. In the first place, it was highly likely that the margins were equally perilous all the way around. In the second place, I wasn't at all certain that my notion of a whirlpool in the middle of the lake had been a figment of near-hysteria. It would be taunting fate to repeat that escapade. There had to be another way to see that ruin.

That evening, after I was warm and dry again, and after I had hungrily wolfed down Mrs. Rory's supper of home-cured ham tasting deliciously of peat-smoke and served with buttered french-cut green beans, I took another crack at trying to resolve the problem. While Mr. and Mrs. Rory worked on their accounts, I reread the description in the *Book of Ancient Monuments*. But it had nothing to tell about such crucial matters as rights of egress and ingress, and I quickly closed it in favor of the map. There I noted that through the wood rising behind Tur Bran Beag and stretching back into the hills ran a small stream called the Derry. The thin blue line was broken and difficult to trace through an area dense with tree symbols, with hachures denoting cliffs or escarpments, and with contour lines. But it seemed to pass beside the tower at its apparent point of entry into the lake.

Remembering how the stream had washed the lower walls of Thoor Ballylee, my interest rose. What if the stream were shallow enough to wade, and its bed firm? I could pick it up somewhere in the wood and follow it down until I reached the tower, couldn't I? I at least could try.

My final action of the evening was to compose the letter to my grandfather requesting the name and address of the realtor, and copies of the correspondence that had passed between them—all items I'd believed to be included in the envelope he'd handed me before I left. I said honestly I wished to know the measurements of the lot, access, rights of way, *et cetera*. But I tried to make it sound as if this information was needed to take care of minor routine details only. I dashed off the final copy in a hurried hand, hoping it would suggest that my reason for saying nothing about the tower's condition was simply lack of time. Until I knew the score, there was no point in worrying him.

It was also necessary to allay the Rorys' fears for me, so I decided to say nothing of my newest plan. When I dropped Mrs. Rory off at Mr. Meaney's house next morning, I acted as though I planned to do some more exploring over a wider area.

In actual fact, I went first to the cottage of Sean's cousin, where I pressed on the woman the ten pounds I figured to be more than fair value for the loss of such a leaky tub. Then I swiftly doubled back to pick up a lane on the far side of the wood.

In the usual way of Irish side roads, it turned out to be no wider than a cart track, so I parked the camper and once more took to my feet. The weather had improved some over the day before, which I might have viewed as a good omen as well as a practical advantage, except that you could tell the dense clouds hovering above were only waiting their chance to drop their heavy loads.

I cut across a slope of furze and heather, startling a large chickeny bird, which rose on rapidly beating wings to skim the purple and yellow blossoms. With wings bent downward as though ready any moment to alight, it disappeared in a long glide into the mist.

My gentle grandfather's predations were confined to fishing, but my father and his brothers shot quail and chukar in the open seasons. On the basis of this flapping fowl, which I took to be a grouse, they might have been won over even to the point of putting up money for reconstruction, if circumstances had only put us in the tower.

I went down into a dip, its heathlike cover strewn with rocks, to where I thought I would pick up the stream. But there was no stream bed to be seen. I carefully picked my way transversely around the hill through thorny scrub and bramble, and again drew a total blank. Puzzled and frustrated, I must have walked a mile or more before it began to dawn on me what the broken blue line on the map might mean. It was probably due neither to imperfect printing nor to overprinting of woodland symbols after all. My limestone-happy Kris had taught me something inadvertently. Perhaps the Derry meandered somewhere far below my feet in limestone vaults. Perhaps it ran through something comparable to the underground cave that Yeats called "Raftery's cellar" between Thoor Ballylee and Coole.

With new eyes I surveyed the landscape, noting the relative baldness of the area I searched compared with the lush woods below. Surely that must mean a difference in soil, or drainage, or rock structure, or perhaps all. Lush vegetation would argue for a geologic formation more impervious to water than was limestone. If Kris could have heard my reasoning, she'd have been proud of me.

I headed downhill to the trees. When I reached the edge of the wood, a flash of movement in the shadows caught my eye. Something very fast and furry dashed out of the undergrowth straight toward me. I let out a yell and almost climbed a tree.

But the creature stopped dead within a half a dozen feet, wagged its long, incongruous tail, and lolled its silly tongue. It was the scruffy terrier I had met on the beach the previous day, giving me a buddy's welcome. I had some Marie biscuits in my pocket, and he said please like a pampered poodle. When I fed him one, he crunched ecstatically.

By this time the dog's master had emerged into the open, his freckles almost jumping from his face with apprehension in the brief instant between seeing and recognizing me.

"What do you know!" I smiled in surprised delight. "We meet again. This is getting to be quite a habit."

His lips twitched in a phantom smile.

I said: "Let me say thanks again for yesterday."

He stood awkwardly, trapped by my gaze.

To change the subject for his comfort, I said: "What are you doing here now?"

"Nothing," he said quickly. His watery eyes panned the trees and underbrush in a two-hundred-and-fifty-degree arc.

"You can tell me," I said confidentially. "It won't go any further. You're my friend."

"Looking for mushrooms," he murmured swiftly.

"Find any?"

"A few."

His lively eyes still darting everywhere like a poacher's, he beckoned with his head for me to follow. He led me to a spot a yard or so from where the stream gushed from a thicket shrouding a rocky incline. My deductions had been sound: the stream's appearance coincided with the growth of trees.

The boy said: "Look." He pointed at a pile of the most weird mushrooms I had ever seen. Accustomed to the standard domesticated pasty beige-and-tan affairs sold in grocery stores, I was startled at the wide variety of shapes and colors sitting in the middle of a red-and-white-spotted kerchief. Thin, long-stemmed things with tiny heads shading to inky purple; flat fluted brownish ones; a delicate pink branched variety resembling coral; mummy-brown umbrellas; and snuff-color buttons with cameo gills.

"Wow! Are those all edible?" I pointed to my mouth. He nodded.

"How can you tell?"

"I know."

"But they *look* like poison toadstools. How can you be certain that they're not?"

"I know," he said again. "You want to learn?"

"I'd love to. But another time. Right now there's something else I have to do."

As on the day before, he asked no questions, as though he had been trained to mind his tongue. But his thin little weasel face ached with curiosity.

I said: "I want to follow this stream downhill as far as it will go. Care to come along?"

Also as the day before, he didn't smile, but the voltage of his eyes increased.

We set off along the bank where a path of sorts had been worn by centuries of poacher-fishermen. Here and there the ground was sloppy wet and it seemed safer and more practical to wade the stream. But it was a choice of evils—the water was ice cold. In his wisdom, the dog stuck to the bank. I started in the lead, but the boy soon went ahead of me.

As we walked, I tried to find out more about him. He told me that his name was Mervin, but when I asked him if I could call him Red, the light went on behind his eyes. The vagueness and reticence which met my other questions about his home and family warned me I'd lose his confidence if I pried too much.

When I asked the names of trees and flowers, however, he was most forthcoming. A country nomad, he was obviously a born naturalist, grasping the nature of living things through the pores of his skin. I learned inside a fascinating half an hour what it would have taken me a tedious age to glean from the clearest tree and flower books.

Despite my concentration on getting to the tower, that excursion through the wood with Red was so absorbing of itself that I almost forgot time and goals. Everywhere dense ground cover grew luxuriantly from the rich bed of leaf mold whose scent permeated the clear, sweet air. Los Angeles and smoggy freeways were very far away.

We splashed together down the stream, which fell at intervals in steps, the water dropping in miniature cascades, bubbling and rippling into deep pools where, every now and then, silver scales flashed. When the gray flutter of a white-patched wood pigeon drew the eyes aloft, the shimmer of the trees was magical.

As we penetrated deeper, the wood grew darker and more mysterious. It was clearly a place not much frequented by prosaic human beings. That there was life there, however, was apparent from sudden scampers in the underbrush. I saw several gray squirrels, and even a shy pine marten that Red pointed out.

We had gone well over a mile downstream when we entered a miniature chasm between head-high rock draped with festoons of ivy, and tufted with green ferns. As I splashed toward it through the knee-deep water of the brook, I stopped dead in my tracks.

A dark hole split the lichened stone. Into this guzzling dragon's mouth the water disappeared.

I stared at it in stunned fascination, my nerve ends tingling in the primeval gloom.

The practical implications of that weird phenomenon came rushing home. "Darn it. Did you know this happened, Red?"

He nodded, his eyes anxious.

As much to myself as to him, I murmured: "But there, you had no idea what I had in mind."

Again he asked no questions with his mouth, but I answered what was in his eyes: "I was hoping the stream went by the tower."

He wrinkled his nose and raised his rabbit lip in puzzlement.

"I just wanted to go past the tower to take a look," I said, not willing to say more.

He watched me as I craned and peered into the shadows of that gulping muzzle. An awesome fall of water sounded deep inside the rock. I said: "I wonder whether we can go through this."

His red hair seemed to bristle. A white line rimmed his nostrils. He began to back upstream.

"What's up?" I said.

He continued backing until he had returned beyond the entry to the chasm.

Alarmed, I followed him. The dog was moving in cowed circles on the bank.

"Don't go," I pleaded as Red speeded up.

But he turned abruptly on his heels. At a dead tree, still sapped by frilly fungus, he dove into the underbrush.

The dog shot after him.

16

"For Heaven's sake," I said aloud, puzzled and dismayed. "Whatever could have gotten into him?" He must be just a timid country kid, easily spooked, to behave so skittishly.

I peered once more toward the grim cave into which the stream was flowing, but did not retrace my steps. I had probably, I told myself, taken the stream hypothesis as far as it would go right then. I was unwilling to admit it at that moment, but Red's reaction had unnerved me. I needed to remuster my reserves of courage before looking down that eerie hole again.

In any event, I rationalized, it might be smarter to climb the rocky rise above the gaping mouth, hike on up through the wood, and find out if there wasn't a way down to the tower from that wall of rock that rose behind it. It was the least likely avenue of all those I had held out hopes for, but I was reduced to trying it.

More than one person had come to the barrier of the gaping hole and decided to climb above it, for a path took off beyond the rock into the trees. It was a different kind of wood, though, from the magical woodland flanking the stream along which we had just come. The oak, holly and arbutus were interspersed with dark heavy evergreens that exuded a bleak, austere air.

I missed Red's company. By keeping my mind exercised with natural lore, he would have kept at bay the unaccountable anxieties afflicting me. Now, all I could think about was the remoteness and sense of isolation I experienced. Perhaps isolation was the wrong word, for I didn't feel alone. The wood had suddenly grown alien. The play of light and the strange, sly movements of the vegetation engendered a sense of brooding mystery that almost persuaded my tough modern wits there were strange, watchful presences abroad. I kept my eyes peeled and my ears pricked. A couple of times I caught a flash out of the corner of my eye. But when I looked in the direction of the movement, nothing could be seen except the trees, the undergrowth and the weaving mist.

The path climbed steeply through the turbid gloom. It was not much more than an animal track, a mulch of mud and rotting leaves mixed with loose boulders that would turn the ankle if you didn't check where you were stepping. The feeling of being watched persisted, but I had to give my full attention to my progress, pushing ferns, suckers and tendrils out of my way, holding back nettles and thorny branches with a stick.

At last the trees seemed to be thinning out ahead. At least more light seeped through the swirl of mist. With any luck, I would soon emerge onto the cliff that overlooked the tower. Eager to find out how the land lay, I speeded up.

A few minutes more and the pathway leveled off. But the mist was thicker now, almost as dense and white as absorbent cotton. It was like living in a cloud, cut off from all contact with reality. This weird insulation of my senses and the spinning movement of the vapor disoriented me.

Adapting rules of Western woodcraft, I made a special point of looking carefully ahead before I put the next foot forward.

A few seconds later, without warning, I was flung full length into a stand of nettles beside the path. Stung in a dozen places, I leapt up yelping like a hurt pup. What a stupid thing for me to do. If I *had* to trip, why hadn't I gone sprawling on the nice soft cushion of mud and leaves along the path? Huge blistery bumps were rising on my hands and face where my skin had come in contact with the stinging hairs.

As I licked the fiery hives across my knuckles, and held a wet leaf to a hot welt on my cheek, I began to wonder how I could have taken such a heavy spill. Hadn't I been watching very closely where I trod?

Baffled, I inspected where I'd walked. A deep hole pitted the path. How odd for me not to have seen it when I'd been so wary of my step. I could have sworn the path had looked intact. Had the hole been covered up with leaves? When I tried to reconstruct the mishap, I had a sense of having caught my heel. Apparently, I had rocked off balance backward, which had somehow sent me flying sideways.

But what was the hole doing there? Perhaps it was a disused exit from a rabbit warren or a badger's set that hadn't been disturbed for years. For all I knew, it might even be some kind of poacher's trap.

Well, the fall had taught me something. If I intended to go on, it would pay me to be even more cautious than I'd been before.

I took the stick with which I had been pressing back the bushes and used it as a probe to test the ground. For the next couple of steps the path was rock-firm. But caution paid off. Next time I prodded what looked like solid ground, the stick sliced through the leafy carpet into empty space.

Kneeling in place, I scooped away the leafmold. It rested

lightly, like a canopy, upon runners of vine and ivy which spanned a yawning crevice. A few prods more, and I discovered what I had already started to suspect: the path itself had ended leaving only this false surface. My poking stick dislodged some earth and stones. They went tumbling a long way down. I knew then that I must have reached a crumbling indentation in the cliff's edge. Behind that woolly bank of mist billowing like steam out of some giant cauldron was a sheer drop equivalent to many stories.

Only at that moment did I realize my luck in having fallen into the bed of nettles. If I'd stumbled forward onto the path itself, I'd surely have gone crashing through that crust of leaves, pitching headlong where the loose stones had just plummeted.

17

I lost no time returning to the camper. This latest escapade reinforced my earlier feeling of being slightly hexed. True, if you looked at it from another angle, I'd been lucky. But the next time I got myself into a tight spot would the pattern hold? That's if there was to be a next time. I was running out of likely ways to reach the tower.

Well, it was no time to be trying to figure my next move. I had promises to keep. Since it was Saturday, a heavy day for business at the shop, I had arranged to take Mrs. Rory home at noon. I had volunteered my services for clerking in the store, but my ignorance of inventory and prices, coupled with my unfamiliarity with Irish currency, made it more sensible for me to stay with Mrs. Rory's father until his son came home from work.

After driving Mrs. Rory back to town, I returned to Mr. Meaney's cottage for the lunch of tongue and garden salad that Mrs. Rory had prepared for us. My place was laid on a scrubbed oak table flanked by ladder-back chairs with seats of sugán, coiled rope made out of hay. The recumbent Mr. Meaney ate his meal off a potato basket used as a lap-tray.

My visit proved to be a case of casting bread upon the

waters, for it turned out to be of far more use to me than to Mr. Meaney. The poor old dear was in need of little more than company. He sat up against a stack of pillows on his ancient settle-bed built into a hearthside recess, his huge dropsied feet sticking out from the bottom of the covers, the weight of even a sheet too much to bear.

Yet he accepted his affliction with absolute good humor, even making little jokes about it, as though to free me from excess of pity. "It is all the port that I have drunk, Jan. And all the steak I've eaten." He pronounced it "steek." And to be sure I got his witty point: "They say the gout be a rich man's disease."

He bore my attempt at making tea with humorous patience. "It is hot and wet," he said. "That's three parts of the pleasure right there. Besides, my *eyes* have more need of a treat than does my palate." It was his gallant old-world way of paying me a compliment, especially to compare me with his wife long dead. "My Mary had long, dark, shiny, silky hair like yours. She was not so slender, and maybe a mite shorter. But her eyes were every bit as bright and lively. And her wrist as small and dainty."

I said: "If you keep it up my body won't be able to support my head."

He thought that very funny, repeating it a time or two, as though savoring a *bon mot,* and perhaps recording it for future use.

I cleared lunch and washed the dishes, restoring them to the huge dresser ranged against the wall. The bottom section, which in the olden days had housed straw and wattle coops for hens, and stave-built wooden piggins for milk and water, now stored a variety of modern cookware. But the top shelves still contained relics of an older way of life in the shape of crude wooden kitchen tools and precious bits of "delph."

Perhaps impressed by my domestic talents, Mr. Meaney asked me: "Have you got a young man yet, Jan?"

I shook my head.

"Have you not met anyone you fancy, then?"

"That's not the problem," I said ruefully. "The problem is getting those I fancy to fancy me."

He laughed heartily again, as though I were a grade-A wit. Inspired to match me, he said: "You know the saying: a bull pursues a willing heifer, not a shy one. It's up to you to jump the fence."

The analogy was so outrageous, I had to join him in his own delighted laughter at himself.

There were a lot of bachelors around that area he told me as I built the fire with turf stacked under a stone seat to one side of the fireplace. A similar stone box on the other side turned out to be the place to put the ashes that I swept up from the pebble-and-flagstone hearth with a heather besom. As pretty a girl as I, in his estimation, could take her pick, and, if I played my cards right, be wed within the year. He was so old, of such another age and culture, that I could not be irritated by his sexist patronage. According to his lights he was paying me the highest tribute.

Settled at last on the "creepie," a three-legged stool made out of bog oak, I discovered he spoke Gaelic, and I had a grand time learning corny phrases like *Erin go braugh,* "Ireland forever," and useful ones like *Conas tá tú,* "How are you?" and *Fáilte,* "Welcome." He took a real delight in coaching me. "The young ones now don't show much interest in the old ways," he said regretfully. "They only want excitement. The bright lights of the city. We raise them up, and they go off to England in droves for their enemies to have the benefit."

"If the land's so poor it can't support them, what can you expect?"

"Aye, there's a fact." He sighed heavily—a man caught between two equally despairing situations.

"Take my great-great-grandfather," I said. "We still have some letters he wrote to his mother, full of longing for the old country. But he had a good job in America. He couldn't afford to return to the old life."

"If he had stayed here, he likely would have died," the old man said. His face, so young in mirth, looked worn and heavy. "He probably left in the famine of 1842, when blight destroyed the whole of the potato crop. A million died. A million took off for foreign parts—damned if they did, and damned if they didn't. The Protestants stood by and let it happen. The British didn't raise a finger."

"Things are better now you've won your freedom, though."

He spread his calloused hands. "Even so it's been a struggle. No sooner did we get our independence than depression fell."

Most of his life he had been a farm laborer, but his son's prudence had enabled him to buy the small holding he had farmed alone until his recent failure in health. His son worked at a flour mill in Ballymor and could help out with the farm chores only evenings and Sundays. The land would have to be leased out if his health did not improve. Possessing the typical Irish esteem of numerous progeny, he lamented the lack of grandchildren to take over from him.

We talked about land usage since the establishment of the Republic. I had gotten the impression, mainly from the fate of Coole, that the old Protestant demesnes had been broken up. But many were still intact, he said. The Morton estate, for example, a little farther east, consisted of many hundreds of acres of wood and relatively virgin land, and a fine house used for little more than a shooting lodge.

"Talking of those old estates," I said, "I guess the tower was originally part of some demesne."

He jerked his thumb toward the window. "The tower over here, you mean?" And when I nodded, he said: "Hand me my pipe from the bole, please, Jan," pointing to a keeping hole, a small recess beside the fireplace.

He began to work a fluffy white pipe cleaner down the stem of his clay pipe to ream it out. "The tower," he said, reflecting. "That must be part of the old Aranmore demesne."

He described the old Protestant house whose ruins I had come across the day before. "A lot of acreage was sold before old Lady Grayson died, like this holding here of ours, and some strips to the Herlihys. The rest has been tied up in legal problems since her death."

"Why would the tower be called Tur Bran?"

He withdrew the pipe cleaner, stained dark brown with tobacco juice, and sucked the pipe to see if it would draw. By his slow and careful actions, he seemed to be avoiding a response.

I prompted: "Could it simply be descriptive—like maybe the crows or daws flock round there?"

Apparently not yet satisfied with the pipe's performance, he now began to scrape the bowl with a gadget from his smoker's kit. "There's quite a rookery among the trees," he said, tapping the scrapings into a large ashtray. "But it isn't on account of that, I doubt."

When he volunteered no more, I said: "Should it be Tur Bron, perhaps, rather than Bran? That's what your daughter called it."

He said: "In any case, it adds up to the same thing," and sucked his pipe again. This time it made a hollow gurgly sound, which must have been the right result, for he reached for his tobacco tin. As he filled it with his thumb, he said tangentially: "A crow perched on our roof for half an hour the day my father drowned."

His meaning thrilled along my nerves. Black wings swooped through my head.

He said: "Herself often changed into a corpse-eating crow."

"Herself?"

"The Morrigan. She of the three heads. Always there in the shape of a carrion crow in battle or at death. Just as when Cuchulain fought and died."

"Are you telling me the Morrigan's connected with Tur Bran?"

"The old tower is her haunt."

"Is she the wailing lady, then?"

He tossed his head. "White lady or black crow, she means no good."

"Have you ever seen or heard her?"

"Last time I heard her moan was about a year ago, boding young Siobhan O'Brien's death."

He was out of matches. Returning with a new box, I had another topic ready: "You know those woods behind the tower, Mr. Meaney?"

"What about them?"

"Do you know them well?"

He eyed me warily. "Why should I now? Only them that poach have cause to enter."

"It's a lovely place for picnics. Or to walk there on a summer evening."

"Aye, maybe. But prudent folk prefer to do their walking and their courting somewhere else."

I was all ears. "Why would that be, Mr. Meaney?"

He gave his full attention to the lighting of his pipe, puffing elaborately, expelling the smoke out of the corner of his mouth.

Gently, not to sound impertinent, I nudged: "What do you have against the woods?"

"Never you mind," he said irascibly.

"But they're beautiful. I was there this morning. I followed the stream until it disappeared down a hole. Has anybody ever been down there?"

His reaction was electric: a jerk of the head as though I'd slapped his face, and a sharp intake of breath. He burst out: "Who in his right mind would want to try it?"

"Why not?"

"Why not!" he said indignantly. "Some of the host of St. Patrick hides down there."

"What kind of host?"

He was shocked that I didn't know what every Irish child learns before it is knee-high to a duckling—the famous story of St. Patrick's fasting forty days and forty nights like Christ Himself in the mountain wilderness on what has ever since been called Croagh Patrick. At the end of the fast, the legend went, St. Patrick rang his bell and purged himself of demons. Most of them fled into the sea beyond Achill Island, where they were engulfed. "But a few escaped this way," Mr. Meaney said, "and crawled into the cave in Derry Woods."

"How do you know?"

"They've been seen there in the shape of snakes and worms."

"But aren't creepy crawly things quite natural in a dark, wet place like that?"

Mr. Meaney laughed dryly. "If it's proof you want, you'll find it down at Tober Tullaghan."

"What's that?"

"St. Patrick's Well, of course. The one down yonder on the shore."

I guessed it was the stone-built demi-beehive topped by a cross I'd seen in the cove the previous day.

Mr. Meaney said: "Even when the tide comes in high

enough to cover it, you can always ladle out sweet water there. So pure, it's medicine. A cure for all sorts of ailments."

"How is the well proof of the demons in the cave?"

He gave an exasperated cluck. "By time the stream has journeyed through the earth to Tober Tullaghan, all the demons are cleansed out of it. Just as St. Patrick purged them from his blessed self."

To his annoyance, he had almost let his pipe go out during this unsettling exchange. He applied the empty match box as a lid to improve the draw.

When he began emitting smoke again, I said: "Is that the only reason for the wood's unpopularity?"

He eyed me closely as he puffed, as though judging my sincerity. Finally he said: "There are Druid enchantments in there, too."

I didn't know much more about the Druids than that their pre-Christian priesthood practiced arcane rites in sacred groves. "Druid enchantments. What are those?"

"Druids trapped in certain stones and oaks."

"How do you know that?"

"By the halo surrounding them at night. It's the Druid spirit struggling to get out to do some mischief."

"Have you ever seen such lights?"

"Many times," he said, his eye mirroring remembered fear. "Just the other night when I had a sleepless bout, I saw one through that window."

I twisted around to look where he was pointing through the tiny casement. "Where?"

"Up there on the Leap."

"The Leap?"

"The height behind the tower. About where Siobhan O'Brien fell last St. John's Eve."

"Fell?"

"Went off the edge into the lake."

Bristlingly attentive, I said: "What do you mean? Did she throw herself over?"

He was appalled that I could even entertain such an explanation. "Siobhan would never have committed such a sin." It was an insult to her memory, his tone implied.

Chastened, I said: "So how did it happen?"

He sniffed skeptically. "They *said* the cliff edge crumbled."

"But you don't believe that?"

"She was heard screaming and running like a wild thing through the woods before she plunged."

Hackles rising, I listened to his thory that some evil deed must have released a Druid from its stone to drive her to her doom. The hostile energy I'd felt lurking in the woods took on a chilling new construction.

Was it possible that my own fall up on the Leap hadn't been an accident? Could I, too, be the quarry of some sinister supernatural force?

18

That night I did so much running from the goblins and specters that filled my dreams, I awoke exhausted Sunday morning. But opening the curtains to a cheerful sky, I said my little blessing as the Irish do, and looked forward to a better day.

The nearest Protestant church was several miles distant near the ruined house of Aranmore. When the Rorys recollected that regular services had not been held there since her ladyship's demise, I accompanied them to their local parish church instead.

That the church was full to overflowing was an immense surprise to me. Growing up, I had acquired a general sense of the norm of church attendance as half-emptiness. Moreover, in my few days in Dunderg, I had received the distinct impression that the area was sparsely populated. Either the parish covered an extraordinarily wide area, or, since that seemed unlikely, every man, woman and child served by the church must, amazingly, be present and accounted for.

While Father Flanagan, in flowing vestments, shuffled up and down the aisles sprinkling holy water, I stole as good a look around as I could manage without appearing ill-mannered—duly aware that as a stranger I'd be singled out for close critical attention. My sweeping gaze picked out the Herlihys sitting across the aisle, the old woman garbed in black with a scarf draped peasant-style about her head, holding her beads. The son, his profiled lower lip hanging loose and wet, his neck as thick as a young bull's, held his hands palm to palm, finger to finger, in an attitude of prayer. From where I sat I could see that his boots were still plastered, and undoubtedly pungent, with bog mud and manure, contributing to the heavy odor wafting on the air whose other elements I analyzed as sour milk and sweat aged in wool.

Over on the other side Sean Danaher shared a crowded pew with his cousin, his cousin's wife and their stair-step children. When my glance slid past him, he acknowledged me with a barely perceptible lifting of his clean-cut chin.

Holding my head as motionless as possible, I surveyed the church during the first part of the Mass. The plaster flaked in patches between the beams of a ceiling ribbed like the keel of an inverted hull. The nave was paved with gray stone, giving way beyond the chancel to crude colored tiles. Around the wall ranged a series of garish reprints of the Stations of the Cross. The graceless pews, painted with an ersatz grain and heavily varnished, the unadorned windows, and the simple altar were a far cry from the sumptuous, sensuous appeal I had always associated with Catholic sanctuaries. But during my few days in Ireland, I had come to learn that the older churches, with their magnificent craftsmanship and priceless art objects, had been appropriated by the Church of Ireland—the Protestant Anglican denomination imposed on the Irish by the ruling British since the Tudor period. Most Catholic parish churches dated only from the nineteenth century, when the harsh penal laws, which had forbidden Catholics to worship as they chose, were finally relaxed.

I have no great yen for sermons, but I prefer sitting down—even on a narrow wooden pew—to kneeling on cold stones. So when Father Flanagan climbed into the gaudily rococo pulpit, I was almost willing to endure the threatened half-hour or so of boredom. The good father's wizened, leprechaunish, Arthur Godfrey face radiated as much cunning and smugness as piety, and I wouldn't have been at all surprised if he'd preached like a carnival pitchman. But if he *looked* worldly and faintly pagan, he sounded positively puritan.

Announcing his text from Chapter Seventeen of the Second Book of Kings, he began to read it in forbidding tones, gesturing dramatically where he needed emphasis:

> This came about because the Israelites sinned against the Lord, their God, who had brought them up from the land of Egypt. . . . They adopted unlawful practices toward the Lord, their God. They built high places in all their settlements, the watchtowers as well as the walled cities.

Usually, at the first sound of the text my mind automatically goes into neutral and idles for the duration of the commentary. But I became gradually aware that the text was running beyond the normal verse or two. In fact, it seemed less a thesis for a sermon than an additional Reading from the Scriptures, perhaps introduced because the set one for the day didn't fit some situation the reverend father wished to raise.

> They set up pillars and sacred poles for themselves on every high hill and under every leafy tree. There, on all the high places, they burned incense. . . . They did evil things that provoked the Lord, and served idols,

although the Lord had told them, "You must not do this."

By this time I was as attentive as a losing matron at a parish bingo game. It was not so much the text itself that I found compelling, nor yet the priest's delivery—for all his histrionics. It was rather something extraordinarily galvanizing in the air around me, as though the parishioners were all sitting on the edges of their pews holding their breath. Even the scratch of hobnails against flagstones had completely ceased.

Did this flock always respond so ideally? Did the good father always command such incredible attention?

I had heard about the Church's powerful influence, but this absorption hit me as quite extraordinary. They were all as rapt as village gossips vacuuming up a bit of top-grade scandal.

The priest went on:

And though the Lord warned Israel and Judah by every prophet and seer, "Give up your evil ways and keep my commandments," they did not listen, but were as stiff-necked as their fathers, who had not believed in the Lord, their God.

About then it struck me that this was not going to be any canned, run-of-the-mill sermon. The words echoing down the nave were clearly charged with sizzling relevance.

They rejected his statutes. . . . They disregarded all the commandments of the Lord, their God, and made for themselves two molten calves; they also made a sacred pole and worshiped all the host of heaven, and served Baal. They immolated their sons and daughters by fire, practiced fortune-telling and divination, and sold themselves into evildoing in the Lord's sight, provoking him till, in his great anger against Israel, the Lord put them away out of his sight.

So silent was the sanctuary when the reading ended that the little plop he made closing the Book rang out like a slammed door.

Father Flanagan took off his wire-frame Ben Franklin reading glasses and coughed politely into the barrel of his fist. "Dearly beloved," he addressed us, "we are already beginning to look towards the celebration of the feast of St. John the Baptist. What does it mean to us? It means we should pay honor to one who was the Lord's messenger, preparing the way before Him. As we are told in Matthew, St. John is that voice crying in the desert: 'Prepare the way of the Lord, make straight his paths.'"

He paused, panning the audience from wall to wall from back to front, peering intently as though to bore into the very soul of each of us. The intenseness of the silence was dramatized by a small, harsh cough that some nervous man was unable to suppress.

"Dearly beloved," Father Flanagan continued, his voice several notes deeper, "there are those who in times past did not heed the example of the saint. Who hewed themselves paths a long way from straight."

So far it was all Greek to me, but I hung on every word as if he revealed a formula for making gold brick out of beer cans. The so-called text and the commentary he was now delivering seemed not to bear at all upon each other. But beside me Mrs. Rory's hands were clenched in a white grip, and a red tide began suffusing the back of the neck in front of me.

"Brethren," Father Flanagan went on, "let me remind you of our blessed Patrick. You all know the story." He held up his hands, one directed to the east, the other to the west. "Here is Tara. Here is Slane. On this hill sits the King; on this the Holy Patrick. 'Tis coming up time when the Druids will be holding their spring festivals. No fire must be kindled until the royal fire is lit. You know the rest: On Easter Eve, in defiance of the heathen rule, St. Patrick lights his Paschal fire on the Hill of Slane. Across the river on Tara, the angry King sees its triumphant blaze. His Druid prophesies: 'If we do not quench Slane's bonfire now, it will never more be quenched in Eire.'"

The good father paused again, glowering from under beetling brows. Mr. Rory picked intently at a soiled spot on the rough tweed of his sleeve. You could hear the wasps buzz in the flowers outside.

"That was *one* heathen seer who saw and spoke the truth," Father Flanagan resumed. "Those old heathen fires have been extinguished for fifteen centuries and more. Let them not be lit again. When we build our bonfires these coming days, let our intentions be only to prepare the way of the Lord and make straight his paths."

A subtle release of tension could be felt throughout the church. The reprimand was drawing to a close. Soon the children would be off the carpet, dismissed to return to carefree play.

But I experienced no such relief. Struggling through a spawn of unhatched clues, I grew slightly chilled at the hypotheses beginning to take form inside my head.

The lecture wasn't over yet. There was the final admonition: "His Holiness Pope Paul VI has exhorted us to be ever aware of the cracks through which the Devil can easily penetrate and work upon the human mind. One of these ways is giving credit to unwarranted magical or popular superstitions. Let us heed his warning that 'this dark and disturbing Spirit of the Devil really exists, and that he still acts with treacherous cunning,' this secret enemy, this fatal tempter, this enchanter.

"Dearly beloved, let us not be like the children of Israel who went astray worshipping false gods in high places under green trees, provoking the Lord to anger. Let us rather follow John, the voice prophesied in Isaiah, crying: 'Make straight in the wasteland a highway for our God.'"

With the end of the rebuke came an immediate slackening of the remaining tension. The Mass continued in an atmosphere of eagerness for absolution, as though a batch of chastened kids were rushing to get back into good books again.

This load-lightened spirit extended beyond the ending of the Mass. Meeting the sunlight at the exit, the congregation became positively festive, talking and laughing its leisurely way along gravel paths among gravestones, mounds and yews. Clearly nobody was in a hurry to depart. While the young shouted and played, and the adolescents paraded in their smartest clothes, executing various tactics in the mating game, their parents promenaded, deploring prices and the weather, and the old folks stood in knots, bemoaning the dead and dying and their own declining health. On a pleasant day like this, the after-Mass communion was obviously a social highlight of the week.

Mr. and Mrs. Rory introduced me to a number of local families, and once again I philosophically endured the tedious routine of telling who I was and how much I enjoyed my visit. As I talked, I kept my weather eye open. Over by a Celtic cross, whose intricate spirals and interlacings were worn dim by a dozen centuries of lashing rain and wind, stood Sean Danaher. Lean and suntanned, he stood as tall as the crossed circle of the ancient monument. He was casually watching a group of pretty teen-agers, all very much aware of him and behaving with a mixture of flirtatious provocation and shy awe. In practical, financial terms alone, he would no doubt be considered a superior catch. With the powerful sexual appeal he exerted, he would be irresistible to all the eligible girls throughout the area. I would bet competition for his favors to be cutthroat.

The minute I got free of the last inquisitive group to whom the Rorys introduced me, Padraic Herlihy accosted me. "Bygones be bygones, is it?" he said ingratiatingly, exposing his furred teeth and shoving his huge paw in mine. His palm felt as stiff and rough as an old baseball mitt, but for a pleasant change he smelled of hay instead of barnyard dung.

I felt ashamed for having harbored such serious suspicions of his character and conduct. He might be gross and gauche, but he was hardly menacing.

I shot him a faint smile.

He shook me by responding: "Would you care to take a walk?" His expression suggested he was offering the elusive product at the rainbow's end.

I would have put up with a great deal to see the tower—if that was where he had in mind to take me. But he had already overreacted to my fleeting smile. I didn't dare risk appearing to encourage him—above all not in front of the whole village. "I'm sorry," I said, trying to sound gracious for the sake of future harmony, "I'm going home to lunch with Mr. and Mrs. Rory." I closed in behind Mrs. Rory, hoping she'd catch on to my predicament and bail me out.

"Don't worry about that, love," she said so accommodatingly I could have kicked her. "The joint will not be done till two o'clock at least. Go off now and enjoy yourself."

I had no time to think. I grabbed at the first straw. "If I'd realized that," I said, "I needn't have said 'no' to Mr. Danaher . . ." I trailed off, trying to avoid a blatant lie. "Thanks anyway," I said apologetically, to let Padraic down as gently as I could.

But he looked more surprised than damaged. Smiling knowingly, he turned to gaze at Sean, who still stood at the cross, one foot on the stone plinth, a casual elbow propped against the sculptured shaft whose panels depicted scenes of the Temptation in the Garden. "So that's it, is it?" Padraic said good-naturedly enough. "He's a sly one, that one. Ah, well, good luck to him."

I didn't have time to worry what I was going to do about the lie I'd told. Almost as if Padraic gave him the high sign, Sean strolled across the daisied turf and offered me his arm. Falling in step beside him, I told Mrs. Rory I'd see her in a couple of hours.

The glances of the teen-age girls were poised harpoons.

19

We walked under the lych gate and along the road. Parked beside the ivied ruin next door to the church was a fairly recent Land Rover. "I thought we were going for a walk," I said, as he helped me into it.

"And so we shall be when we reach a spot that takes your fancy."

He followed the road leading eastward in the direction of Tur Bran, but before we came to it he cut off along the hilly side road, past the wood and on toward the higher hills. His hands, of as smooth and brown a texture as pecans, were capable and confident on the Land Rover's wheel.

He caught me looking at him, and I hurriedly returned my gaze toward the road. After a moment he said: "How did you like Mass this morning?"

"I found it very interesting."

"I gather you're not a Catholic."

"How did you gather that?"

"You didn't cross yourself."

So he had been watching me. I wondered how devout he was himself, and why he'd date a Protestant, if you could call this ride a date.

After another minute's silence, I said: "What was that sermon all about?"

He had to concentrate on passing an old plaidshirted man astride a heavy work horse. When he was past, he shot me a penetrating look. "Ah, yes, I suppose it wouldn't make much sense to you."

"I realized there was some very relevant and telling point Father Flanagan was trying to get across. But I couldn't figure what."

A donkey and a rough two-wheeled cart, loaded with turf, loomed into view, competing for scarce space on the narrow road. The skinny boy, who might have been my Red, but wasn't, crushed the donkey and himself against the hedge.

"I wonder where he stole that," Sean said as we sped by.

"Why do you say that?"

He turned to eye me with surprise. "He's an itinerant. A trickey."

"So?"

"So begging and stealing are a way of life with them."

Thinking particularly of Red, I said: "I don't go much for blanket indictments of whole groups. I prefer not to prejudge."

He smiled. "That's a nice sentiment. It becomes you. But it'll get you into trouble." When I didn't respond he went on: "Once is once too much to trust a tinker, as the saying goes."

To change the subject, I resumed where we left off. "About that sermon. What were all those hints about worshipping false gods?"

"Oh, that," he said, in a tone of humorous depreciation. "The father was just giving us our annual caution to behave ourselves on St. John's Eve."

St. John's Eve. Wasn't that when Mr. Meaney said

Siobhan O'Brien had fallen from the Leap? Agog, I said: "What happens on St. John's Eve?"

"I don't know what you do to celebrate it in your country. Over here we have fun and games."

"Fun and games like what?"

"We build bonfires along the hills and dance around them."

I'd never heard of any such contemporary celebration in the States. But as a student of mythology my curiosity began to twitch like a divining rod. "Tell me more."

He laughed at my enthusiasm. "I don't know what you want to know. It's been going on for centuries. In fact the country folk built bonfires on Midsummer's Eve long before Christianity arrived."

"Midsummer's Eve?"

"June twenty-second is St. John's Day."

"But that's the summer solstice—the beginning of summer."

"Same thing. It's *called* midsummer because it's the midpoint of the year, the longest day."

"Of course!" I said, connecting. "The Midsummer revels like in *Midsummer Night's Dream*." I was beginning to understand the reverend father's admonitions. He would look askance at the tumbling in the hay, the joyous abandon—remnants of ancient fertility rites traditionally practiced on Midsummer's Eve.

"Clever girl," he said. "Just as the Blessed Patrick turned the pagan rites of spring into Christian rejoicing of the Easter Resurrection, so the old Midsummer rites were transformed into a celebration of Christ's forerunner, St. John."

"Midsummer madness into Christian piety," I said. I was in my element. To think that these old customs had survived and I was here to witness them. Frazer's *Golden Bough*, my bible since Mythology 100, was becoming vibrantly alive. The ritual fires had always fascinated me.

I said: "What's the purpose of the fires?"

"Just high jinks." His dark eyes left the road to seek mine briefly. "To dance around and keep lovers warm when they stay out all night."

"I meant originally."

"Some say to give the sun more power. To stop it turning round and shortening the days."

My memory stirred. "I saw this picture once—a giant wicker basket full of human offerings being burnt alive. That was supposed to be to appease the sun, to keep it coming on and climbing higher in the sky—"

Even as I said it, my flesh began to crawl. Before Sean even had a chance to answer, I burst out: "Good grief. You don't suppose . . . ? But no, I'm being silly."

"What don't you suppose?"

"Father Flanagan couldn't have meant . . . he doesn't suspect a revival of that sacrificial pagan business?"

He did not reply immediately. The road had narrowed, so his attention could have been pre-empted by the need for careful driving. On the other hand, I could very well have sounded slightly off the beam to him. I said defensively: "That's not such a way-out thought. I mean all kinds of weird practices are being revived these days. All kinds of primitive and pagan cults. Witchcraft, satanism, stuff like that. I thought maybe—"

He pulled into a recess where a gate was let into the hedge, a convenient parking place. Across the road was a turnoff onto an even narrower lane. "We can't make that in this," he said. "But it's a nice walk if you'd like to try it."

"Fine," I said. "It looks inviting."

The lane, no more than a path to start with, soon dwindled to a sheep track. It wound across a densely covered area that I was now experienced enough to recognize as bog even before I saw the occasional water-sodden trough with brick-patterned walls attesting to the ministrations of the slane. Up there the air was tingling-fresh and as heady as Cold Duck.

We had sauntered several hundred yards before either of us spoke. Sean was refreshingly laconic, not shy but deep, the type who always made me sound like a hare-brained chatterer. But how could I keep quiet when there was so much to know? Like what bird made that bubbly song? The whimbrel or the curlew. And was that a skylark soaring out of sight? It was.

After a little while, I picked up where we left off in the car: "About those bonfires—"

"What about them?"

"Could Father Flanagan be making veiled accusations against people in the neighborhood?"

"What sort of accusations?"

"Like I was saying, pre-Christian rites being practiced hereabouts."

He shrugged, his sole reply.

"What's that supposed to mean?"

He finger-combed his dark, springy hair which he wore just long enough so the collar of his cashmere sport coat turned the neck strands up into soft curls. "There are rumors," he said vaguely, keeping his eyes on the trail ahead.

To get the proper answers out of him was like pulling molars. "What sort of rumors?"

"Just gossip," he said, sounding as if I had begun to tax his patience. "I doubt anybody has any actual information."

"Tell me anyway," I said, "or I'll think you're deliberately frustrating me."

Preoccupied, he kicked a white rock embedded in the thick turf. It jumped and flipped, leaving a pallid socket across which a wireworm scurried. "I daresay anybody'd tell you if you asked them." He spoke as though this was the

only reason he would take responsibility for telling me.
"There's supposed to be a secret brotherhood operating in
this area that goes in for ancient ritual."

"No kidding. Like what?"

He sighed as though burdened by my curiosity. But with
well-placed verbal nudges, bit by reluctant bit, I began to
prise the story out of him. I couldn't tell whether his
reticence was a superstitious avoidance of unholy facts, a
reluctance to wash the community's dirty linen before a
stranger, or a delicate concern for sensibilities which he
didn't know I didn't have until I shamelessly pestered the
whole story out of him.

"How big is this brotherhood? Do they have many
members?" I was thinking of something like the Rosicru-
cians, or the Masons even.

"I've heard thirteen. Twelve and the leader."

"Like Christ and the Apostles!"

He made a twisted mouth, ruefully conceding, though
apparently disliking, the blasphemous parallel.

"And what do these apostles of the New Millennium *do*
Midsummer night?" I said, my flippancy more a whistling
in the dark by now than a display of skepticism.

He looked at me intently, as though I had said something
with a special meaning. But after a few seconds he
responded: "They choose a tanist, so I've heard."

"A tanist?" I had a faint recollection of having met the
word before, but its sense eluded me. "What's a tanist?"

"A successor to their reigning king."

This was getting more and more interesting.

"What kind of king?"

"The Oak King, I believe."

Vague stirrings, something I had read in Frazer,
prompted me to ask: "What happens to the old king?"

"He's killed before the new one's crowned."

The sun was warm, but the down rose along my arms.

I said: "Not *really*. They wouldn't dare get into murder, would they?"

"Oh, I was speaking of the *ancient* ritual, not the current group. Hearsay has it they substitute a surrogate for the stricken king."

"What kind of surrogate?" My voice was hoarse.

"A bird, it's rumored. Perhaps a raven. That would be appropriate."

"A raven!" Even before my experience on the battlement of Thoor Ballylee, the notion of a black bird serving as proxy for ritual murder would have curled my hair.

But he seemed not to have noticed the horror in my tone. He went on: "Then the next king reigns until the winter solstice when the Holly King's reborn."

"Wow. The seasonal myth. Of course. Six months' darkness, six months' light." The dread went out of me as intellectual enthusiasm flooded in. This was fabulous. "I ought to write it down," I said, hoping I didn't sound too much like Haines in Joyce's *Ulysses*.

"If you do, you'll change into a pumpkin," he said wryly, "or the paper will burst into flame."

He distracted my attention for a moment to point out a plant with spatulate leaves haloed with glistening hairs. It was the notorious sundew, one of the sinister wonders of the vegetable world engineered to lure and trap insects.

But I wasn't going to be sidetracked. I gave another prod: "What else do you know about the Oak King ritual?"

"What else do I know about it?" he said, affecting weary patience at my single-mindedness. "There's a queen—in the ancient ceremony at least."

I said dryly: "And what role does *she* play?"

"Through her, in the old ritual, the continuity of kingship was maintained between the dying monarch and his tanist." His smoky eyes held mine a moment. "Apparently the old king goes to bed with her before he dies. The new one takes her after he is crowned."

"Very interesting," I said sardonically. "You seem to know a lot about it."

"It's common knowledge."

"If it's common knowledge, why don't the authorities put a stop to it?"

"There's no crime committed that anybody knows about."

With heavy irony, I said: "How about the lucky girl? I assume they wouldn't pass up *that* bit of the ceremony."

"If she consents," he said, "who is there to object?"

I had a sudden nasty thought. "I wonder," I said, thinking of Mr. Meaney's account of Siobhan O'Brien's fall from the Leap last St. John's Eve.

"What do you wonder?"

But I was jumping to absurd conclusions. I changed my tack abruptly: "Who does the grapevine say is the current king?"

"No one you'd know." Pause. "But you may be interested in who the grapevine puts in line to be the *next* one."

"I'll bite."

He cast a sly, sidelong glance at me. "How does Padraic Herlihy strike you?"

With heavy sarcasm, I said: "I'll offer to play queen."

We were above the bog now in a moorland area of bilberry, furze and heather. Rocky outcrops were lichened on their sheltered sides with a palette of colors—lime, lemon, black and vivid orange splotches, like a psychedelic skin disease. The area was sprinkled with the dry pellet droppings of the black-faced sheep, who negotiated crags as if their dainty hooves were suction-cupped. It was a wild romantic landscape with a matching skyscape of scudding mountainous clouds.

The sum of exotic and shaking experiences of the past few days and the chilling story with its shock ending that Sean had just finished telling me conspired with these wild surroundings to evoke quite alien emotions. In just one week I had grown a subtle new identity. Or was it truer to say I had uncovered a latent, more primitive self carried undeveloped in the genes until at last it had found its native ambience in which to germinate and flourish?

I said: "I guess we should be getting back."

"Sure," he said, grinning his handsome amicable grin. "There's no need to retrace our steps, however. We'll circle down this other way."

As we descended, I could indistinctly see a good deal of the bay. But the distance was too hazy to pick out the fabled mountains of Ben Bulben and Knocknarea, which I had learned about through Yeats's poetry.

We went down through varying shades of green to a bushier, more meadowed area grazed by cattle now resting and chewing the cud in a little copse. Several brown skewbald cows turned their lazy heads to stare at us with unbatted, liquid eyes as we went by. As far as I could make out from the view beyond, we were perhaps a mile above the highest limit of the Derry Wood where I had walked yesterday with Red.

A few steps farther and we came upon a sight that brought me to a gaping halt. Beyond the copse, in a verdant clearing, stood a circle of standing stones.

Instinctively, profoundly, I recognized it as a place of mysteries, arcane and primitive and slightly sinister. As I stared, it came alive with figures of a distant past, an ancient tribe performing rites at dawn or sunset, or on some other "boundary of time"—an equinox or solstice. In actual fact, the only living thing, besides the grass, within the ring of "druid stones" was an old oak tree, pollarded to an extraordinary shape. Many of its branches had been lopped away leaving only two huge leafy branches stretching out to form a giant T. Below the maimed oak lay a round flat stone atop four chunky pillars. A few feet in front of the stone table the makings of a campfire of considerable size had been assembled.

Sean said: "They're already gathering the bonfire, by the look of it."

As I approached the pile, I saw it was composed of sticks and turf and what presumably was wrack gleaned from the beach—flotsam and jetsam in a tangle of dried seaweed. Among this mass I identified an assortment of white bones. Repelled, appalled, I sprang away.

"Keep calm," he said. "They're only butcher bones."

"Butcher bones! Why on earth!"

"It's an old trick of bonfire builders. They make an evil-smelling smoke."

But this rational explanation didn't do much to soothe me. There was a smack of the satanic about those white bones gleaming in that smelly, fly-infested heap. They made you think, even if only symbolically, of animal—even human—sacrifice on a ritual pyre.

The next instant, with a little thrill of horror, it occurred to me what that place might be. Not anthropologically, nor historically speaking, but in contemporary terms. The round, elevated stone resembling an altar could have been there millennia ago, of course. But the lopped oak had only recently been polled. And it had the aura of a sacrificial tree, a demonic cross—a heathen travesty of the Crucifix.

"It's so blatant," I said. "You wonder how they get away with it."

"There's nothing actually *wrong* with it, however." And when I made a grimace of disgust, he said defensively: "It's no different from a hundred such bonfires being gathered throughout these mountains. They do no harm." He sounded resentful, as if I'd disappointed him by acting like an ignorant tourist disdainful of time-honored local customs.

Perhaps, in the usual abandoned way of my hyped-up imagination, I *had* rather overreacted. Still, the influences of the place and my bumpy flesh continued to persuade me that, if not actionably illegal, whatever was enacted there must be something pretty sick.

But it had been good of Sean to show it to me after I'd been such a plague to him with my unbridled curiosity. I said: "Thanks, Sean, for bringing me by. It's fascinating."

"Maybe you'd like to see it lit," he said.

I laughed at his macabre and deadpan humor.

He flashed me a sardonic smile. "St. John's Eve, then. Remember, it's a date."

20

But St. John's Eve was more than a week away, Sean said. He must see me before that. By the time we reached the post office, he had offered to take me in his boat around the bay and along the coast later in the week. I accepted eagerly, not just because it was a trip I wanted very much to take. I was attracted to him. He was vibrantly exciting, educated and urbane, and if I hadn't recently suffered the let-down of an unrequited crush, I might have gone for him in a big way. He was, I gathered, extremely enterprising. Without either arrogance or false modesty, he told me he had tripled the family business since he graduated from college. In addition to his other qualities, he was an ideal date, keeping a casual, friendly distance as though the main reason for his seeking my company was pleasant camaraderie. He was clearly not a person to rush relationships. In a context that seemed to grow more threatening by the hour, such an attitude was especially welcome. More than anything right then, I needed the comfort of a solid friend.

While I was still in the Land Rover thanking Sean and firming up our date, Mr. Rory appeared on the doorstep, beckoning me and miming a telephone receiver to his ear.

With another speedy thank you and a "See you Friday, Sean," I rushed inside.

As I expected, Kris was calling. But my hopes of seeing her were soon dashed when she said in her contorted English: "It is another week yet until I am planning to leave the Burren. But I phone for fear you are expecting me."

"That's bad news," I said. "I had a job lined up for you."

"A job? What do you mean?"

"There's this cave I'd like to have you take a look at."

"What cave?"

"It looks like the only entrance to a place I want to get to."

"What place?"

"Our tower."

There was a tiny silence. "I don't understand. You can't get *to* your tower?"

"There's a bog all around it."

She made a small explosive guttural sound. "I get the picture." It was an expression she'd picked up from me; it sounded comical rolling off her stilted foreign tongue.

I said: "But there's this cave in the woods where a small stream disappears. I'd like to try to follow it through to the other side. Could the job be tackled alone?"

"You mean by me? Yes. I am expert. You mean by you? No. Risky business. It requires the special apparatus and techniques."

"What equipment would be needed?"

"Nailed boots, ropes, torches, a pick and pitons—"

"I'm not going mountain climbing."

"You very well *might* be. Underground, of course."

Her list was beyond my immediate ability to produce, and, even if located, beyond my expertise to use. She was rattling on: "You have to think of topography below ground like there is no ceiling but the sky. You think like you are mountaineer. The water fall over maybe underground cliffs into ravines. There may be crevices for to climb down. After you reach goal, you have to make it back to home. Maybe to scale sheer faces. Think about it."

"I've thought about it."

"Do not do anything ridiculous. Be patient. Wait for I come next week to take charge of the expedition."

"You bet."

"I do not say good-bye," she said. "That sounds too . . . too . . ."

"Ominous?" I said.

"Too ominous."

Next time I saw her, I would hear the word again. "You can say 'so long,' " I said now. "So long, Kris."

"So long, Jan. Behave yourself."

As I was about to replace the receiver, I suddenly remembered I wanted her to bring a postcard of the hostel for my file on Yeats.

"Hey, Kris." The line was still open, but there was no response. "Kris, are you still there?"

The operator's voice came on the line. "The other party hung up. Shall I call her back?"

"No, it's okay, thanks," I said, a bit nonplussed. "It's not all that important."

So the telephone connections in and out of this tiny place were operator-mediated. For someone brought up on direct dialing to all parts of an enormous continent, this small fact was at once amusing and unnerving. I'd seen ancient movies on the late-night show depicting nosy, loose-lipped, long-tongued, small-town operators. It was pretty much like being bugged. Henceforth if I had a private message to communicate, I'd find another route than the telephone to send it by.

A delicious smell of roast lamb and pungent mint sauce permeated the Rorys' house. Either I was just in time for the sumptuous Sunday dinner, or they had waited, these generous people, to make it appear so. As we sat down to the meal, they were full of good-humored joshing about my finding a "young man" so soon.

"Don't arrange to have the banns called yet," I joshed back. "I'm very fickle."

"He's such a nice young man," Mrs. Rory said. "The handsomest man in seven counties." As if there was a cause-and-consequence connection, she added: "He was Mr. Rory's pupil at one time, wasn't he, dear?"

Mr. Rory always masticated every mouthful very carefully, so there was the usual lull before he answered. "Clever lad. Sharp as a tack. Good head for business."

Mrs. Rory said: "There's not a girl around wouldn't give everything in her dower chest just to be seen walking out with him. You had some envious looks today."

Mr. Rory laid down his knife and fork. "His father owns an ironmonger's shop in town. When Sean joined the firm after he came home from college, he developed his own side of the business, going around the county, delivering bottled gas. Then he began promoting farm machinery and supplies on hire purchase. Visiting the farms like that, you see, he could advise the farmer what would help him. Then he'd take the order, deliver it, and give the farmer training in its use without the farmer having to lose time going into town to shop, or worry about which or what."

"He knows everybody," Mrs. Rory said, "and everybody likes him. He and his father must be worth a pretty penny, but there's no side to him. He'll turn his hand to anything—cutting hay or turf if anybody needs a hand."

"He has a way of winning people's confidence," Mr. Rory said. "He's trusted and looked up to."

I said: "You sound like a pair of marriage brokers," and they laughed delightedly.

Mrs. Rory passed the vegetable dishes for second helpings. "So, did you have a nice walk, then?" She was obviously fishing for vicarious tidbits to sweeten her romantic tooth.

Her question put me on a track I wanted to pursue. "We walked along the mountain to the stone circle above the tower. Do you know it?"

"Do I know it!" Mrs. Rory laughed. "That's the Bed of Diarmaid and Gráinne. Just the place for a courting couple."

I let the reference to courting couples pass. Mr. Rory donned his figurative mortar board to tell me the tragic story of Gráinne, a king's daughter, and her lover, Diarmaid. Pursued in their doomed elopement they found shelter in stone monuments.

I said: "I'm afraid the associations from the stones this morning weren't that romantic. Sean took me by to see the bonfire and the lopped oak inside the stone circle. We'd been discussing the ritual murder of the seasonal king at the summer solstice."

There was a silence broken only by the click of Mr. Rory's knife and fork on Mrs. Rory's best, leaf-bordered china.

I explained: "I asked him what Father Flanagan's barbed hints were all about, and he told me about the rumors of the Midsummer pagan rites."

Mrs. Rory scrambled to her feet muttering something about checking the rice pudding. She rapidly wiggled her fingers as though making a small protective cross over herself.

Mr. Rory masticated five more times before swallowing his last bite. He carefully placed his knife and fork together on his plate, prongs up, blade in, and patted his napkin to his mouth. "I don't know that I would take much notice of such tales if I were you," he said. "I'm surprised Sean bothered telling you."

"It was like pulling rusty nails to get it out of him," I said.

"But any self-respecting student of mythology has *got* to find things out like that."

"Those things are better left unspoken."

"But everybody *knows* about it. That *had* to be Father Flanagan's assumption or he wouldn't have delivered a whole sermon on it."

Mrs. Rory returned looking distressed. "Don't let's spoil our Sunday dinner with such things," she begged, setting down a delicious brown-topped pudding as though to buy my silence with a bribe. "Let's forget it, now."

Mr. Rory skillfully changed the subject with a topic he knew would successfully divert me: "Incidentally Jan, I looked up a Chamber pamphlet before lunch. It lists different businesses in the area. There are not so many estate agents that you couldn't canvas the whole crew inside a morning. You might be able to track down your man by phone and clear the whole thing up."

21

Mr. Rory's suggestion was ingenious, but it would be soon enough to think of that next morning when the offices were open. Right then, when I went up to my room ostensibly to take a nap like my good hosts, I remained deeply preoccupied with the stone circle and the Midsummer rites. My mind felt like the insectivorous sundew Sean had shown me on the bog—all greedy, sensitive antennae.

My curiosity, however, was more than the intellectual hunger of a student of mythology as I had claimed. More even than common-or-garden nosiness. I found myself developing a morbid fascination with this startling manifestation of the dark, irrational side of human beings. There was even more to it than that. In some way that as yet I couldn't fathom, the stone circle and the satanic rites supposedly performed there merged with my reactions to the tower to increase the sense of personal threat. Perhaps my apprehension rose out of Padraic Herlihy's possible connection with both the tower and the rites. Or maybe something similar in the troubled reactions of the Rorys had made me bring both things together.

In the *Book of Ancient Monuments,* which I had brought

upstairs, I found a reference to a stone circle at a location roughly corresponding to the place where I deduced that Sean and I had walked. The text described it as "twelve orthostats and a recumbent on the west side." The account continued:

> The portal stones, set radially, are seven feet high. At the summer solstice, the axis points to sunset. One legend claims the stones are the petrified remains of a druid coven spellbound when St. Patrick robbed them of the holy fire. Some archeologists maintain that the circle is a temple (a simpler version of Stonehenge) used for sun worship by a civilization many centuries before the birth of Christ. According to another legend, this monument is the "Last Bed of Diarmaid and Gráinne," being the lovers' final resting place before Diarmaid was killed by the Enchanted Boar. Local legend also speaks of a tunnel leading into the bracken-covered hills behind. Another such tunnel has been said to connect the monument to Caisleán Bran below. An early nineteenth-century account tells of excavation inside the circle of a rock-lined cyst, in which were found fragments of cremated bone and ash.

This brief summary contained a number of goose-pimpling features. The twelve stones—I hadn't thought to count them on the ground—conformed to the twelvesome of the brotherhood, the thirteenth separated stone perhaps symbolizing the doomed king. One thought of Arthur, twice betrayed, and his Knights of the Round Table, especially with the rounded altar stone; and then of Christ and his twelve apostles—which evoked suggestions of a black-Mass inversion of the Christian grouping, the demonic thirteenth stone off-center and outside the ring. The cremated bones and the alignment of the axis to the summer solstice raised another bump or two. And the connection of the circle to the tower by a secret tunnel all but turned my scalp into a stiff-bristle brush.

I got up from the desk and prowled around the room to discharge some of the tension this information generated. It had put me on the saw side of the seesaw, going down to a hard thud. The faster I discovered our realtor and annulled the dead, the happier I'd be.

As if to match my mood, the room was darkening. I parted the curtains to look outside. After such a lovely day, the sky had suddenly turned mean. Swirls of steel-gray clouds trailed tatters from their undersides like straggles from the coats of lumbering yaks at the San Diego Zoo. Officially night wouldn't fall for hours, but we were in for another of those long Celtic twilights jointed between day and night. The village looked deserted, one scurrying figure in the distance the only sign of life.

While I watched the sky close in to meet the sea and form one great blob of striated gray, I caught a nearby movement out of the corner of my eye. A cat, maybe, sensing the threatening storm and scuttling for cover beneath my camper.

A second later I saw the crown of a shock of rusty hair. Red. What on earth was he doing? Something obviously not too . . . too regular, judging by his furtiveness. He was keeping very low.

Surely he wasn't trying to steal something from my car? And yet, why not? He was a tinker child. Everybody said they were light-fingered. Living off the land and other people's property like gypsies, parasites. What had Sean said: Once is once too much to trust them.

I didn't think twice. It couldn't have taken me more than half a minute to streak downstairs and out the door. But already the little brat had disappeared. I scoured the area with indignant eyes but could see neither hide nor hair of him.

Irked, I turned back to the camper to see what he had lifted, or what damage he had done, perhaps for the sheer hell of it. I expected the hubcaps to be missing at the very least.

But the vehicle was intact, watertight and shipshape.

Except: under the windshield wipers I saw a bunch of flowers. Wild blue stars, pink bells, purple tufts, in a bundle of leaves and stems.

Nor was that the full extent of the embellishments. Pressed into each hubcap and the radiator were other tiny blooms.

I stood there going weak with shame. How unforgivable of me to have jumped to such prejudiced conclusions about someone who had shown nothing but good will toward me, even saving me from the lake.

Perhaps I had needed to have myself cut down to size in my own eyes in order to see the boy as he really was. Like some kind of wood sprite, he had touched my life with a natural benignity. If that was a funny way to put it, it was only because I could find no other words to express his unique influence. These flowers, for example. What an extraordinary gesture for a child. What did they express? A compliment? A blessing? A charm?

The flowers and their bearer were, however, put out of my mind the next moment when Mrs. Rory appeared in the vestibule to summon me to the phone.

This time it was Michael Cunningham. He said: "I have to go to Sligo in the morning. I wonder whether we could meet for lunch."

"You must be picking up my frequency. I was just thinking about going there myself tomorrow to try and find the realtor who sold my grandfather the tower."

No sooner had I said it than I remembered large ears were undoubtedly pricked along the line.

Michael said anxiously: "I hope that doesn't mean you're having problems. I was just going to ask you what you'd found."

"It's a complicated story," I said guardedly. "I'll tell you about it over lunch tomorrow."

22

The next day was one of those charmed spots in time that flower in Ireland like windblown milkmaid blossoms in a bog, not beauty of a static sort but of an ever-changing shape and shade and pattern. As I drove to Sligo, I saw the wind had "bundled up the clouds high over Knocknarea." And on top of that mountain of the kings, an enormous truncated cone of limestone of a thousand or so feet high, Maeve's Lump stood out in bold relief—the huge cairn beneath which, legend says, lies the pagan queen.

I hoped the glory of the morning was a portent of the day.

Having faint recollections of the name of Boland, the only name on the list of estate agents that rang a bell, I went there first, and chalked up a hole in one. Himself wasn't in his office at that moment, but the bony lady with earphone hair style remembered the transaction when I gave my name. She steered me to an adjoining office to talk to the solicitor who'd drawn up the deed.

Mr. McGreevy unrolled a battered survey map across his desk and established once and for all that Tur Bran, Tur Beag, and Caisleán Bran Beag were one. Riffling through an abstract to show how the title had descended from time immemorial, he confirmed the title to be now in my grandfather's name. As Mr. Meaney had conjectured, the tower was part of the ancient demesne of Aranmore. Hit by hard times in the economic slump of the twenties and thirties, most of its lands, except unproductive plots around the old house and the tower, had been sold to adjacent farms and smallholders. The recent belated and final settlement of the last remnants of the historic old estate had released the tower for sale.

Of course there was access to the tower, Mr. McGreevy said, laughing paternally at my silliness. With his tortoise-shell and silver letter opener, he tapped the yellow paper of the survey map. "Right here."

"Yes," I said cuttingly. "Across a bog."

Up shot his curly brows. "Dear me. Is that so? I haven't seen the actual premises, of course."

I said: "You're *sure* these boundaries are correct?" My finger traced them on the map. "We don't own any of this higher land?"

Mr. McGreevy looked distressed, shaking his head. Then he brightened visibly. "However, it wouldn't cost too much to build a footbridge to the road. Better yet, drain the land."

All ears, I said: "How would you do that?"

"The cheapest way is to cut ditches for the water to drain into. Or there are outfits in the business of pumping bogs and reclaiming land."

His suggestions were ingenious. But they were no help at all in solving my more immediate problem of getting to the tower. "Meantime," I said, pointing to a dotted line across Herlihy's field. "we wouldn't have a right-of-way through here by any chance?"

Mr. McGreevy pursed his lips unhopefully. "It's *possible* it's a public pathway. It would take a bit of research to find out. Though knowing the land's history, I think it most unlikely." The space between his curly brows increased. "However, if the path's a good way in, I dare say as good neighbors they'd be glad to let you use it."

I didn't bother to enlighten him of the pointlessness of that suggestion. I said: "If you haven't seen the premises, I assume you don't have any idea what condition the tower itself is in?"

At that moment a face colored tippler red peered around the door followed by a portly tub of tweed. "Matt Boland," the intruder said, thrusting out a hairy hand. "I see now why Timmy didn't let me know you'd come. My cousin Timmy Bourke down at Dunderg," he added parenthetically. "We were expecting just your granddaddy." And hardly waiting to draw a breath: "So you wouldn't have picked up the caravan I booked for you?"

"You mean the camper? Yes, I did. It's parked outside."

As though in disbelief, he craned to look into the street.

Mr. McGreevy said: "Miss McDonagh was enquiring about the condition of the tower."

Mr. Boland pulled his head back into his set of chins and put on a look of pained regret. "I'm afraid I have sad tidings, Miss McDonagh. They've condemned the place."

"What's that supposed to mean?" I had visions of an imminent demolition with cranes and iron balls.

"It means it's deemed unsanitary or unsafe by the authorities," Mr. McGreevy said, "and boarded up."

I turned on him, saying icily: "That had better mean that the contract is null and void and my grandfather will get his money back."

Mr. McGreevy's face crumpled as though he were about to cry. "I'm afraid . . ." he started.

But Mr. Boland cut in. "Oh, much better than that; I'll resell it for your grandfather. He'll turn a tidy profit."

"Who'd want to buy it if it's in such bad condition?"

"One of our local landowners. He didn't know it had

come on the market. He was most put out at me for not giving him first chance."

"Why would he want it any more than we do?"

"Sentimental value," Mr. Boland said expansively. "To preserve it as a local monument, not to live in it."

23

After that disturbing interview, I was lucky to have Michael's visit to look forward to. When I met him at the train, I almost forgave him for belonging to Cathy, I was so glad to see him. We clasped hands like long-lost friends, as indeed we seemed—so much had happened in the intervening days.

We ate in the Silver Swan overlooking the amber froth of the Garavogue River. It rushed and eddied around the pillars and under the arches of a stone bridge signed like a sculpture with the builder's name.

Over leek soup, I brought Michael up to date on the story of the tower. The longer he listened the more serious his expression grew. When he heard that Mr. Boland had a buyer, he said firmly: "You must write your grandfather urging him to sell at once."

Amazed at his intensity, I said: "Not until I've seen the inside of the tower."

"You already know it must be pretty awful for it to have been condemned."

"If someone wants it bad enough to give a lot more than we paid for it, I've got to know what's so attractive."

"That agent gave you a good reason. This is not the first time local potentates have woken up belatedly to the loss of a landmark in their bailiwick."

"We're not going to remove it stone by stone!"

"It's another kind of loss. They're resentful of a foreign purchaser."

"How do you figure that?"

"It's just an educated guess." He spelled out what I'd intuited already, that a good deal of ill feeling was harbored by the Irish against acquisitive foreigners, especially rich Germans and Americans. After all, the Irish had been serfs in their own country for eight or nine centuries, through the foreign occupations of the Anglo-Norman barons, the Tudors, Cromwell's Puritans, the Orangemen, and the British Protestant Ascendancy in general. Now, in the twentieth century, though they had won political independence, quantities of economic power still lay with foreign overlords.

But surely a modest private purchase of a crumbling ruin wouldn't fall under the general indictment of encroaching strangers?

Michael smiled ruefully. "Those lucky breaks, as you've been calling them. You don't really think they're accidents? They sound to me suspiciously like deliberate harassments. Acts of communal mischief, maybe, against somebody who's not too welcome in the neighborhood."

My soup was cold. I laid down my spoon. I said: "Don't think I haven't thought about it. Especially since you'd put me on my guard. I mean when incidents pile up like that you have to wonder whether there's anything intentional behind them. But I don't see how."

The waitress came to take the plates.

I said: "I walked myself into that bog. The cyclist who gave me vague directions was just a casual passerby. He couldn't have had the slightest notion who I was, or what I was doing in the neighborhood. The same goes for the fellow who lent me his leaky curragh. It was purely at random I happened by. And nobody, not even me, knew I was going to the Leap. That was a spur-of-the-moment impulse, allowing no time for anyone to fix a trap. In fact, the only guy who's been unfriendly is Padraic Herlihy, and I can sort of understand his reasons."

Michael said: "You've left out the incident of the exploding stove."

"All I can say is that I was a big surprise—a total stranger—to Padraic Herlihy." And then I stopped. Something had just clicked in my head. Mr. Boland had booked the camper. His cousin Timmy Bourke had kept a lookout for my grandfather's arrival in Dunderg. Guinness is good for you said the sign on the wall across the bridge. J. Kilfeather, Thomas Connolly, said the name boards on the shops. Gulls swooped. Ferns and moss grew in the high stone bank. We had definitely been expected.

Michael was watching me. As though he glimpsed my thoughts, he asked: "What is it?"

If I told him, he'd only overreact, darkly misconstruing a bit of casual trivia that undoubtedly held no significance at all.

Fortunately, our order came: stuffed roast chicken with new potatoes. While we sampled it, it was easy to change the subject. "You haven't told me what you're doing here."

Finishing his bite he said: "You remember me telling you about that group of passage graves in Sligo—the ones I was finagling to get a crack at if the funds came through? Well, they got the go-ahead for preliminary examination of the sites. My bid was in, so I got first refusal."

It was futile to be thrilled about it, especially now I knew his reason for wanting to come west to work. "That means you'll be sticking around this area awhile?"

He nodded. "Another chap, Dick Brown, and I are to

pitch camp at Lake Arrow. They've equipped us with a caravan hitched to Dick's Vauxhall. Dick's installed already. He's coming to pick me up when I phone him after lunch."

I had a marvelous idea. "Why can't I drive you over?"

Irishly reluctant to be any trouble, he said: "It's a bit out of your way."

"I've got an ulterior motive. I was going to try to coax you into going to Lough Gill this afternoon."

"Why not," he said, his ironic mouth and the deepening highlights in his eyes provoking useless wishes that he was not off limits.

The day was a cornucopia of thrills for a Yeats fanatic. To our left as we traveled east lay the famed Ben Bulben, an awesome hulk of treeless limestone looking like a loaf which had risen to break its crust. Yeats had climbed it in boyhood days, dreaming of Diarmaid dying on the tusks of the Sacred Boar. Ahead, Sleuth Woods led down to the island-studded opal waters of Lake Gill—five miles of incredibly blue surface faithfully reflecting skies garnished with whipped cream. Parking the car to climb through ash, oak, hazel, arbutus, and an ecstasy of flowers to Dooney Rock, we squinted across leafy islands scattered in the lake to distant Drumcliffe, Yeats's final resting place.

The highlight of our expedition was a visit by rowboat to tiny Heather Island, the world-renowned Lake Isle of Innisfree, where Yeats had conjured up a pastoral utopia à la Thoreau.

Walking around the tiny island, we listened to the water lapping with low sounds on the rock-and-pebbled shore, and to the drowsy hum in the fragrant meadowsweet. At the far end of the island, we climbed a cliff and returned along a steeply wooded path into a central glade. There in a shower of birdsong, new-coined sunlight, and leaf-shadow I found the hub of time, the world's omphalos, the magic circle within the ever-enlarging circles of the Lake Isle, the

Lough, the island of Ireland, and the spinning globe. The only flaw was that I couldn't share the experience with Michael. It was pointless longing for absolute perfection, even in a spellbound moment of suspended time.

That was not the only bittersweet moment that the day produced. Later that evening Michael and I climbed to the nearest of five parallel ridges running roughly north to south, in the area where Michael was to work. From east to west across the grain of these five ridges rose the thirteen magnificent cairns of Carrowkeel. From the top of the first of these mounds of loose gray stones we viewed the impressive sheet of water of Lough Arrow and the prehistoric battleground beyond, where the Tuatha De Danaan were said to have defeated the Firbolgs.

Sauntering among ling and cowberry and cross-leaved heath, beneath the kestrel winging on the evening air, Michael spoke of Ireland's ancient people. He had come to know them by their differing tombs: passage graves, court graves, cruciform chambers in a round cairn, forecourted galleries in a long cairn. It was a short course in Neolithic and Bronze Age archeology.

My enthusiasm didn't extend to sharing his pleasure when we entered an opened cairn, scrunching under the huge rock slab that formed its lintel. The awe-inspiring fact that it was built a thousand years and more before Christ's birth couldn't persuade me to linger in its chilling dark.

Outside again, I asked him: "How are these cairns associated with Druidic rituals?"

"They aren't."

Puzzled, I said: "What about stone circles?"

"Are you thinking about those claims that Stonehenge and such are Druid temples? That's just popular confusion. There's no evidence of any connection."

"What *do* you know about the Druids, then?"

"Not much. They're really not an archeologist's concern.

What's actually known about them—tangible evidence—would go into a thimble."

"So how are they known at all?"

"Various writings make reference to them—accounts from the Roman occupation of Gaul and Wales. Then some people argue for the theory of folk-memory as a method of transmission."

"Do you buy that?"

"It's really not my thing. I prefer objective, scientific proof. Still, one does have to wonder how this mystical irrational stuff gets perpetuated—why it surfaces every now and then in a sort of cyclical regeneration."

"What do you think accounts for it?"

He laughed. "It would take a psychologist, a theologian and a sociologist rolled into one to tackle that. Maybe offbeat beliefs lie dormant in the social psyche through a more or less rational period. Then the wheel turns and the irrational stuff comes to the fore again. Strange beliefs stored in old people's memories, or written down in esoteric books, are suddenly revived."

"But what causes them to burst out again?"

"Perhaps their revival is triggered by some kind of psychic poverty. Or maybe there's a latent urge in us for the demonic and irrational—an urge that can only be suppressed so long before it has to ooze out somewhere."

"Could this cyclic of the irrational have quite physical causes—like the moon's influence on the tides, or other astronomical phenomena? Is there even something to those theories of the New Millennium, like Yeats's theory of the phases of history? Here the two-thousand-year cycle of the Great Year is soon coming to a close, and we have all this frightening preoccupation with the occult and satanism."

He said: "What are those famous lines in Yeats's 'Second Coming'?"

" 'Things fall apart, the center cannot hold.' "

In the slanting rays of a weird evening light, the landscape spread before us, fantastic and surreal, broken horizontally as well as laterally by steep rock-faces, as though some giant had built himself a model of a relief map in contoured steps. There was a moonscape starkness about the whole terrain that made the hackles rise. In that bizarre context, in the dying light with the dark mouth of the cairn yawning behind us, any theory seemed credible. Despite myself, I shivered.

"You're cold," he said, concerned, putting an arm around me.

I clung to him like a scared child.

The next second his arms encircled me and we were kissing.

For a moment, I was aware only of his mouth, his body, and my whirling senses, as excitement coursed through blood and nerve.

Then I remembered Cathy.

I pulled away.

How could I let myself be kissed by a man committed to another woman? How could I have possibly responded to the sort of man who played two girls at the same time? How dare he try to use me in that way! Good luck to the girl who got him if he could not resist a fleeting impulse. She was welcome.

I turned abruptly and started back along the sheep track up which we had climbed, slithering in my haste and almost tripping over the tangled heath.

He kept pace with me a couple of feet behind on the single track. But we said nothing to each other until we reached the camper parked on the sand road. The brief ride to Castle Baldwin was strained and silent.

But just before I dropped him at his trailer campsite, he said casually, as if the aborted embrace had never happened:

"Incidentally, I meant to ask you when you brought it up. Why your interest in the Druids?"

I was glad he asked. It gave me a chance to let him know that he was not the beach's only pebble. "A fellow I'm dating in Dunderg was telling me yesterday about the revival of some Druid rituals on St. John's Eve. We walked to a stone circle where they hold their secret ceremonies."

I assumed I had spoked his wheel for he was silent a long minute. Then he said mildly: "Cathy wrote a paper on the Druids once. I can ask her for it when I see her Wednesday, if you like. I'll drop it off on my way back Thursday morning."

24

I had only one thing on my mind when I returned to Dunderg late that evening. How could I carry out the speediest inspection of the tower? If it really was as bad as everyone made out, the sooner I got the wheels in motion to dispose of it the better.

Why shouldn't I go to Padraic Herlihy and ask permission to cross his land? I could imply that my request was mainly a gesture of acceptance of the peace pipe he had proffered Sunday after church. And if I carefully pointed out that there was no question of a long-term favor to cause him inconvenience, how could he refuse?

Yet I couldn't bring myself to go and talk to him. My internal buzzer kept sounding at a low and steady pitch each time I tried to pull myself together and drop in at the farm. I persuaded myself that my repeated postponements were due to the deterioration in the condition of Mr. Meaney, discovered Tuesday morning semicomatose, poor dear, and rushed to hospital. The crisis *did* eat a big hole in my day with my having to drive Mrs. Rory back and forth. But there was plenty of time left over for somebody less craven to have knocked on a door and exchanged some words.

By Wednesday I had battled my way to the conclusion that I would sooner brave the unknowns of the underground-cave route on my own than ask a favor of Padraic Herlihy.

Still and all, throughout Wednesday I suffered increasingly cold feet as I began uneasily collecting some of the items of equipment Kris had suggested on the phone—a "torch," i.e., a flashlight, a hammer, and a length of hemp rope that didn't look too sturdy but was the best I could lay hands on. The closest I could come to a piton was a roofing nail. Without any faith that they'd be any use, I bought a half a dozen. Matches, a ball of string and some chocolate bars completed my purchases, all made secretly in a general store close to the hospital while I waited during visiting hours for Mrs. Rory and her brother. The Rorys would be bound to stop me, one way or another, if they got wind of my projected escapade.

I didn't need their protests anyway. The shortfall in my preparations increasingly convinced me of the hazard of the enterprise. What if I fell and broke my leg? I would die a death of slow starvation, locked in perpetual night in the bowels of the earth. Against such an exigency I could leave a letter on my bureau to tell them where to look for me if I didn't return. But that wouldn't help me if I stumbled into a subterranean chasm and broke my neck.

My doubts accelerated at such a rate that by the time I picked up Mrs. Rory and her brother for the return trip Wednesday evening, I had practically sold myself on the prudence of waiting for Kris to lead the expedition. If necessary, I would drive down to Kinvara and prevail on her to return with me without delay.

Great was my pleasure, therefore, when I returned to Dunderg that evening to find Kris installed in the bedroom next to mine.

"Am I glad to see *you*," I said, giving her a hero's

welcome. "I thought you weren't coming up until next week."

"I am very worried all the time. I have, how you call it, the foreboding. I keep seeing you drowned in a syphon."

"What's a syphon?"

"A sump."

"A sump?"

"A narrow passage filled with water."

"You don't have a very good impression of me, do you? I may be stupid, but I'm not such an idiot as to try anything *that* dangerous."

"Sometimes you are in such spots before you know it," she said bossily. "You can find yourself wedged in corkscrew shaft before you realize. Even with plenty help, strong men have died in such situations."

"Well, it's nice you think so much of me to forego your precious Burren."

"It is not alone your welfare that has brought me here," she said, wagging her finger like a governess. "I more and more curious become about this cave of yours."

"Thanks," I said dryly.

"It is off the beaten track," she said. "It is not likely speleologists are aware of it. What is more, if she is place of superstition and suspicion, few will have try to penetrate her."

"What would it matter if they had?"

"The treasures might be gone or damaged."

"Treasures!" She sounded like a child whose head was stuffed with Robert Louis Stevenson.

Unruffled by my hoots, and disdainful of my ignorance, she said: "Bones. Bones of prehistoric men and animals. Implements. Maybe Neolithic art objects."

She really was a dreamer, my sweet Kris. Men had been around this place for eons. I couldn't believe they had left any stone unturned. I told her so.

She snorted. "Of course you haven't even *heard* of the Lascaux caves in the Dordogne."

I made a stab. "The famous caves where they found prehistoric drawings?"

She milled her long arms up and around creating a great cavern in one sweep. "Huge animals. Red, black, yellow. Horses, stags, bulls. Painted by Cro-Magnon Man. *Twenty-five thousand years ago.* And only discovered in 1940 by boys looking for lost dog!"

I threw up my hands in mock capitulation.

Her huge haversack bulged with climbing gear—impressive first-grade Alpine stuff such as nylon rope that would hold a man suspended over the sharp lip of a crevasse without fraying out. She said: "We start at dawn tomorrow. I promised to be back on Friday. A German group come to hostel at the weekend—a group of specialists that would like my help."

"Not so fast," I told her. I had commitments in the morning to run Mrs. Rory to the hospital. Moreover, dawn activity might be conspicuous. I expressed these reservations. "Why not tonight?"

To my surprise, she consented readily. "It is always night below ground anyway."

My heart began a rapid beat that didn't slow for many hours. It was almost more than I could bear to sit through supper and the long-winded rehearsal to the Rorys of the facts of Kris's life. I had a tough time keeping our mission secret, concealing the mounting excitement that might have given it away.

But at last, on the pretext of a sightseeing tour around the neighborhood, we left the house, and with a fast swing along the low road for Kris to gape at the picture-postcard tower she was assisting me to reconnoiter, we headed for the lane behind the wood.

Lost on us that evening were the shadowed siftings of the

leaves, the tumultuous birdsong. The wood's thick carpet and dense coverts were more hindrance than pleasure. With a singleness of purpose almost sacrilegious, we blundered our way through to the fern-and-moss-grown opening resembling more than ever, in the somber gloom of evening, a dragon's mouth. I was glad the prosaic Kris was my companion, not the spook-prone Red.

Kris waded in the stream, less full, less forceful, than when I had last seen it, to survey the aperture no more than two feet high by three feet wide. Shocked and shivering in that liquid ice, I craned around her as she shone her flashlight down the hole. Though the water spilled over a lip to disappear into a roaring well below, a vault of sorts lay just a little lower than the level where we stood. The beam of light picked out its damp walls, which curved concavely down till they converged to form a "floor," loose boulders plugging the narrow gap. This strange formation was what Kris termed a "diaclase."

She said: "We can lower ourselves over side down to level of water. Or we can try this upper level. Which we do?"

I was quaking, but I hoped not noticeably. "You're the boss."

"Without diving equipment, water can be hazardous. Of course, the stream is not very big. But we do not know what else drains down there. The noise she makes is loud."

"On the other hand," I said, "the stream is what I want to follow, if it runs beside the tower."

"This top story will lead roughly the same way," she said authoritatively. "It is stream's old course. Since you are novice, we are wise to start out on fossilized system. We can drop down to active system when she looks more promising."

Only to baby me, she gave me very much to understand, she tied one of her nylon ropes to a nearby tree. Holding on to it, I lowered myself after her into the vault. My eyes were everywhere at once, watching where Kris put her feet—as close into the wall as possible—watching for footholds for my own feet, and occasionally peering down the gaps to the dark roar below. I'd been smarter than I realized to have given up my plan of trying it alone.

Farther along we moved into a passage with a firmer floor. But it was only one loop of a complicated maze, and I was more than ever grateful for the rope. It looked easy to get very lost in there. "She is like Swiss cheese," Kris cried enthusiastically.

A few feet more and the passage curved. A pile of rubble barred our way. A quick peek into adjacent cavities giving off the main gallery, plus a glance at Kris's pocket compass pinned to her shirt, revealed two possible routes forward, neither very promising. One was a narrow cleft at a limestone joint. The other was what Kris referred to as a "chimney," an irregularly walled shaft down to the active system of the stream below.

Scrutinizing the cleft, Kris bit her lip. "This might be no more than a catrun." And misreading my apprehensive face: "You call such a crawlway, maybe?" She made wiggling motions to explain. "To go through on all fours."

"It's not that I don't understand," I said. "I'm remembering your dream about my getting wedged."

She laughed. "My shoulders are the problem. If *I* get through, you are a cinch." It was another of her overworked expressions she'd picked up from me.

"What about the shaft?"

"He looks tempting. But I am not sure about you. You have tried chimneying before?"

"What do you mean, 'chimneying'?"

She spread her feet apart, moving from right to left, motioning perpendicularly with her hands to suggest the shaft.

I began to sweat. I took the flashlight from her, peering down into the black depths.

"It is very small circumference," she said. "Not far to stretch. And plenty footholds. Almost like a stairs."

"Let's try the crawl first."

"Okay. But if that no good, we have only two choices. Chimney or go back." It sounded like a threat.

Returning to the cleft, Kris shone the beam along the crawl. It ran only a short length before it veered. The ground of the tunnel, however, seemed kind enough: smooth rock, a little loose sand, and no projections.

Kris entered feet first, the correct position for a fast return, she explained to me, if the crawl got dangerously snug.

"I see," I said, my voice the consistency of partially set jello.

"You are cold?" she said.

I was indeed. It was like an ice house deep inside that hill. But it was not on that account I shivered. Every cautious word proceeding from her mouth sapped my ebbing confidence. I said: "No, I'm chicken."

"What is chicken?"

"Never mind."

She gave me one of her forbidding Lutheran looks. "Now listen and remember. Do not follow me until I call. If I out of earshot and I yank three times the rope, you must pull me back. Is that understood?"

The next minute she had wriggled out of sight, and I was left in quaking blackness.

In a moment her voice came echoing back. She was swearing, apparently in Dutch.

I called: "What's up?"

"I have hit bottleneck." The sound of labored breathing filled the hole.

"Come back," I croaked. "Let's give it up."

"My hips are through."

"But I'm scared," I said. "What if you get stuck and I won't be able to budge you?"

Sounds of more exertion in the narrow tube.

"Please come back," I begged her. "I'll go to pieces if you don't."

A long minute more and her head emerged into the small oasis of the flashlight, her blond hair covered with sandy debris. When she scrambled out, I saw her pants were torn.

She put on her parson's look and said: "Some fine spelunker."

I hung my head.

She said dourly: "I suppose you not even game to try chimney now."

In a mouse's voice I said: "If you think we should."

She shrugged. "It is not *me* who want to see the tower."

But I was thinking that maybe after all I didn't need to *ask* Herlihy for permission to cross his land. I could just *do* it. He would hardly take a rifle to me. And that wolfhound of his was probably more bark than bite. Perhaps I should even forget the tower for this year, as Michael had suggested, and wait until my grandfather could look it over. Who was I to make such big decisions in any case?

Kris said: "You *are* chicken." She learned very fast.

That spurred me to show some kind of spirit. I had the responsibility of a national as well as a personal image to maintain. "It's just I'm new at this. Give me another chance."

Staring down the chimney, taking stock, she said: "He looks like child play. But just in case, I drive piton in to secure a rope. Then you have not excuse to fall or throw a fit."

The honeycomb of caves reverberated with the sound of

metal hammered against rock. I don't know what or who I feared might be alerted by the noise, but each blow made me wince.

When she had secured the rope, she started down the chimney, straddling the void, expertly moving hands and feet in coordinated grace and confidence.

When the scuffling ceased, I anxiously called down: "Are you all right?"

"She pretty damp down here. Otherwise I'm fine."

"Do you want me to start down?"

"Wait until I look around."

I waited. Once more the silence of the cavern got to me. It had a quality that had to be comparable to living in a padded cell—all natural noises filtered out of one's experience. It seemed the lesser of two evils now to descend the jagged shaft to be with a human being.

After a few moments I couldn't bear it any longer. "Are you there, Kris?"

A moment of sheer panic. Then her voice came floating up: "She look quite promising if you prepared to wade the stream."

"I'm prepared," I said, "if I can make it down."

"You shall make it down. You not even need the rope."

The inside of my mouth felt lined with chalk as I lowered myself over the edge. There was room for both feet on the first projection. All I had to do was lean across the void, and with hands braced, lower myself to the next foothold. At one spot I found it necessary to brace my back against the wall and "walk" down the other side. Satisfaction bathed me when I put both feet on the ground.

"Ground" was not exactly the right word, however. The floor of the small cavern in which I found myself was a damp mix of silt and sand into which my feet sank to the ankles. The stream swirled through the middle of it, carrying the particles suspended in its ochre brew.

Kris pointed to a scum line on the walls. "We have luck today, she is not flooding. She recently rise up to here. In cloudburst she could swell up to the roof."

Once more I was grateful that a surge of rare good sense had stopped me trying it earlier alone.

Kris said: "Ahead chamber narrows to passage, so water deepens." She looked at me intently, hanging a question on the air between us that made me swallow back my heart.

"Lead the way," I said.

The walls closed in, the water backed up behind the narrowing outlet like a funnel, and the level rose above my waist. The temperature, barely above freezing, rattled my teeth.

Kris appeared to be made of the same stuff as the walls. She strode blithely on, prattling like a tape recorder. "Jan, earlier you ask me what is sump or syphon. It is what this passage be when storm shall fill her to the roof."

We had to stoop now as the ceiling lowered. The water inched up to my armpits and I grew more and more alarmed. "What makes you think that farther on it's not a sump right now?"

She stopped dead, shining the beam to light my face. "Don't tell me you not swim?"

"Of *course* I can swim," I said defensively.

"Well then," she said, as if I'd been a fool to raise the matter.

But a short way on, the passage miraculously widened, and the water fanned into a pool. Numerous galleries gave off a large central chamber. The whole area resembled a highly magnified piece of travertine with irregularly shaped pores. I felt like a termite in a riddled board.

Kris was obviously itching to do some reconnoitering. She said: "I wonder where *that* branch go?"

"That's not the way the water flows," I said, to remind her of our mission.

"Though she used to flow here long ago until she somehow got diverted," she said, off on her own track. "This channel may bypass lake and run directly to the sea. She is much more complicated cave system than I first suspect. It possible we are first to penetrate it."

"I doubt that," I said, pointing with my toe to a cigarette butt ground into the sand.

Her face fell, but she said optimistically: "There will be parts of such a complex system that is unexplored, I'm sure."

In case she had intentions of poking around right now, I said: "I'd like to see the tower before the light is absolutely gone."

"That's simple," she said, returning to the central chamber and examining the compass pinned to her pocket flap. "In another about thirty yards, I predict we see ahead the light."

And she was right. We had only to traverse another passage with an obvious gradient and the stream tumbled toward the gray glow of a twilight sky.

Leaving the inside of the hill, the water splashed over a shallow fall shrouded by dense bushes. It was a fair guess that the vegetation effectively concealed the entrance from anyone outside.

My heart accelerating, I parted the bushes. There, within a stone's throw, were the foundations of the tower.

25

I stood spellbound for a moment, drinking in the magic of it. The stream eddied and gurgled over rocks and pebbles, lapping the ancient base-batter flaring boldly to form a solid support for the tapered walls above. Only the corners and the arches of the openings were of chiseled stone. The flat expanses of the walls were jigsaws composed of all shapes and sizes of rocks and pebbles skillfully fitted into place with little dressing by the hammer, and fixed with a mortar of lime and sand and clay that had withstood the storms of centuries. The structure stood more steadily, more immutably, than might a mountain along our unstable, faulted coast back home.

In the weird light of the lingering Irish dusk, the stones seemed to give off a muted luminosity of slate blue, beige-rose, moss and olive from their gray, textured faces, perhaps picking up the intense colors of the trees, the sky, the last salmon clouds in the declining light.

I looked cautiously around and waded clear of the bushes. Something splashed and darted along the far side of the stream—a rat, a water hen, Yeats would have speculated, or an otter sliding off the bank. I advanced to touch those beautiful foundations, first tentatively with fingertips, then palms, and finally my cheek. It was a gesture that surprised even myself. To have done such a thing back home would have been mawkishly impossible. But there we didn't have centuries-old towers about which to wax emotional.

From where I stood, looking up the walls toward the crenelated top, the tower seemed as high as any L. A. skyscraper. Almost as high as the surrounding trees. Old ragged elms, old thorns, perhaps, their branches darkly blobbed with masses that looked like nests, and a stand of firs around which swarmed a swirl of wings, bizarre and slightly sinister, flapping and dashing against the foliage. When another black horde flew in across the lake, it occurred to me they were the rooks that Mr. Meaney spoke about, and this copse a rookery at roosting time. Many settled in the branches, yakking to each other, perhaps registering disapproval of us interlopers. The cool, clear air around the tower teemed with raucous sound, and I no longer wondered why the tower was called Tur Bran.

The tower itself was built upon a rocky outcrop, an extension of the mass of rock which formed the stark cliff some way behind. Between the cliff base and the small lake-lapped "peninsula" on which the tower had been built rose a gentle slope of densely wooded land. A quick survey of the tower's position confirmed that access could be obtained only across the Herlihys' meadow, a route highly visible from their farmhouse. Equally clearly, as I'd suspected, all other approaches seemed barred by treacherous bog.

Kris came up behind me: "Some fine place, eh?" she said. I beamed at her. "Let's see if we can get inside."

As I skirted the foundation, I counted on the screen of trees and bushes to hide us from the Herlihys. Padraic hadn't lied about the tower being boarded up. At least the lowest window slits or loops were blocked. Above, small but beautifully shaped windows, which I later learned were a fine example of cusped-ogee, were, without an extension ladder, way out of reach.

Worse yet, the single doorway had been nailed permanently closed with rough, stout planks. As disturbing as the barrier it represented was the damage this structure must have inflicted on the stones. If I tried to pry it loose, the chances were that great hunks of stone would come away.

Peering close, I felt around the boarding to see how many nails attached it to the wall. Several scraped knuckles and a splintered finger later, it began to dawn on me that the boards might not be anchored in the stone. My poor grazed hands took a further beating as I double-checked.

Excitedly, I tugged gently at the rickety structure. It moved, all in one piece. Some harder tugging and it came completely free. It was no more than a fake barricade hinged to a frame of uprights.

Why had it been put there? To fool the curious and keep them out without permanently blocking the entranceway?

The false "gate" creaked and grated open to reveal a stout oak door of venerable age reinforced with iron studs and braces.

Trembling, I lunged for the iron ring that appeared to serve as a handle. But my action remained uncompleted. Below the ring a large modern hasp and padlock barred the way.

26

After I had bruised the air with expletives which I hoped Kris wouldn't copy, there was nothing to be done but retrace our steps.

With everything reversed, and so many red-herring turnings in that giant warren, it was trickier going back than coming in. In the ascent the chimney shaft was harder to negotiate, requiring more bracing, more calculation before making moves, hence more energy. I was already very tired from the unaccustomed exercise, and where before I had been propelled by the zest of anticipation, I was now slowed down by disappointment.

But at last we emerged into the night wood. Spooky enough in the daytime, it was positively unnerving now, its magic became negative and menacing. The wind soughed way up in the branches, and stirred the undergrowth along the woodland floor. The harsh cry of some night bird sent centipedes along my spine. Nor was the hoot of a responding owl more soothing for its softness. Even Kris started at a scrabble in the brush before our feet.

A few more steps and she stopped dead, her restraining hand upon my arm. We stood there listening, all our energy concentrated in our ears. Not knowing what had alerted her, I dared not speak. I strained so hard to catch what she was waiting for that my hearing became scrambled by interference from a thousand night noises emitted by each leaf and blade of grass, mingling with the splashing water and the pounding of my heart.

At last I felt Kris relax. She said: "I guess it's nothing."

"What was it anyway?"

"I thought something, somebody, was prowling over there."

Instead of reassuring me, her explanation scared me rigid. "Where?"

She motioned vaguely to one side of us.

"For pete's sake," I said, my voice rough with alarm. "Let's get out of here."

We forged ahead, Kris in the lead, me following. Each second I teetered on the rim of a small panic, so my movements weren't too well under control. Brambles scratched wherever they found a bit of me exposed. My wet feet were constantly resoaked from misstepping in the brook. But since it was our leading string to the safety of the road, we put up with stubbed toes and turned ankles from loose boulders.

A scalp-prickling ten minutes more, and we cleared the wood. Kris said: "That is better," the only indication she had given of having lost some of her own aplomb. "Back to the civilization."

"Not quite," I said. "We're still pretty isolated." The dark, lonely hills above us had their own particular brand of eeriness.

"There is a cottage over there, at least," she said.

"Where?"

She pointed up the hill in the direction of the Druids' circle.

"There's no cottage there," I said, shrinking into myself.

"I see a light a few steps back. But he is gone now."

Again alarm raced along my nerves. When I had walked that way with Sean there hadn't been a single cottage within miles.

It was a relief to reach the car and hit the road. Under a bleak moon, lashed by a sharp wind, the lake gleamed like the scaled hide of a dragon as we passed. Kris said: "We know now how the lake is filled. I wonder how she drains."

"I'm not interested in that tonight," I said. All I wanted was to get safely home.

But the conversation she was having was with herself.

"The road runs right along edge of it. There is not outlet on the surface or a bridge would be. She must have the subterranean drainage also, to the sea."

Now I *was* interested. Remembering Mr. Meaney's story of the demon-ridden water emerging purified after passing through the earth, I said: "A spout of water gushes out at what's regarded as a holy well down at the cove. Is that any help?"

She gave a small approving grunt. "In the morning we shall check it, and see how smart you are."

But in the morning I overslept. I had forgotten to pull out my alarm button. When I jumped up in a flap and went to call Kris, I discovered her bed empty and a note propped on the bureau. "You are sleep sound," it said, her writing more atrociously eccentric than her speech. "I do not like it that to wake you up. You shall find me at the shore to investigate if lake drains out at passage at the sea."

I skipped breakfast to rush Mrs. Rory to the hospital as promised, telling Mr. Rory I'd be back to eat as soon as I'd retrieved Kris from the beach.

But when, a half an hour or so later, I drove to the cliff above the cove, she was nowhere in sight. Perhaps she had already returned to the village on foot. But I'd better make sure.

I climbed down the cliff path, and scrambled over the rocks to the holy well, where I expected her to be. But she was not poking around that weird demibeehive out of which a gush of crystal water welled. Nor was she anywhere along that horn of the crescent, at least as far as I could see. She might, of course, have penetrated some subterranean hole by now, according to her style. If so, it was hopeless to try locating her. Besides, I was famished. If she didn't make it back to base under her own steam, I'd return later on a fuller stomach to look for her.

As I turned to head back to the camper, I scanned the sands, the rocks, the cliffs from my new vantage point. My sweeping glance stopped at the dangerous black holes which Sean had cautioned me from entering when I was looking for a boat. What if, with no one around to warn her, Kris had gone inside? It would be just like her to want to find out what was in there. She couldn't stand to pass up any interesting phenomenon in limestone.

The thought filled me with alarm. My God. What if the ceiling had fallen in on her? She might this very minute be pinned under a pile of rubble.

With winged feet I rushed down onto the strand and toward the holes.

But before I got there, a bundle of clothes dumped in a basin of rocks below the cliff registered on the corner of my eye. How strange. I turned to look at it directly.

I went still closer.

Horror spurted along my veins.

As limp as a rag doll, spread-eagled, face down on the rough, gray limestone blocks, lay Kris.

I didn't have to touch her to know that she was dead.

27

In our imagination we fight dragons, but in life itself we crawl into the nearest crack. Under the shock of that unimaginable experience, I folded so completely, I hardly knew what I was doing.

I must have fled sobbing from the scene, tripping and falling over the pebbles in my desperation. This much I deduced later from the bouquet of bruises on my knees as well as from a playback by my offended ears of a harsh keening sound that could only have come from my own throat. I barely remembered, afterward, stumbling up the steep path in the bluff.

The first thing that registered was a blurred flurry up on the green clifftop. It resolved into two figures running toward me. They were distorted out of all recognition by my streaming tears. A long time seemed to elapse between my seeing them and recognizing them.

One of the figures turned out to be Sean's cousin. He must have heard me from his nearby cottage. The other man was Michael Cunningham.

All recollection of Michael's intention of dropping by Dunderg that morning had gone right out of my mind. But it didn't seem the least bit odd he would be there. I needed him. He was answering a call for help. Babbling my awful news, I let him lead me to the Vauxhall where I collapsed shuddering on the seat. Grim-faced, he drove me to the village to get help while the other man remained to oversee the situation in the cove.

I was beside myself. But Michael managed to extract the story out of me. I finished brokenly: "Why didn't I listen to you? Why didn't I have the sense to leave well enough alone? If only I had, Kris would still be alive."

He said sharply: "You mustn't blame yourself like this. Going to the cove this morning was her own idea."

"She wouldn't have gone if I hadn't told her about the holy well. She wouldn't have been curious about an outlet to the sea if I hadn't taken her through the cave." Worst of all to bear, I tried to tell him between racking sobs: she wouldn't have been near Dunderg at all except for me.

"Even so, you can't hold yourself responsible for her falling to her death."

"Can't I?" I said self-scathingly. "I didn't even warn her her life might be in danger. I could at least have told her to be on her guard."

Horrified, he said: "What are you saying? You're not suggesting it was anything . . . other than an accident?"

"Accident?!" I said with bitter scorn. "She was an expert climber. She never took unnecessary risks. It was broad daylight. She could only have been deliberately pushed over that cliff."

He said sternly: "You're jumping to an awfully wild conclusion."

"Look who's talking!" I said in harsh astonishment. "Who was beating the alarm last Monday? Why the sudden change of tune?"

"It was you I was concerned about. What has Kris to do with it?"

"I don't know for what reason or by whom, but Kris was killed because of me."

After a little silence, he said gravely: "Listen, pet. In a minute you're going to have to talk to the police. Murder's a pretty serious charge. You can't go around voicing suspicions without solid evidence. It might boomerang."

But his cautiousness enraged me. I refused to listen. At the police station I demanded an investigation of foul play. When it was clear I had neither proof nor reasonable grounds, they began treating me as a hysteric, and finally, the more strident I became, as a borderline paranoiac.

Ravaged by guilt, frustration, grief, I had nowhere to go but into that state of numbness which shock mercifully induces. Unlike the lapse in consciousness which blanked me out when I found Kris, I experienced everything that followed with full awareness, but as a jumbled montage of impressions flickering across me as across a movie screen, without soaking in. It was the only way my mind could handle such ghoulish details as the whispered consultations about the disposal of the corpse, culminating in Michael's phone call to a representative of the Netherlands in Dublin, who flew in by private plane to take charge of the arrangements.

There had, of course, to be an inquest before Kris's body could be released for shipment back to her home in Holland. That event turned into its own particular brand of nightmare. Too late I saw the wisdom of Michael's warning not to level unsubstantiated charges about Kris's death. Serious questions had been raised, the coroner said, about the possibility of foul play. Three people were at the scene at or about the crucial time. My own explanation for my presence was weak enough. Michael's sounded fabricated out of whole cloth. He had come very much out of his way—"en route" from Galway Bay to Lough Arrow yet!—to let me know that he had forgotten to bring me a promised essay on the Druids! He had glimpsed a camper in the distance and detoured off the main road on the off chance of it being mine, to arrive at the cliff at the psychological moment of the accident. If Sean's cousin hadn't testified that he had seen Kris clambering alone along the cliff a short time earlier, we might have found ourselves shot down by the ricochet of our own charge. After some tart comments from the coroner about coincidences that were very hard to chew, Kris's death was ruled a self-caused, one-man accident.

After it was all over, the numbness continued to cushion me for several days. I caught a dreadful cold, which provided me with a good excuse for what I needed very much to do—to withdraw and get myself together. Michael showed the right kind of concern, dropping by occasionally to bring me magazines and books, but only staying a few minutes. The generous Rorys honored my need for privacy by leaving me alone. Sean sent me a bouquet of white roses and a touching note of sympathy.

Most of the time I stayed upstairs in my room, aware that my precious vacation was running out, but incapable of doing anything about it. What ailed me was not just the aftermath of shock—though that was sizable enough, particularly since it was the first fatal accident I had been involved in, and the first dead body I had ever seen. I had not thought it possible to have grown so fond of an acquaintance of such a short duration.

There was more to it than just a personal sense of loss. I was gripped by a sick unappeasable frustration that a mind so bright and talented, a disposition so bold and cheerful, a body so healthy, a life so vibrant had been so casually snuffed out. It was beyond my powers to comprehend, much less accept, the awful wastefulness of death.

But the most persistent reason for my wretchedness continued to be my pressing sense of guilt. I could never hope to free myself from the feeling of being deeply implicated in her death.

As the days wore on, however, it occurred to me that I might find some peace if I succeeded in transferring the main burden of responsibility to where it properly belonged—the unknown persons who had murdered her.

Michael must have sensed the way my thoughts were heading before I was even sure myself. "It's time to leave Dunderg, pet."

"When I'm ready."

"You're even worse off now than you were before Kris died."

"Maybe."

"Especially since you made those accusations."

There was nothing I could say.

Taking my hand, he said: "I've got to go to Galway the next few days. I don't want to leave you here."

"I'll be all right."

"I'm afraid you'll go and do something silly."

I snatched my hand away from his. "I'm not a child."

He was quiet for a moment. Then he said in a placating voice: "I didn't mean you were. It's just the whole thing's been a rotten shock for you. You're so far from home, with no one to look after you."

The soothing, protective act infuriated me. "I can look after myself, thanks." I nearly told him to save his blarneying for Cathy, but bit my tongue in time.

"I'll phone you when I get back, to see that you're all right."

It was too much. I flung myself away from him, saying rudely: *"Good bye."*

A few seconds later I heard him leave the room and descend the stairs.

28

Michael was right, of course, about the peril I was in. But our exchange had clarified things for me. I now saw that I had greater needs than mere safety. I had to solve Kris's murder before my life could start again.

The solution couldn't be all that difficult to find. It was focused on the tower—that much I was certain of. What secret did that ruin hold? A secret so important that it had to be hidden at all costs—even by the taking of a life? What kind of sinister forces operated there? It was no longer a matter of self-interest or curiosity to storm that tower. I owed it to Kris and myself to see justice done.

From that moment I bent my whole attention to that single goal, beginning with the problem of the padlock on the door. How was I going to force it? It was out of the question to call in a locksmith—even if one existed in that area. I dared not try to buy a hacksaw. So unusual a purchase by a girl in that male-chauvinist society would be bound to draw attention to itself. More than ever now I must court secrecy.

Obviously what I needed was a picklock. In the first instance I meant an instrument to pick locks, then realized

I'd have to find a person-picklock to supply the tool and show me how to use it. After all my pious protestations, it was shameful that my freckled red-headed friend should flash to mind. But, I justified myself, a deprived people couldn't be blamed for fending for themselves. One shouldn't apply one's own affluent standards to those living the precarious existence of impoverished itinerants. Besides, the main reason I had thought of him was that I trusted him.

How could I get hold of him? I hadn't seen him since he'd garlanded my camper. But Michael had talked to him the day before our quarrel, when the child had stopped him with a gift for me. The tiny four-legged creature whittled crudely out of bog-oak might have been a cult object—boar, horse or bull, all sacred animals in Celtic ritual. The boy no doubt had meant it as a talisman, and Michael had returned the compliment with the gift of a retractable steel measuring tape—the only thing he happened to have on him that would interest a small boy.

Where did the tinkers usually camp in this vicinity? Driving the main highways, I had seen tinker colonies monopolizing lay-bys especially at the intersections of main arteries. But out here in the country individual families must have their own private little spots to which they'd come and go. I had a vague impression that Red and his family might hang out somewhere farther up the Derry brook from Mr. Meaney's cottage. First thing tomorrow I'd try to track him down.

But that evening Sean telephoned to ask if I felt well enough to take a motorcycle spin next day around the neighborhood. He had customer-friends to see, to whom he'd like to introduce me. It would do me good. It would blow away the blues.

The following morning was a perfect one for riding pillion. The bike, a modern British-made affair, with spit-and-polished chrome, rode beautifully. With my hands around his waist, my canvas knapsack bouncing lightly on my back, and the wind just fresh enough to slap the color back into my washed-out cheeks and to stream my hair deliciously behind me, I began feeling my old self again. This was exactly what I needed to complete the recuperation begun the night before. The honeysuckle in the hedges wafted a heavenly fragrance under my nose, and even the barnyard smells spoke only of summer and the country.

A few miles along a lane running south, then west, and new to me, we came to a small farm comprised of the usual thatched cottage and outbuildings that dotted the country-side. Sean shouted something back indicating this was our first port of call.

We parked the bike at a five-bar gate and walked into a pleasant pasture. Beside a barn a man was shearing sheep. He was so intent upon his task, and the hum of the powered shears so masked the sound of our approach, he didn't notice us. A teen-ager standing by a pen to regulate the flow of animals touched his forehead, and an older man tucking in and rolling up a fleece on an old oak table nodded an acknowledgment.

We waited quietly at a distance to allow the shearer to complete the sheep on which he worked. With his brown head bent over his bleating subject, his hand guided the shears under the thick fleece, pushing and releasing it in rhythmic spurts to prevent the wool catching in the teeth. It looked so easy, but I guessed how difficult the knack had been to learn. Like dirty detergent foam scooped from an over-bubbled tub, the fleece peeled away under the shears all in one sheet.

At last the sheep stood naked among clumps and tufts of wool and desperate sheep droppings, its eyes wild, its skinned coat patched and lumpy where the shears had skipped. The shearer released the animal for branding by the young assistant, and tossed the fleece to the old man who was bundling.

At that moment the shearer noticed us. He jumped up and came toward us with a puzzled smile. "Ah, Sean! What brings *you* here this soft and blessed day?"

"Isn't it enough that I'm here to gladden your eyes with this grand sight?" Sean said, smilingly presenting me.

Suppressing my amusement at the Irish blarney, I tried not to behave too much like the liberated woman I like to think I am, and accepted with a straight face the shearer's claim that he was honored by my presence. It was the cue for a long spiel of who I was and where I'd come from. It wouldn't be the only time that day I'd wish I had the whole routine on tape.

After a few minutes more of friendly chatting about the prices of wool and mutton and the costs of tacking, Sean said: "We'd better go now and see Jimeen."

"He's over yonder at the dip."

We walked up a rise and down into a hollow, where, between two hillocks, lay a pool crudely walled with field stones, an obvious ox-bow diversion from the stream which followed the lower contours. Two men herded bleating sheep along the gulley, forcing each animal into the dirty pool.

With a long-poled shepherd's crook, a husky black-haired man prodded the animals, dunking them in over their heads. If any animal got into difficulties, he would yank it out with the hooked end of the pole. The poor sheep looked sick with panic when they emerged. Pot-bellied, bird-legged, skittishly clumsy on their dainty hooves, they scampered off into a natural pen beyond the dip where shrill yapping collies herded stragglers back into the flock.

The dipper seemed to be having himself a ball immersing the sheep in the filthy brew. The expression on his face came close to sadistic glee. When he saw us he shouted: "Hang on a minute. I'm nearly through with this bunch." His accent sounded vaguely American.

In a few moments he came toward us, clomping in his gumboots, his hands huge and dirty when he took my hand to greet me. He smelled of lanolin and creosote.

"Have you come to help me out?" he said.

I said: "Isn't that cruel to sink them in over their heads?"

He laughed. "Doesn't hurt them. Maybe makes their eyes smart for a while. But they don't know anything."

"Actually," Sean said, "it's being cruel to be kind, Jan. If you don't submerge them, the ticks and lice run to their silly heads and nothing's gained in dipping them. They'd be bitten alive and fester if it wasn't done properly. It's government regulations anyway."

The dipper, who had been eyeing me unabashedly as Sean gave his explanation, said: "Who do my poor eyes owe this treat to, Sean?" This time the false and flowery tribute had a nasty fawning sound, and I limited my routine recital to a reluctant minimum.

When I could divert the talk away from me, I remarked that from his accent I'd gathered he had visited America.

He thought me clever to have picked up what was but the slightest slurring of the consonants. "I lived in Chicago as a boy," he said. "My mother brought me home when my old man got chewed up in the city meatgrinder. Ireland's the only place in all the world where a man's a man. But I daresay you've discovered that already." He stooped to scoop up a handful of dirt, letting it trickle through his fingers. "All those rotten years in that crummy concrete jungle when I could have had this under my feet."

I'm not fanatically patriotic but his arrogance and unfairness aroused my anger. I would have uttered a choice comeback if Sean hadn't hurriedly interposed by saying we must be on our way.

"Is it Tom you'll be having to see next?" Jimeen asked as he walked with us a little way toward the motorcycle.

It was indeed. We found Tom at the next farm in a cowshed strewn with dirty, trampled straw and old and new manure stinking to high heaven. The place had obviously not been mucked out for a week or more. A young, brawny fellow with a heap of tousled hair, Tom squatted on a milking stool, his knees wide, a pail canted between them, pulling at the udders of a brindled cow. While her milk pinged in white spurts against the bucket's sides, the cow stood doggedly in her stall, flicking her filthy tail to clear away the swarms of flies that kept lighting on her hide, nonchalantly munching strings of hay pulled from the stall in front of her.

As we approached, stepping gingerly through the barn-yard gunk, the milker raised an elbow, and with his forearm brushed the chestnut cowlick out of his eyes to look at us. The eyes, with caked, inflamed lids, looked familiar.

"Well, hello. Sean is it?" he said, squinting out of the darkness of the cowshed into the bright rectangle of the doorway where we stood. "Half a tick. I'm nearly done with Bessie."

He pulled the udders between thumb and forefinger, stripping them of the last ounce of milk. I was intrigued to see him deliberately squirt the last squeeze on the ground. Then, before rising, he dipped his thumb in the frothing milk pail and made a wet cross on the cow's flank.

He kicked the stool out of the way as he got up, wiping his hand on his thigh before offering it for shaking.

"Have we met before?" I asked as we were introduced.

He frowned and shook his head.

As soon as Sean had finished explaining who I was, I asked Tom why he made the thumb-cross on the cow.

"To make her safe against the little people." He was dead

serious. "That way she'll continue to give milk, and her butter'll turn."

"And the milk spurted on the ground?"

"For them to drink so they have no call for spite against me or mine."

I shook my head in the ironic gesture that says one's ears must not be working properly to have heard what has been heard. But there was no one with whom to share the joke.

While Sean talked quite ordinary small talk about crops and the weather, Tom darted sidelong looks at me, and I, still puzzled by his eyes, darted them right back again.

He blurted: "I was at the inquest."

"Ah. Then I must have seen you there."

"That chap Cunningham done it," he said gratuitously.

I stared open-mouthed.

"Everybody thinks so," he said nodding.

"But that's ridiculous. The victim was his friend. He had no more opportunity or motive than I did." I wouldn't even try the theory on for size—it was too disloyal and preposterous. Besides, Michael's only reason for keeping me from the tower was concern for me.

Tom wouldn't hear of us departing without taking some refreshment. He went to get a measure from a lean-to shed, dipped it in the pail and offered me a drink. Brought up as a food-and-drug-administered American, I took a sip less out of appetite than courtesy. I was expecting it to taste as if the cow had flicked her tail in it. But it had a flavor like no milk I'd ever drunk before, like the way one might surmise that nectar tasted—sweet, yet not sweet, warm yet pleasant, redolent of clover and new-mown hay.

At the "bohreen," a cowpath or a back lane to the next small farmstead, Tom paid me quaint respects by thanking Sean for having given him the pleasure of my company. Doffing an imaginary cap, he took his leave.

Across another barnyard we scattered the fowl foraging around a jumble of old hoes, rakes and battered milk cans. A stooped white-haired woman hauled a steaming bucket to a pig pen. A sour ferment of mash made mostly from potato peelings wafted toward us as she slopped the swill over the fence. It splashed and gurgled as it hit the trough. Bald pink-and-mottled porkers, with albino lashes and muck-fouled backs, hoink-hoinked toward it.

The woman straightened. "Hello, Mr. Danaher. It is a brave day ye've brought with ye."

" 'Tis that," he said, lapsing into country talk in the natural charming way that I noticed he fell into when he wanted to put folk at ease. "And how have you been keeping?"

She tossed her head and clucked. " 'Tis no good grumbling. We are born into this world to work and suffer. That's the middle and both ends of it."

Sean introduced me briefly with no explanations. "And where is Dennis?"

"Turning the hay over in the river meadow. Will I go and fetch him?"

"I'll go myself," Sean said.

In a field separated from the barnyard by plots planted in green rows of turnips and potatoes, a tractor roared. An attachment of spoked discs tossed, turned and spread the cut grass to hasten drying. Thistle and dock and nettle mingled with the yellowing stalks and shafts of the long grass, soon, Sean said, to be raked into small cocks, then pitched and trampled into hayricks, and later carted to the yard for building into one huge garden cock. In the uncut fringes at the verges, bees dipped and hummed.

A young man wearing a light, open-necked shirt stopped the tractor when he reached the hedge and climbed down from the high saddle. Blowing the stray wisps from his face, he came toward us, shouting a greeting of pleased surprise.

"Have you come to help me with the haying?" he said teasingly.

"You have twenty pair more hands than last season," Sean said, pointing to the attachment on the tractor. "You don't need me. The next time the river rises and washes Sullivan's cocks downstream when yours are already in the garden, it'll have paid for itself."

While this exchange was going on, the young man flicked an appreciative inquiring glance or two in my direction, and once more we launched into the usual routine with the usual dollop of Irish schmalz.

Ten minutes later we concluded what apparently was our final call, and Sean and I rode off into the hills for lunch. Up there with the hovering hawk and the scissoring snipe, and the magic distant view of Ben Bulben and beyond, and a breeze whistling way above, and water trickling deep in the brown bog, we munched the marmite and bloater-paste sandwiches that I'd prepared. Drinking in the view, we said little to each other until lunch was finished.

While Sean lay back against the ferns, his eyes closed, a comfortable smile flipping the corners of his mouth, I lazily thought back over the interesting encounters of the day. Altogether a fascinating experience, lifting my mind out of the doldrums. I was glad Sean had had to make his rounds to talk business with them.

But he *hadn't* talked business. All he had done was briefly pass the time of day and exchange a little banter. There had been no deals transacted, no exchange, however brief, of information. I had thought he . . . didn't he say . . . but perhaps he had only wanted to give me some distraction from the burden of the past few days by taking me to see those interesting country occupations.

Still, I couldn't help feeling that the real motive for the circuit had been to show me off. More than wanting me to see his friends, he had been concerned to have his friends see me. But why would he have wanted them to look me over? All those sentimental touches of romanticism, were they customary, or had they thought, maybe, that Sean and I? . . .

I cast a swift look at him lying so relaxed in his fern and heather bed that he had apparently dozed off. His long, strong brown arms in his short-sleeve shirt, the marvelously modeled hands, the handsome profile and lean line of the jaw . . . he was like some young blood-stirring god. What if he? . . .

And if he did, what did I think about it? As the Rorys said, he was quite some catch. Even by American standards he must be quite successful, not to mention his charm, his confidence, his stillness, his reticence, his poise, his strength. He had especially the particular fascination of an unknown entity and a sort of bridled power.

I pulled idly at the tight curl of a shooting fern. It was a bit arrogant of me, wasn't it, to be jumping to conclusions that Sean had wanted to show me round as someone special. He had never made the slightest pass except to pay me verbal compliments. It was possible, of course, that this was all part of the courting mores of the area—a hands-off, pedestal-type respect. If so, it was, ironically, extraordinarily seductive, a quality that had all but disappeared from the mating game back home.

As if he had become aware that I was staring at him, his eyes opened suddenly and wide. When his glance met mine, he smiled and said: "What are you thinking?"

I said: "About all those fellows I just met."

"What about them?"

"I picked up a pattern. They didn't have a wife between them. The only women we saw were a generation older."

"That's right," he said, shifting his long, lithe body into a more comfortable position. "Didn't you know, Ireland is a maiden's paradise. It's full of bachelors."

"Some of them seemed to be well over thirty."

"That's right," he said again. "In Ireland we don't rush into marriage."

"Really," I said, amused at what he must consider rushing. "Why not?"

He shrugged. "I suppose we tend to place responsibility to parents first. Filial duty comes before frivolity."

I digested this. "I wouldn't have thought marriage was considered a frivolous affair, certainly not in a Catholic country." When he didn't respond, I went on: "I mean isn't holy matrimony a sacrament? I thought it was the Church's duty to encourage marriage and procreation."

"It's not as easy as all that. Economic considerations enter into it. Many chaps can't afford it."

"I don't get it," I said. "We *are* living in the twentieth century—as I have to keep reminding you."

"This isn't an industrial urban society like you're used to. The average farm is usually only large enough to support one family—and that not too well. The eldest son has to wait to take over from his father. The way women are, you can't put another in a tiny house. And his mother is the average Irishman's first love."

"The parents could move out and let the son take over."

He laughed. "We care about our old people. The family spans the generations here. We don't put the old ones out to rot in nursing homes."

"All right," I said. "So the son could get an outside job."

"How? Outside jobs are hard to come by. Even if he migrated to the city, he'd have to work a long time to save enough to start a home. But, in any case, the son is *needed* on the farm."

I found this very poignant, this crunch of poverty, and told him so.

"Save your pity," he said crisply. "It's better this way than all those broken marriages we hear you have across the ocean. Hordes of fatherless kids growing up in Jimeen's meatgrinder."

But then his tone changed, and he playfully threw a sprig of heather in my lap. "Besides," he said, "you shouldn't pride yourselves too much, you ladies, that we have a hard time living without you. We bachelors have a good time in our way. There's a lot to be said for the close camaraderie of a group of single fellows."

Which may or may not have been meant to put me in my place.

29

I saw some of that bachelor good time that evening. We called in at a village pub, a noisy, jovial place, resounding with good-natured banter. The liveliest action was coming from the public bar. But that was an all-male domain, and I was shepherded into a room on the far side of the bar they called a snug. Crammed full of chairs and tables, it had a composite effect of shiny toffee-apple brown. The fireplace grate contained festoons of curling ivy, with a jelly-jar of wild flowers on each hob. Across a counter of polished wood, the fat, white-bibbed landlord beamed expansively.

In one corner, a group of hunting-and-sporting types spoke in confident, firm, upper-crustish voices that marked them as rather high in the pecking order for that neck of the woods. A couple of them called out to Sean, and one of them, a young man, detached himself to join us. Sean introduced him as Jack Morton, whose name I recognized from Mr. Meaney's mention of the Morton demesne, one of the large estates in the vicinity.

Most of the other guests were quaffing "jars" of a thick, dark brew—Ireland's famous Guinness stout. And for the next five minutes, while I sampled it, Sean and Jack sounded like a couple of Hamm's beer salesmen in Guinness clothing touting its unique formula of malt and barley and pure crystal water from the springs of County Kildare. The thick sweet-bitter tangy stuff was very easy on the palate and got more so as the rings of froth descended down the "jar."

It was also very easy on the senses, as light and soft and bubbly as the crowning head that foamed so high over the glass when the stately publican pumped it from the barrel that he had to scrape the top to level it. As the evening progressed the snug grew snugger, almost bursting at the seams with laughing, wisecracking people, mellowed by the brown elixir or peat-aged Irish whiskey.

Even in the snug, there were far more men than women, and I got gobs galore of male attention. Conn, the shearer, Jimeen and Tom stopped in from the public bar long enough to share a jar. It was quite an experience to be the focus of a group of half a dozen virile, vital men. It was the closest I had ever gotten to playing Virgin Queen with Courtiers, except that I didn't have red hair. But although they were all courteous, even deferent, never the least bit out of line, I felt more unsettled than flattered by their interest, and I was glad when the threesome retired to their male domain beyond the bar.

Sean was involved with a group of people at another table, working something out on paper, so I seized the opportunity to find out more about Jack Morton. He had stayed attentively beside me since we first sat down. His family's interest included flour mills, beet-sugar processing plants and fertilizers, so I gathered they were pretty well-to-do. As his accent indicated, he had been educated at a famous public—which meant a high-class private—school in England, and then at Oxford. And since he had come down from there he had been successfully engaged in breeding race horses on their nearby demesne.

What I found particularly refreshing about him was that

despite his obvious social advantages he was no snob. He self-mockingly acknowledged himself part of the Protestant Establishment that had oppressed Ireland for seven centuries, from the time Henry Plantagenet had divided Ireland between his Norman barons up to the long persecution of the penal laws.

I thought he sounded like the son of a rich white Protestant businessman back home, joining the American Indian Movement to turn back the clock at Wounded Knee and return the country to the Indians. When I told him so, he seemed pleased by the comparison. "Any decent Anglo-Irishman in his right mind can't help feeling guilty for the raw deal the British have given the Irish."

"However," I said, "if you carry that too far wouldn't you have to argue that the Republic should have dispossessed the Protestant landowners when they won their independence? Then where would you have been?"

"If I had been an Irish Catholic, I would have argued for expropriation of what the Protestant Ascendancy had robbed me of—land, wealth, industrial power. It rather makes one sick to see the way the old aristocracy still has their vast estates, their fox hunting, their stables, their huge bank balances. The common Irishman is still socially and economically beyond the Pale. For many, independence is a farce."

It was a bizarre position for somebody so privileged. "What makes you so pro-Catholic?"

"Oh, I'm not pro-Catholic. That silly squabble between Protestants and Catholics, that's just a stupid choice of evils, both Christian."

It was a hair-straightening remark. I struggled to make sense out of it. "You mean, what's happening up north, you don't see it as a religious problem at all, but rather an economic and political one?"

He shrugged. "Even that's too narrow a construction.

The problem goes much deeper. There'll be no peace, no
final settlement till we get back to first principles."

"First principles?"

"What Ireland needs, and needs desperately," he said,
toying with his glass, "is a return to Irishness in the oldest
sense. Both here and in the north."

"To Irishness," I said. "I'm not sure what you mean."

"I mean to a way of life practiced by the ancient Celt of
the heroic age. Pre-Christian Irishness."

It reminded me of what I had read of the Celtic
Renaissance in Yeats's *Autobiography*. But perhaps Jack
Morton was only advocating the narrow goals of Irish
nationalism. "Does that mean you'd like everybody to go
back to speaking Gaelic?"

"I'd like to see everyone return to the high values and
mystic view of life we lost when the first Englishman,
Patrick, landed on this island and subverted our native
values."

His argument was outrageous, but his zest was real. And
chilling. He went on: "This island won't be one again until
no one gives a hang whether or not there's a Pope in Rome,
or even whether Christ was born."

I have to admit I'm not too terribly religious—at least not
in any formal or orthodox sense of the word. But his words
jolted me with the force of blasphemy. I kept thinking of
Yeats's poem "The Second Coming":

Surely now some revelation is at hand;
Surely the Second Coming is at hand.
The Second Coming! Hardly are those words out
When a vast image out of *Spiritus Mundi*
Troubles my sight: somewhere in sands of the desert
A shape with lion body and the head of a man,
A gaze blank and pitiless as the sun,
Is moving its slow thighs, while all about it

Reel shadows of the indignant desert birds.
The darkness drops again; but now I know
That twenty centuries of stony sleep
Were vexed to nightmare by a rocking cradle,
And what rough beast, its hour come round at last,
Slouches towards Bethlehem to be born?

This beautifully groomed and dressed, this elegantly mannered, urbane and cultivated man sounded, paradoxically, as if he were the herald of some frightening New Millennium a mere quarter of a century away, a black-mounted crusader calling to arms those:

                    hoping to find once more,
Being by Calvary's turbulence unsatisfied,
The uncontrollable mystery on the bestial floor.

30

I was up early the next morning, feeling better able to face the world and with my emotions less volatile over Kris's death. With his usual considerateness, Sean had taken me home as soon as I had mentioned I was tired the night before. There had been none of the usual hassle before saying goodnight. When I thanked him for a splendid day, he said he couldn't think of any nicer one he'd ever spent, except the one he planned to spend with me tomorrow, if I'd honor him with my company for the boat ride we had planned the previous week. His old-fashioned gallantry was very comforting, and I said that I'd be privileged.

My suspicions about Kris's death, however, had not evaporated with the soothing of my spirits, and I was determined to find Red before my afternoon date with Sean. The ambulance had brought Mr. Meaney home the day before, and I had first to drop in briefly to see how he'd improved, when I delivered Mrs. Rory at the cottage.

As soon as I was free, I followed my intuition and drove as far as I could go along a road that I figured paralleled the Derry Brook. Predictably, it was soon negotiable only by one vehicle abreast. It was well-rutted, so I knew some sort of conveyances had been there before me. I put the car in first and jogged along at not much more than walking pace. The beech and hawthorn hedge scratched at the paint; buttercups and purple vetch were beheaded by my wheels.

On a hill so round I suspected it to be one of prehistory's man-made mounds, the path petered out completely, and I had to park and walk. Down below me in a little dell, I saw a flash of blue and red. A gaily colored cart stood with its shafts empty and resting on the ground. Its barrel top reminded me of the covered wagons like the one in which a pair of my great-great-grandparents, lured by the glint of gold, had rumbled west in the eighteen fifties across parching desert and freezing Sierras to the Promised Land.

As I approached, however, I saw that the wagon was different from the pioneer Conestoga. Instead of a covering of arched canvas, the top was of curved, molded, corrugated metal with a tin chimney stack protruding from the top. The flat front, and I presumed the back, was enclosed with wood containing a Dutch door. Through the open top, white curtains billowed. Scrollwork borders of stylized flowers trimmed the cart's red paint.

The bushes at the margin of the brook near which the caravan was parked were decked with washing spread to dry. An assortment of junk cluttered the ground, reminding me of how the tinkers got their name, from their traditional trade of mending metal.

Between the cart and the brook browsed a spavined, piebald horse, keeping judiciously aloof from a group of cattle churning fetlock-deep in the bullrushed mire at the water's edge. Two speckled, red-headed little boys sat playing quietly in a pool of mud between the shafts. A sandy terrier lay near them, lazing in the sun.

The dog pricked his ears and sat up at my descent toward the dingle. He woofed a couple of times, and the kids stopped playing and scrambled around in place to take a look. The wagging of his long wavy tail confirmed him as Red's canine friend. But he made no move toward me when I slapped my thigh and made elaborate kissing sounds. He had apparently been set to guard the children and was sticking to his post.

I didn't want to make a point of heading straight toward the caravan to ask for Red. His parents might be antisocial. They would undoubtedly regard it as highly irregular, if not suspicious, for anyone, much less a foreign girl, to be wanting anything to do with their young son. They might think I was trying to corrupt him. And the last thing I wanted was to get old Red in trouble.

I tried to give the impression that I was going for a casual walk along the stream, and pretended to be indifferent to the wagon's occupants. The spavined horse cast a mean eye in my direction, whinnying softly as I approached the water's edge. The cows nonchalantly raised their heads.

From the deep, still pools which alternated with more active stretches of the lovely stream, I could tell there would be excellent fishing. To prove my hunch a spotted trout leapt up to bag an insect. Creatures with legs like lunar landing gear, and strange iridescent dragonflies with beautiful veined opalescent wings darted and hovered among clouds of gnats above the silver surface.

I strolled along the bank upstream past the caravan. To alert Red to my presence while at the same time appearing footloose and fancy free, I hummed a rock tune, which sounded absurdly alien in that rural setting. I'd do better, perhaps, to whistle the bird call my Sioux Indian friend Zed Ironcloud had taught me. Bird and animal calls were used as signals by most people who lived close to nature.

A second or two following my whistle, there came a whistle of response, the piercing note of two curved fingers in the mouth.

In a shady nook of willow, birch and hazel, I found Red

fishing. His pole was a peeled sapling with a string tied to the end of it. And at the end of that was a bent pin he was loading with a squiggling worm. Three beautifully stippled pewter trout lay on the grass beside him. Red's face was still and steady, locked into an intense preoccupation with immediacy.

His eyes lightened in recognition when he saw me. His brows, which normally frowned protectively against the sun, momentarily uncreased.

"Hi, Red," I said. "Thanks for the present you sent up with Michael Cunningham. Did you make it? It was beautiful."

He shyly ducked his head.

"I haven't seen you since you put those flowers on my camper. It was a nice thought. Thanks a lot."

He hung his head still lower over the job of baiting his already baited line. I didn't have the heart to add to his embarrassment by asking what the present meant or why he'd plied me with the flowers.

I said instead: "Are your parents home?" I jerked my head toward the caravan.

He shook his head.

"You're baby-sitting your kid brothers, are you?"

He looked up at me sideways, his eyes glinting with amusement.

I sat down beside him with the shiny bodies of the trout between us, and watched him jerk the sapling up, back and forward in a skillful, continuous movement. The baited pin dropped into the dark reaches where the waters broke in feathery ripples like silver arrowheads. I waited, silent, not wanting to alarm the fish.

In a few moments, a trout basking in the shallows took the bait, and in a twinkle Red had yanked it high above the water and over to the bank. The trout flipped and flopped as Red hauled it in. While he unhooked the pin I turned my head away. He laid the fish, still struggling, in the basket of the grass.

When he began to bait his line again, I took courage in both hands. "I expect you wonder why I'm here. I came to look for you. I have another problem I hope you'll help me solve."

He looked up, squinting, his red brows knotted. Curiosity must have gotten the better of him. He said: "What?"

"You remember how I wanted to go by the tower? Well, I went there through the Demons' Cave before my friend got killed."

His alarm was instant. His fingers worked too fast for me to fathom what kind of sign he made over himself.

To reassure him, I said hurriedly: "That wasn't where she fell. It was pretty easy going through the cave. It's just a subterranean passage."

Amazement with a seasoning of terror passed across his face. What he feared were obviously not natural hazards.

I said: "But when we reached the tower the door was locked."

His face turned impassive, shutting me off as though he had drawn the blinds upon himself. Perhaps superstitious fear had made him tune me out. Perhaps he sensed my mission and wished to close me down before I uttered such an insult.

But it was now or never. Whispering in order not to scare the fish, I said: "I have to bust a padlock. I was hoping you could tell me how."

He sat stolidly watching where he had cast his bait. The seconds ticked away.

I whispered: "The tower *is* mine, you know. At least my grandfather's. We paid for it."

The line jerked. Once again he yanked the pole high into the air and back across his shoulder, so fast the trout could not have known what hit him. In a second the poor creature was thrashing, palpitating, on the bank.

While he took care of the business of hauling in the line and unhooking the fish, I said: "It's not just that I'm curious anymore, you know. I think something's going on in there. I've got to find out what."

He began to pack up, meticulously winding the line into a hank. Then he strung the trout on a twig stake through their heads.

I said: "I have a funny feeling it might even be connected with Kris's death."

But nothing drew a reaction out of him. He stowed his wound-up line and his tin of bait in the pocket of his sloppy jacket and stashed his fishing rod in the middle of some bushes.

I said despairingly: "You're mad at me for suggesting you'd know how to pick a lock. But you're the only one I know that I can trust."

Shooting me a puzzled look as he picked up the fish, he beckoned with his head for me to follow him.

Hope surged. "Does that mean that you'll help me?"

He shrugged, bracing the stake of fish across his shoulder.

I pleaded: "Just lend me something to do it with, and show me how. I don't want you to do the dirty work."

I trotted with him to the caravan. The dog came up waving his muddy tail like a plume, nosing tentatively around me until I patted him. The hands and overalls of the beaming, apple-faced urchins were thick with mud—it was even in their brushy, ginger hair. Their grins were so appealing, I wished I had the time to join them patting mud into a muffin pan and turning out the sticky mounds they made believe were "tarts."

Red disappeared into the caravan and emerged carrying a wooden crate, a makeshift toolbox. As he rummaged I said breathlessly: "What are you looking for?"

"A jemmy."

"A jemmy? What's that?"

He pivoted his closed fist at the wrist, making levering motions. When I didn't get it, he said: "Crowbar."

"Ah. Yes." But I couldn't figure what use a crowbar'd be to pick a lock. "What good will that do?"

"Prize the staple."

That was gibberish to me. I frowned, shaking my bewildered head.

He gave a burdened sigh. "Staple," he said, making a horseshoe with his thumb and forefinger against his arm. "Prize," he said, repeating the prying motion.

"Red, you're a genius."

Another short hunt and he produced an iron bar with a forked chisel at the end. For extra measure, he loaned me a pincers and a screwdriver. Then he hammered a staple in a piece of wood and demonstrated how to take it out. I wasn't at all certain I could manage on my own.

I said: "You wouldn't like to come with me this evening?"

He shrank back, his eyes wary.

"There's nothing to it," I said more blithely than I felt. His reactions sapped my confidence. "Well, if you change your mind, I'll see you at the cave around nine or so. Thanks for the help."

I had already turned on the ignition when he came racing up the hill with something trailing in his hand. It was a long tendril from a vine bearing a death-white, bell-shaped flower like a convolvulus. It rather turned me off.

When he shoved it through the window, I said: "What's this for?"

"To bind around the jemmy when you go into the hollow hill."

"Good grief. Whatever for?"

"Iron and bindweed keep the *sídhe* away," he said.

In my rearview mirror I saw him looking after me until a tall hedge came between us. Only then did I remember that I should have asked about the flowers he'd put around the camper.

Could those, too, have been intended to protect me from some harm? And if so, what?

31

As planned, that afternoon I went aboard Sean's boat at Ennis. It was a sleek cabin cruiser of very recent vintage. He had named it *Lugh* after Ireland's most ancient, most all-embracing pagan deity, and the name reflected his obvious pride and pleasure in the craft. He gave me an instant grand tour, imparting such technical details as the storage capacities of the water and gasoline tanks both in liters and imperial gallons, the location of the bilge pumps, and many more of the boat's specifications that I was supposed to be enthralled to hear.

The appointments of the cabin, which extended over the greater part of the boat's deck, were a different story, compelling my attention. The galley built-ins included a modern stove and refrigerator, fueled by bottle gas, stainless steel sinks with hot and cold water, and fine custom cabinetwork in polished teak. Forward and aft of the living area, cosy bunks were fitted to accommodate a half a dozen crew. A shower and head completed the conveniences.

Sean coached me, as though training a new recruit, as we got under way. He obviously enjoyed the process, perhaps deriving double pleasure out of putting every movement into words. Or perhaps casting me as a student gave him leave to put a coaching arm around me, which was not at all unpleasant.

From the nonchalant way he handled that forty foot of vibrant power, he was clearly an expert. Edging from the jetty, skillfully maneuvering port and starboard throttles, he headed for the buoy marking the channel to the sea. The spirited wind blew from the west, kicking up jaunty whitecaps. The curls of dense white foam looked like dollops of fluffy lather from an aerosol can.

The highly varnished, sharp-edged prow sliced neatly through the water, throwing a convex curve of carved and polished jade each side of the stem. My exhilaration was reflected in Sean's face when he returned my smile.

But soon the bow began flinging up festoons of spray, which hit the cockpit screen to momentarily obscure our view. If we ran parallel to the crests, they slapped our sides, rocking us alarmingly as we dropped into the troughs. In seas like that, Sean said, fitting action to his words, the trick was to steer at the correct angle to the waves.

"Where are we going?" I asked him as the shore receded, not at all easy about heading into open ocean with the sea so rough.

"Innis Ree," he said. "A small island off that western tip."

"I know Innis means island," I said. "What's Ree?"

"Some say King's Island. One of our early kings is supposed to have retired there and become a monk. Other people say it means Grey Island."

The sky, which had been so beautiful, turned moody, like a spoiled, capricious child, until it matched the changing sea. At first overcast, it deteriorated to a turbid woolly wetness halfway between rain and mist, completely blanking out the universe around us. It gave me the feeling of plunging into a barrel of dirty sheep shearings. If it made it cosy on the inside, it was scary on the outside, not knowing whether, beyond the murk, there was anything with which we might collide. Even at arm's length I felt the tenseness in Sean's muscles, but the confidence that he exuded convinced me that he knew what he was doing. If anything, he was enjoying the slight edge the weather put upon the expedition. It increased our intimacy and gave our junket a conspiratorial flavor. Reassured by his expertise and our warm camaraderie, I began to find the whole experience exotic and exciting, completely off the beaten track of all my prior experience.

Now navigating by compass, he told me we would shortly pick out land to starboard. He had set course to slightly overshoot the island, compensating against a total failure of visibility. When we sighted land we would come about.

In a few minutes more, the mist miraculously began to clear. A pale light broke through the gray. Ahead, a great gray rock loomed out of the gray sea, and I personally plumped for Grey Island as the meaning of Innis Ree.

With a slight correction of his course, Sean nosed toward a point about the middle of the shoreline that presented itself to us. The mass of rock may have had the effect of a local dissipation of the mist, for I could see pretty far inland, even making out the ragged outline of monastic ruins. The main sign of habitation was a column of smoke rising from the beach.

As Sean throttled back the engines and steered alongside the jetty built out along one arm of the natural harbor, a tall scraggy man came loping from the direction of the fire. He hailed us in a booming voice that masked the words. Sean responded warmly.

When we went ashore, Sean introduced him only by the name of Brendan. He was so thin as to seem almost a cadaver, his hands like a skeleton's, every joint visible through the blue-veined skin. His skull almost bald, his cheeks sunken, he put me in mind of a starved ascetic who might have inhabited the ruins beyond the beach in some bygone day when the buildings must have formed the nucleus of an active early Celtic church. His skin, however, was tanned and leathery.

Sean and I walked and chatted with him as he returned to his turf fire burning in a pit built of large pebbles in the sand. On the fire bubbled a vat of tar.

He waved at a small hide-covered native craft resting bottom up on flotsam timbers. "I was about to tar the pucan."

"Don't stop on our account," Sean said. "Let me mix the wax through while you get her ready."

While Sean stirred the wax into the boiling tar, Brendan briskly rubbed the pucan with a piece of burlap to remove loose dirt. Next the gaunt man took a dauber, a knob of rag tied to a short pole, and, dipping it in the smoking brew, mopped the shiny substance over the taut hide in long even strokes.

When the tar began to thicken, Sean flashed the fire and added more wax to the tar. In next to no time, Brendan had one side of the pucan glazed a glossy black from head to stern.

As they worked and talked of what the news was on the mainland, snow-white gulls and terns wheeled around us. And in the ledges of the dark cliff cormorants faced the rock like black-robed monks staring at the blank wall of their cells in silent meditation. At the base of the black drop, waves hissed and creamed.

Sean said: "Better go and see the others. Time's getting on."

We rounded a rocky promontory to another tiny beach where stood several small crofters' cottages. Someone had been patching one of the roofs. The dry, gray stalks of the old thatch contrasted with the sunny rushes of the new.

Thatching tools lay around on the thin grass, a bat like a lacrosse stick for beating the bundles into place, and an old-fashioned sheep shears which had obviously been used to trim the reeds, so that the overhang resembled the neat ends of a cornstalk whiskbroom.

We found the thatcher on the far side of the house engrossed in the last stages of the job. With sugán rope he was pegging down the thatch to stone projections at the eaves, anchoring the roof against the strong winds from the west, whose incipient force one felt even in the small blow of this summer day.

As soon as Sean had introduced him as plain Luke, I congratulated him on his handiwork. He laughed. "I keep dreaming that one day we'll be able to afford a slate roof."

I groaned elaborately. "Don't even think of it. This is the only roof that looks right in this setting."

Luke tested the ropes V-ed against the gable and climbed down. "That should hold us through a blow or two. And if it doesn't, it won't be the last time we've had to throw a fishing net over the top held down with boulders." He waved to the large whitewashed stones forming an enclo-sure around the pathetic "garden" coaxed from a thin film of soil which barely covered the stony land. Everywhere you looked the landscape was as spare as the men who won a living from the rocky island. Like the Aran islanders, they had carted the scarce dirt from elsewhere on the island, or shipped it in in sackfuls from the mainland in quantities sufficient to enable them to grow their own vegetables and potatoes and even their own grain.

I began to gather that their ideal was total self-subsist-ence. It was a matter of pride to wrest their every need from that inclement isle. The few necessities that still held them from their goal, such as oil for lamps and basic medications, were financed by kelp-making.

It was quite evident they weren't customers for Sean's

elaborate farm machinery. What then could his connection be with them? I'd bet their meager need for oil would hardly justify the journey from the mainland to deliver it. It must be something other than a business relationship. It was plain they held each other in esteem. But what a weird kind of friendship it must be between a sophisticated, well-heeled, urban businessman and a bunch of frugal islanders.

And why had we come today? Just for a social call? Once again I had the feeling that more than wanting me to meet them, he wanted them to meet and approve of me.

Our next stop was a smokehouse in the village. There Dan McGee sat on a slab floor among fishing gear and creels, opening and gutting a new catch of pollack, cod and wrasse. He told us they were to be smoked or salted down in a huge barrel for times when fierce storms would hold them land-bound weeks at a stretch. "We do our eye good on crab and lobster, dining as well as any hotel on the mainland," he said, smiling. "And we never want for mackerel. There are always schools of them to be netted out on the banks." In early summer their quarry was the basking shark, whose skins were used to cover their curraghs as in the olden days.

As I watched and listened, other matters than that immediately preoccupying me seemed to be gestating deep inside my brain. A half-formed question pushed against my skull, but wasn't ready yet to be expelled.

The question went away, leaving only a frail ghost of unsatisfaction when Sean headed us toward another section of the beach. There we found a wiry-looking fellow called Paudeen Colm raking dark, slithery ribbons and bulbous strands of tangled seaweed into piles. These cocks of laminaria, as he called them, were the valuable income-producing crop which bought them oil and medicines. Harvested from the ebbing tide and heaped in the shore garden, the kelp was hauled farther inland to the main stack for drying and bleaching. Some kinds of algae were used for iodine and phosphates; others to make the emulsifiers and thickeners called Irish moss or carrageen that I had seen so many times on canned milk labels without knowing what it was.

Like the others, Paudeen wore a knitted cap they called a "gansey," and a short coat, or "bawneen," of off-white flannel homespun. Black gum boots covered dark blue trousers to the knees. They seemed so like peas out of the same pod, these men, I had a hard time keeping them apart. I had to concentrate on lengths of noses, condition of teeth and blemishes like warts to individuate them in my mind.

Sean took off his coat to lend Paudeen a hand. I said: "I'd like to take a stroll around the ruins, if you don't mind."

"Okay," Sean said, pitching a slithery forkful onto a cock. "Don't wander off too far."

Obviously spanning many centuries, the ruins were impressive. A stone dry-wall, higher than my head and as thick as it was high, encompassed three clocháns, the beehive cells of corbelled stone where early monks once eked out their devout, austere lives. I walked into a ragged, roofless chancel carpeted with weeds, and the building grew around me stone by eerie stone until I had a sense of being present at its raising rather than its ruin.

I was startled almost to the point of scuttling by the movement of a shadow beside a strange upstanding slab of stone that looked less Christian than Druidical, incongruous in its setting. I gasped involuntarily as a figure stepped out of the shade. A thin, ethereal young man confronted me. He was dressed exactly like the others, but his features were distinctive, quite un-Irish.

Ridiculously, I said: "Hi!"

"Hi," he said back. "You're not supposed to be in here."

"In where?"

"This chapel."

"Why?"

"You're a woman."

I made my nasty little spitting-cat sound that I reserve for MCPs. "That's funny. Nobody told me to keep out."

"*I'm* telling you. Not even *you* are an exception."

I said disdainfully: "Why might I *almost* have been elevated to the male élite?"

"Because."

His accent, his manner, and his bludgeoning forthrightness marked him as an American. Not a hybrid this time, but a hundred-percenter, natural born. I said: "Where are you from stateside?"

"California."

That figured. "South or north?"

"Los Angeles."

"Whatdoyouknow?!"

His perfect teeth and strong tall frame suggested he had had the affluent advantages of at least a middle-class background. I said: "What do you figure you're doing on a bleak, impoverished rock like this?"

But when he came farther out of the shadows, I saw that his eyes were deep set and dark circled, his cheeks sunken. He looked almost tubercular. His large black pupils bored into mine, giving me the creeps. In case my sardonic humor had irritated him, I said: "No, seriously. How do you come to be here?"

"Would you like to see some of my work?" he said evasively.

"What work?"

He led me to the nearest of the clocháns. From the dark interior he produced a piece of stone on which my eye picked out the tracing of a fern. On another was engraved a snail; a vertebra on yet another.

I said: "You *made* those?"

He laughed derisively. "Of course not. They're found objects."

"Fossils?" I said, feeling ridiculous. Had he been trying to put me on?

"Isn't it incredible," he said with childlike delight. "They're all over the place. You can pick them up without even looking."

He ducked into the clochán and brought out a sand dollar.

"Do you know where I picked this up? Big Sur." He laughed self-deprecatingly. "In a tourist gift shop."

"What were you doing in Big Sur?"

"I joined this commune for a while once."

The strange, inchoate feelings that had exercised me earlier returned. There was something here that I couldn't put my finger on. Something that prickled the bumps behind my ears.

I said: "My name's Jan McDonagh. What's yours?"

"Julius Steinberg."

"No kidding. What's a nice Jew like you doing with a bunch of Catholic Bogtrotters?"

"I'm not a Jew," he said. "And we're not Catholics."

The impression I had gained that their clothing, although casual, looked like a uniform of sorts was reinforced by this suggestion of a collective identity. I said: "What are you then?"

He dived into the clochán, emerging with a shamrock immured in plexiglass. "Look at this."

"Did you do that?"

"Nh-nh. The Japanese. That's why I like it. It's so kitsch. Do you know why it's called a shamrock?"

"No, why?"

"Shamer, that's s-e-a-m-a-i-r, means 'clover' in Irish Gaelic," he said pedantically. "Og means 'little.' See?"

"Yes," I said, genuinely intrigued.

"I'm full of interesting useless bits of information. You know why it's the emblem of Ireland?"

I knew that. "St. Patrick used it to explain the Holy Trinity."

He sighed impatiently. "That's just a bit of light-fingered Christian expropriation of the sacred knowledge of much earlier cults. The shamrock was the Druid symbol for the triple goddess. The triumvirate of the Earth Mother."

I gave an automatic grunt of acquiescence, my mind hot on the trail of another thought to explain his weirdness. "Are you into mind-expanding drugs?" I said.

He flicked a piercing glance in my direction, then retreated once more into the dark precincts of the hut. The carved stone that he emerged with looked like a gargoyle with a spout for a mouth.

"Did you find it in the ruins here?" I asked.

"I made it in Ceramics at LBU."

"No kidding. It looks genuine."

He laughed sardonically. "Mescaline, speed, LSD. Wow. What a trip."

He had jumped backwards a few questions. I asked: "Did you crash out?"

"Did I crash out?! Wow."

"Are you clean now?"

"I got into this occult thing at Big Sur. I got more highs on it per square inch than on anything else I'd ever tried."

A substratum of my mind was involved in a lot of rearranging, making connections. I said: "I've just realized — there aren't any women on this island, are there?" I was doing as well as he at non sequiturs.

"That's what saved me," he said earnestly. "Getting turned on to hermetic Celticism. I met this fellow in jail in Mexico. He turned me off peyote and onto this."

Someone was calling me. Sean's voice.

Julius dove into the clochán and came out with a blown egg.

"For you," he said. "Handle with care. The beginning of the universe." He said something else that sounded like "sanctified at terse."

Sean's voice was nearer.

I said. "Why aren't there any women here?"

"They have their own island." He thumbed westward into the declining sun.

"I don't get it."

"The Bacchae, the Maenads, don't you know," he said. "Tearing Dionysus limb from limb."

"You mean there are actually women on another island?"

"They turn to birds at sunset like the Morrigan. I've seen them flying."

It was very scary. I could and couldn't follow him.

He rambled on: "The Western Isle. The Ladies of the Lake. Queens of Eternal Summer. Avalon. The Isle of No Return."

The calls were insistent now. We left the incredible cashel of stones to head toward the beach. "What *is* this place?" I said. "A kind of a male Lesbos?"

"Vows of silence," he said, putting up his index finger to bar his lips. "Come Midsummer all will be revealed."

32

We had a picnic supper on the beach prepared by a man called Emmett, who, cheflike, had fewer bony angles than the others, but was, for all that, still pretty lean. I don't know whether he had outdone himself for company, but he had prepared us quite a feast.

Than potatoes roasted in their jackets on a fire made of wrack and fragrant turf, there could, I decided, be nothing tastier. We had limpets and periwinkles and delicious giant shrimp called prawns and edible seaweed called *dulse* or *duilisg,* and little speckled eggs, and honey tasting of the clover blossom on dainty griddle cakes. Every bite was an epicurean adventure.

All the island men ate sparingly. I behaved like a real pig, but they appeared to take pleasure in my appetite, watching me enjoy myself with smiling, brotherly, indulgent eyes as though I were something special that they wanted to get fattened up.

I lingered over a good cup of herb tea tasting slightly of the peat, watching evening drawing in, the shadows lengthening, the incoming tide rolling up the sandy slope, savoring the values of this good and simple life, wondering if

I'd be too spoiled to settle for it if I were in Julius's shoes.

The man called Brendan said: "Not to be hurrying you, but sunset is not far off."

What did sunset matter? That far north, at that time of year, the long hiatus between the sun's disappearance and nightfall would be plenty long enough for us to reach the mainland in the light.

But I sensed restlessness among the group. Sean must have felt it too, for he said: "Ready, Princess?" and pulled me up and armed me down the beach toward the jetty with unceremonious speed.

"Why all the rush?" I said, as we climbed aboard, surprised at his unusual lack of courtesy. But he was too involved in getting us under way to pay me much attention.

As we slid from the mooring, I waved back at the group still assembled on the white shingle crescent, the dark ruins behind them, and beyond those, darker yet, the jagged rocks. It was quite a scene, with the sun's top edge disappearing like a red-hot coin into the slot of a brass sea. I was seized with a strange time-transcending awe.

Just then a bell rang out across the water from that sacred and mysterious island.

But, strangely, it broke rather than reinforced my mood. "Wow," I said. "Now I get it. We had to leave by sunset, didn't we?"

He said nothing, ostensibly intent on steering.

I said: "I mean they wanted us to leave." Then I had another thought: "Or was it only *me* they wanted to get rid of?"

He remained silent, still occupied intently at the wheel.

I said: "That's it, isn't it?"

He shrugged almost imperceptibly.

"Oh, come on," I persisted.

He said reluctantly: "It's an old superstition on the island. Like women on a fishing smack."

I turned that over for a while. "No, it's more than that. Take the bell. Maybe they hold some sort of services at sundown."

Checking something, he said abstractedly: "Could be."

I said abruptly: "They're some kind of Order, aren't they?"

"Some kind of order? What do you mean?"

"Look how they dress."

He eyed me sharply. "Like fishermen."

"But more or less the same, I mean. Like some kind of uniform. And the simple lives they lead—practically self-sustaining. Like a bunch of monks."

He laughed. "Monks they're not."

"Well, no. Not like the old Christian chaps. I didn't quite mean that."

"What then?"

"A sort of commune maybe."

"I don't understand," he said. "You don't mean a political community? A cell?"

"I was thinking of the groups back home. Some of them are based on early political and religious communities like New Harmony. Or the Quaker groups, or the Amish for example." Because he still looked puzzled I added: "It's the principle of getting back to nature in a cooperative, self-supporting group."

"They are *that* all right."

"Yes, but are they organized or casual?"

He shrugged.

"I mean do they share some faith or ideology, I wonder?"

He shrugged again.

I said: "Julius was talking about some religious mystical experiences."

Sean put a finger to his temple. "Poor Julius lacks a screw or two. He's been excessively experimental, tampering with his mind."

"That may be. But his ramblings made a kind of sense. I know his type. He's off on some kick he calls Celtic hermeticism, and, yes," I said excitedly, "he's being saved."

Sean confined comment to a few responding grunts. But my mind was off on its own track, sniffing at every fragment of the day's experience. "That word Julius said when he was giving me the egg," I mused aloud. "It was '*terce*.' Of course! Sanctified at terce, he said."

"Terce?" Sean echoed, puzzled.

"Tierce. The third hour after sunrise," I said triumphantly. "The bell must have been for vespers. Or is it complin? I don't know. The canonical hours, don't you see?"

He laughed. "Miss Sherlock Holmes!"

"I'd lay my last dollar on it."

He laughed again. "That sort of routine sounds like Julius. I don't know about the others."

"Just look at them," I said. "As unlike the families of fisher folk you'd expect to inhabit such islands as you could get. No women. No children. There's something artificial, transplanted, odd, about them. They're a cult group, aren't they?"

"Who knows?"

"Well, shouldn't *you?*" I said. "I mean they are your friends.

"Technically, only Dan. I've known him since I was a child. He's always lived that kind of a hard, island life. The others are my friends only through him."

"But you must have wondered about their lives, their relationship."

"I just figured them for misogynists." He paused, seeming to choose his words. "Perhaps a Platonic brotherhood." He looked at me to see if I connected. "It's not something you can pry into, even if they *do* happen to be friends of yours."

"I suppose not," I said. "But I'm curious. They fascinate me. I'd like to know more about them."

"You will," he said, throttling back the engines to bring us into dock.

33

I declined Sean's offer of a drink before he took me home on the grounds of pleasant tiredness after an absorbing day. The fact was I needed the remaining period of twilight for the tricky visit to the tower. Dusk would give me cover from the Herlihys while at the same time providing sufficient light to tackle the lock and make an evaluation of the premises.

At the front door Sean said: "I'll see you tomorrow night, then."

Not so fast, I thought. Two nights in a row and taking it for granted there would be a third. I didn't want to lead him on, particularly since I wasn't sure what his motives were in showing me around. If I saw too much of him he might get a distorted impression of where I stood and try to rush me into something prematurely. It had happened to me before like that and ruined everything. It was true I enjoyed his company enormously. I liked him; he was enigmatic and exciting. But commitments? That was something else again. Especially in view of the fact that he was from another culture, another country, which, for any permanent relationship might necessitate my giving up mine. I said: "Time is running out on me. There are only two weeks left until my charter flight returns, and I haven't done any research for my thesis yet."

Dismayed he said: "But you promised me."

"I promised you? What did I promise you? When?"

"Last week you said you'd celebrate the St. John's Eve festivities with me."

I had, of course. But I hadn't realized the festival was the following evening. This almost made things worse. What if he put the same construction on the event as Mrs. Rory did? Hers had been the classic prototype of Midsummer betrothals. You danced, she had told me, around the bonfire with your beloved, reciting the rosary. Then, dousing the dying embers with holy water, you sprinkled them on fields and gardens, asking St. John's blessing for a fruitful harvest and a fruitful life. The thin veil of Christian ritual could not obscure the underlying fertility rites of a more ancient pagan faith.

Still, I couldn't break a promise. "Sorry, Sean. I didn't realize St. John's Eve was tomorrow night. What time?"

"I'll pick you up at six. The show begins at sunset."

When I went into the house, Mr. Rory said: "You're very popular. Your other young man just dropped in to see you."

"You mean Michael Cunningham? Did you tell him where I was?"

"*I* told him," Mrs. Rory said.

"What did you say?"

"The truth. That a nice young man had taken you on a boat ride. It doesn't hurt to give them competition."

I laughed dryly. There was no point telling her what the situation was. "What did he want?"

Mr. Rory picked up a slim book lying on the table with

some folded foolscap pages sticking out of it. "He left these for you. They look mighty interesting. On the Druids and such matters."

I took the book. There was no note. But the paper and the flyleaf bore the name Cathleen O'Reardon.

At least I could put Michael Cunningham's visit to some use. I had been hard-pressed to think up a good story to allay the worry of my self-appointed surrogate parents when I left the house on my late-night expedition. I said: "Maybe if I hurry I can catch him." I was already on my way out of the door. "Don't wait up for me," I called back over my shoulder. "I may be pretty late."

I went at once to the lane, skirting the wood. When I reached the spot where I planned to park my camper in the bushes, a warm sight met my eyes. Red leaned against a stile, his dainty donkey cropping the grass beside him. I barely restrained myself from hugging him.

Red said: "You just missed Mr. Cunningham."

"Ah, well," I said. "Where did you see him?"

"Down there." He pointed to the connecting road. "I was picking flowers."

"Did he stop to talk?"

"Just to ask me if that road went to Lough Arrow."

"And does it?"

"Not to Castle Baldwin."

"How do you know that?"

"He said before that's where he's camped."

"I meant how do you know where the road goes?"

"We camp south of Lough Arrow in the spring. We come over that mountain."

I said: "Ah, yes."

He eyed me questioningly. Perhaps he sensed my coolness toward Michael Cunningham. As though to put in a good word for him he said: "He gave me white money," and pulled a silver tenpence from his pocket.

"That's nice."

In case he might have given the impression he had begged for it, he added hurriedly: "I didn't ask."

I went to pat the donkey. She raised her sweet, heartrending face to acknowledge me. Her eyes held all the world's sadness since Christ rode her from Bethphage to Jerusalem. In honor of that precious burden, it was said, the dark cross ran along the back and shoulders of her dove-gray coat.

I said: "Is it true they're stubborn?"

He said fiercely: "Only if you put an unfair load on them. They put up with a lot."

His words were a defense of all oppressed and misjudged creatures, including himself. And a rebuke of those like me who thought in stereotypes. Contrite, I pulled up a fistful of tender grass. The donkey trustfully received it, nuzzling my palm.

The hinge-bottomed panniers slung from a wooden straddle were empty now, save for a gunny sack in the side-creel nearest me. Red tossed the sack across his shoulder like a tramp.

I said breathlessly: "Are you coming with me?"

He shook his head. "Only to the Demon Hole."

Well, that at least was something. While he tied the donkey's halter to the stile, I got the tools and flashlight from the camper.

It was unlikely anyone had been along that stream since Kris and I the night before her death. The grass and wild flowers had sprung back high and flexible, unmaimed by stepping feet. And at the cave the delicate ferns gave no sign of ever having been disturbed. All the signs were A-Okay.

I said: "I wish you'd come the rest of the way."

He looked deeply pained at my appeal.

"It would be worth a lot to me if you'd like to earn some money."

He drew back, perhaps in protest at the inference he could be lured by promises of profit, or that his friendship could be bought. I said miserably: "I meant no offense."

In the dim, cool green of beech playing filterings of silver light across his freckles, I saw his face relax.

I had neglected to wind the bindweed around the jimmy. He did it while I stowed my various bits and pieces in one hip pocket of my denim tunic. The flashlight fitted in the other, my belt holding all in place.

"How's that?" I asked when I'd found a place for everything, keeping my hands free. "Am I ready?"

But he was busy doing something with his gunny sack, fumbling in the burlap folds like a diminutive Santa Claus fishing for a present for the next good boy in line. Out came a spray of wilted weeds. He threw it in the water. In a second the current carried it over the ledge into the hole.

"Whatever was that?"

"St. John's herbs, Devil chasers." His hand dove back into the sack. He pulled out a twist of newspaper containing what appeared to be beads, but which turned out to be shriveled berries.

I was flabbergasted. "What's all this in aid of?"

"To bring you luck." He threw the berries one by one into the hole.

Ironically, although I knew his motives were the finest, his actions put my hair on end. The mere implication that I needed the protection of his witchberries was, to say the least, disquieting. But for reasons I didn't care to analyze, I would do nothing to curtail his ceremonies now they had begun. I stood rigid while he hurled last year's crab apples for immortality, hazelnuts for wisdom, and beans, filled with immortal breath, into the Demon's Cave.

It was all more than I could handle. Who knew what centuries, even millennia, of occult lore lay behind these simple, natural rites? The whole thing was so unnerving, I didn't really want to know right then. The detached, good-humored, rational perspective of the student of mythology was fast failing me. That attitude seemed patronizing and insulting now. It had obviously blinded me to seeing through to the real heart of ancient ritual. I had treated the deepest, most arcane of mysteries with a trifler's arrogance.

There was more to come, a confetti of petals, foxglove, meadowsweet, harebell, broom and many others, all with their magical significance, were showered over me and on the water. Then came the power of the leaves: the prickly holly, the ivy, oak and willow. They floated briefly on the water before disappearing into the hole.

It wasn't over yet. The final phase was more solemnly compelling than all of the preceding.

I had read Celtic incantations, culled from ancient manuscripts, of the Welsh Taliesin and the Irish Amergin —incantations resonant of shamanistic transformations of identity. So I knew exactly what was going on when this shy little russet-headed tinker intoned his ancient wisdom over the hole and over me, stirring the pool with a willow twig:

> "I am all plants
> I am all trees;
> All honey
> And all bees.
> I am the grain
> The grape of the vine
> I am bread and barley,
> Manna and wine.
> I am the wind
> The wave in the bay
> I am the rock
> And the sun's ray.
> I am salmon

And eagle
I am horse
I am bugle
I was here on the First Day
I was there at the Fall
I stood at the Cross
And drank of the Gall.
I can save you from Evil
And keep you from Ill
I forgive what you won't
And bless what you will."

As he finished his incantation, he whipped the withy twig three times in my direction to baptize me with the splashes from the pool.

Then, without another word or look, he disappeared back into the woods.

34

In another place, at another time, I might have thought Red's ritual a lot of hocus-pocus. But right then I accorded it the full weight of the celebrant's sincerity. And whether it was his shamanistic powers or only my psychological impressionability which buoyed me through the subsequent hazards really made no difference. All that was important was that my quivering legs walked me through the diaclase as if it were the sidewalk on my block back home. Negotiation of the chimney was an absolute breeze, and the stream below had shrunk so much in the days that had elapsed since Kris and I were there that the water in the "syphon" came no higher than my thighs. Since I had taken off my jeans and slung my shoes by the laces around my neck, I emerged with clothes undampened into the large cavern—no small blessing in its igloo temperature.

I swung my flashlight beam around the fantastic "hall" with its dozens of apertures. But there was no one there to see me put my jeans and shoes back on. The light, however, reflected off a tiny object. I suppose I only saw it because in that arena of matte, light-absorbing surfaces, its miniature gleam was like a hundred-watt electric bulb. It was at the entrance to the passage in the fossil system that had incited Kris's speculations about leading to the sea. When I inspected it, it looked like a sample lipstick case. What was it? What was it doing here? Had Kris dropped it? Or someone else?

Well, this was no occasion to go prowling to find out where that passage led. I forged ahead along the final "corridor" to where light showed dimly through the screen of bushes. Once again, at the prospect of another close-up of the tower, my heart began to race.

With trembling fingers I parted the leafy screen.

The light that evening made the colors even more intense than on my previous visit. The hues the stones emitted were as subtle and diverse as those in Monet's color studies of Rouen cathedral. I forgot all my suspicions about Kris's death. Gone were my trepidations about the supernatural. All fear left me. I was entranced.

The whole place was flooded again with sound as well as color. Up in the elms and around the firs the teeming rooks churned and cawed.

But I couldn't afford to pause and savor the scene this evening. The last light was already beginning to die, and I had very little time left to see what I had come for.

Feeling for the jimmy, I darted for the entrance. The false boarding came away with scrapes and creaks, swinging out on hidden hinges to reveal the formidable door. Concerned to leave the least mark possible, I grabbed the padlock for a close look at the staple to figure how to pry it loose.

Miracle of miracles, although the hasp was closed over the staple and the U-bar of the padlock hooked into it, the shackle wasn't snapped into the padlock's case. Red's charms were obviously still working.

I swung the padlock open and unhooked it. There was a good deal more advantage to this lucky break than the work and energy it saved me. No sign of tampering would remain to alert whoever used the tower. I thanked St. Bridget or St. Brendan—whoever had been appointed to look after me.

I hooked the padlock back onto the staple after I had lifted off the hasp, then turned the ornamental iron ring that served as handle. The great door swung slowly open, creaking on its ancient hinges. Peering gingerly inside, I sniffed the air and listened. But there was nothing to suggest the tower was used as a byre for the bull. Only a centuries-old mustiness assailed my nostrils. Hardly breathing, I waited until I was convinced the tower was empty of anything alive. To keep my presence secret in case Herlihy should happen by, I pulled closed the fake boarding. I also pushed the door behind me, leaving it slightly on the jar, the latch tongue delicately poised, but not depressed, against the plate.

When I looked around, I found myself in a shadowed hallway. Flagstones undulated underfoot, worn uneven and satin-smooth by centuries of moving feet. Facing the entrance, a door led to a room beyond, to all appearances used now, and perhaps always, as some sort of storehouse. I looked carefully around for a worm and vats, or any equipment that might be used in distillation of illicit spirits. But I saw nothing but crates and drums and boxes lining the walls. Perhaps this was the reason Padraic Herlihy had resisted my intrusion. If we took possession, a valuable warehouse would be lost to him.

In the waning light filtering through tiny "loopholes" high up from the ground, I could just make out that the walls were whitewashed and in reasonable repair. A row of pegs held musty old garments—smocks, a shapeless natural woollen cardigan, a plastic raincoat. An old oil cookstove sat against one wall, clearly unused for many a year. A stone sink with a single old-fashioned brass faucet at least assured me of running water. Despite its dirty state I was glad to find a Victorian vintage toilet with an overhead tank and chain set into a recess behind a wooden door.

My heart leapt with joy to see the characteristic "winding stair," the pivotal symbol of Yeats's poems. Narrow stone steps shaped like pie slices hugged the walls, rising spirally around a stem of stone. The embrazured slits which lit the stairwell were boarded near the ground, but through a higher one I glimpsed the sea, patterned and glimmering from that distance like a coat of chain mail. The view was already worth the price my grandfather had given for the tower. At sight of it, all lingering reservations were dispelled.

Through a doorway on the second floor lay a chamber with a small open-hearth fireplace. A hole in the stone floor, which gave a clear view of the lobby, was obviously meant to be there. It was probably a murdering hole through which a spear could be thrust to kill an enemy who forced an entrance. On the same level were several closet-size rooms linked by passages running through the thickness of the walls.

With each additional flight of those turning steps, my spirits rose. On the next story, two oak-floored, oak-beamed chambers would make excellent sleeping quarters.

It was far enough above the ground for the windows to be larger. They were set back in shallow recesses with square-headed moulded hoods, the small lights topped by graceful ogee curves. A vaulted mural passage led to a place called—I'd discovered at Thoor Ballylee—a "garderobe," a dressingroom with an ancient privy whose musty shaft emptied undoubtedly into the brook below. I had read somewhere of an entrance to a secret chamber concealed by a latrine. It was an investigation to be undertaken in more leisurely conditions.

On the next floor was an even more marvelous room. In the last gleam from the western windows, I made out a massive fireplace built out of limestone slabs, its mantel carved and decorated with what my tracing fingers picked out as strange motifs of legendary animals and Celtic interlacings. It was the counterpart of Yeats's magnificent "Stranger's Room."

Two large windows with double lights, deeply embrazured, widely splayed, with stone seats at each side, gave a magnificent view of the sea on the one side and the mountains on the other, so that the outside was as compelling as the inside of the room. The sky over the foxfire darkness of the ocean was violet to indigo, splashed with the last faint flashes of flamingo. In the opposite direction, the hills looked fraught with melancholy, veiled with lavender, and aura'd with a ghostly halo of pale rose and saffron, a muted, ethereal, kaleidoscopic bloom conjured out of Turner's palette. The moment was almost an epiphany. I could not have had a better first impression. My one regret was that my grandfather hadn't been along to share it and feel vindicated.

I detected that the windows I was staring through had wooden shutters, folded now against the oblique slant of the splay. When I unfastened them, they closed, to my delight, flush against the stone mullions and window jambs. It had grown too dark to see much, yet I hadn't dared switch on my flashlight. Now, with the windows blocked, I could scrutinize the room more closely, especially since, surprisingly, the room held furnishings.

As my beam traveled around the awesome chamber, it revealed a floor of wide planks of centuries-scarred oak, stained and burnished until they looked almost like ebony. The beams were black, too, as were the trusses, startling against the gray stone walls. An oriental carpet, threadbare but still beautiful, covered the middle of the floor. Near the south window, twelve straight high-backed, heavily carved Jacobean chairs and a master chair of the dimension and design of a modest throne flanked a refectory table made of magnificent polished lengths and thicknesses of oak. On the middle of the table was a many-branched candelabra resembling a Menorah.

I stood there, speculating about these furnishings caught in my flashlight beam. Did they belong to the former owner? Had he sold them with the tower? Perhaps he meant to come and get them before we took possession. Or, as some people do, maybe they'd been left in place to offer them for sale when we moved in. I would take it up with Mr. Boland, the realtor. They belonged to the room like the moon and the stars to the night sky.

But as I continued to peer and marvel, I noticed that the two iron dogs in the fireplace showed traces of ash and carbon, and tiny chips of blackened wood. Although the hearth was tidy, I had the distinct impression that a log fire had burned there not too long ago. Despite the fact the room was dusty and had a musty, closed-up smell, it seemed cared for, perhaps even transiently lived in. Mr. Boland had been right the first time about the tower being habitable. Those who had thought the tower a ruin had been duped by the false barriers and their superstitious prejudices.

So the situation was resolved. My fears had been misplaced. Tur Bran contained no threats, no secrets. Kris's fall *had* been an accident. My suspicions vanished into thin air. And, mercifully, for a while, so did my guilt.

I was glad I had come this evening. I felt higher than the tower itself. It was worth ten times every penny my grandfather had paid for it. A little careful public relations job with the Herlihys, and some arrangements to have the bog drained, maybe by pumping as Mr. McGreevy had suggested, and we'd be home clear.

I was about to inspect a long wooden cupboard running along part of the wall opposite the fireplace, when I heard a sharp, resounding noise below. At first, alarm scrambled my senses. But after a few frozen seconds when no further sound traveled up the stairwell, I pressed the replay button. I heard in my mind's ear what I figured to be the slamming of a door. Carefully peeping through a window shutter, I saw the usual stiff evening breeze rustling the trees outside the windows. Maybe a gust had caught the front door, blowing it open and sucking it closed with a loud bang.

A few cautious minutes more, and I was satisfied enough to proceed with my examination of the cupboard. Tall and heavily constructed, its doors were of carved linen-fold paneling such as I had seen reproduced in courtrooms and wealthy churches back home. Its copious interior was stuffed with duffle bags that on closer inspection turned out to be rolled sleeping bags. That was strange. Perhaps the tower had been used before we bought it as some kind of hostel. A youth hostel? A Boy Scout camp maybe? But the minimal toilet facilities that I had seen would surely not support such a hypothesis. It would more likely have been "borrowed" by some kind of hippy squatters like those back home who made free with people's summer houses, empty mansions awaiting demolition, and the like.

Suddenly, apropos of nothing in particular, I did a bristling double take. If the front door had slammed shut, would I be able to open it again? What if—but there was no percentage in panic-generated speculations when all I had to do was take a quick trip down and reassure myself.

I sped down those tricky, steep, narrow, cramped, ridiculously shaped steps as if a fire alarm were sounding. And, clumsy, stupid me, on the last flight I went flying, twisting my hip, cracking my knee on the cruel flagstones. It was the same leg that had been injured the previous winter when I was thrown by faulty bindings on my skis. I tried to pull myself erect, but the leg buckled under me.

I swore like a longshoreman, furious with myself, remembering the two handicapped months following the skiing accident, realizing I had just blown the rest of my vacation.

Well, there was one consolation. I now knew that our tower was worth fighting for if any further obstacles should strew our way. I had seen all except the top; that turn around the allure inside the battlements would have to wait. I could do nothing now except hobble out of there and back through the cave as fast as my sprained leg would carry me. Scaling the chimney and negotiating the diaclase were nothing to look forward to. I'd just have to grit my teeth.

Better get going. I limped toward the door, hoping against hope.

My worst fears were confirmed. There was no handle on the inside. Nothing whatsoever by which to turn the lock. A mark or two where a handle had once been, and a hole that just possibly might take a key. But no key in it.

35

Dismayed and helpless, I stood there a few moments like a bump on a shillelagh. What would I do now? Well, the first thing to do was to use my intelligence. Whoever had lived there all those centuries would have had to have had a way to let themselves out as well as in. *Some*where there must be a key.

I searched floor, ledges, cracks around the jambs—anywhere a key might have been tucked away. No luck.

I limped to one of the crates, sat down on it, and rubbed my aching leg. What a chrome-plated idiot I was to have pulled a stunt like this—to have gotten myself imprisoned by a gust of wind. What an absolute fool not to have checked whether I could get out of there as easily as getting in. But who would ever have thought of a one-way lock? I had never heard of such a thing—except in a . . . jail.

The mere idea roughened the skin along my arms. Because when you thought about it, that wasn't at all an unlikely function for an ancient tower. I shivered involuntarily. Even to be a prisoner by accident in such a place was, to say the least, unsettling.

I struggled to take a closer look at the loop high up

toward the ceiling. It was opaqued by dust and webs and now only the dimmest blob of gray. If I only had a ladder, I could break the glass. Maybe I could pile the crates.

Encouraged by the thought, I tested several for weight. They were very heavy. Even if I managed to drag a couple into place, could I lift successive ones to build a high enough stack? Assuming that I could, and that the loopholes were large enough, and the broken glass not too jagged for me to crawl through, how would I get down the other side? Jump? On my bum leg? Even more undermining was the almost photographic imprint held in my mind's eye of a barred grid outside the glass. I couldn't be certain I had seen it, but it would explain why an opening close to the ground wasn't boarded up.

I sat back on my crate feeling absolutely stymied. What on earth should I do? Try shouting for help? But the tower walls were arm's-length thick. Perhaps some of the windows on the higher stories would open to enable me to call from there.

Dragging my hurt left leg behind me, letting my right do most of the work, I climbed the twisting stair again. None of the slits or windows in the second story could be opened. The same was true for the larger windows of the next two floors. It was a mystery to me how the place was ventilated until I realized the chimney and the drainage shafts gave direct access to the air. Holding my nose, I carefully inspected the shaft of the long-disused latrine to see if that might provide an exit. But there were no footholds in the wall.

My last hope was the parapet. I certainly could call from there, even signal with my flashlight beam.

I started up the topmost flight in good resolve.

But a few tedious steps up, I began feeling apprehensive. There seemed no sensory reason for it. It was no more than a bubble of uneasiness brewing in my marrow.

Yet after another painful step or so, I stopped. I stood stock still wondering if my senses had become subliminally alerted. After a few seconds I became aware of a strange whispering sound. A sort of rustling. Perhaps it was the wind.

I climbed a couple more steps then stopped again. If it *was* the wind, it was blowing in a way I had never heard before. The sounds were more like expirations . . . more animate. Dear God.

Once more I stopped dead, listening hard. How could I be sure that those phantom sounds were not inside my head? Perhaps it was no more than a surge of blood from straining too intently, or the shushing susurrus of fright.

So clammy was my hand, the flashlight nearly fell out of my grip. At last I found the courage to depress the switch and aim the beam. The yellow circle of light hit a stout oak door, the kind of door one sees in dreams, its blank, intimidating façade hinting at a threatening hinterland.

I knew at once it was a door I didn't want to pass through. Fear is a conjurer which turns interest to repulsion, curiosity to flight. At the first wave of its wand, I backed down the narrow, treacherous steps as rapidly as my injured leg could carry me without making any noise.

Back in the Stranger's Room I picked up a fire iron. While I weighed it in my hand my head weighed the wisdom of using it to break a window. But the same bud of terror that had driven me from the roof-top door restrained me now. There seemed suddenly an overriding need to keep my presence secret. From whom? From whatever might be on the floor above—if anything. I carefully returned the poker to its stand.

I sat down at the table and tried to talk some sense into myself. I was acting like a superstitious peasant, as though I'd never known a practical, commonsense culture like my own, much less received a modern, scientific education.

But even, said my rational, new-world mind, even if I were to break the window and yell to the four points of the compass, the tower was so remote, the road so little traveled, it was unlikely anyone would hear me, except, possibly Padraic Herlihy. And that would seem like stepping off the griddle onto the burning turf. Moreover, even if a passing villager *should* hear my cry for help, he'd probably run a three-minute mile in the opposite direction, believing it had emanated from the *Bean Fhionn,* the Fairy Goddess.

The mere thought of the White Lady set my teeth on edge. What had been a fascinating legend when I had first heard it, assumed in the spooky room in that ancient, isolated tower, the dimensions of a real and terrifying threat. Those weird rustlings above, could they have? . . . but no. I was being absurd again about what was merely the soughing of a west wind straight off the Atlantic blowing in and out the battlements. Even so, a primitive kind of common sense and prudence advised me to observe due caution, to act rather like a ghost myself.

I propped my throbbing leg on the heavy ornamental crosspiece which secured the trestles beneath the table, and considered my situation. My only alternative was to stay put for the night. Maybe I should settle for doing just that. In the morning I'd have a better chance of alerting somebody's attention. In the light of day the locals wouldn't be so likely to mistake my calls or signals for some supernatural emanation. I felt so dwindled, so averse to calling attention to my presence, the decision to sit tight was almost a relief.

The first thing to do was to open the shutters and conserve my flashlight battery. Consistent with my sense for caution, I moved furtively across the room. A dim, crepuscular light poured through the gracefully curved windows to silver and silhouette the contents of the room.

With any luck the wispy clouds would not grow dense enough tonight to obscure the half moon.

Well, if I was going to ride out the night, I had better make myself as comfortable as possible. As I limped over to the cupboard, the boards squeaked alarmingly, as did the hinges of the cupboard door. I pulled out one of the sleeping bags and unrolled it close to the north wall. Smelling damp and musty, it wasn't too inviting. But I was lucky it was there at all. It would pad my bones and keep me warm.

I tossed restlessly, unable to turn off my thoughts. But I must have finally succumbed to a twilight doze, for I found myself being jarred into a heart-hammering alertness, my senses as acute as the antenna of a moth. I lay straining for a repetition of the sharp noise that had roused me, but none came.

Ah, well. Maybe it was a beam contracting in the chill night air. But I couldn't trust the place enough to sleep. All I could do was lie like a mummy, watching the moonlight brightening and dimming through the room.

I was beginning to relax again when another sound came from below, staccato-sharp above the shushing of the wind. I sat bolt upright, sweat breaking out all over me, and scrambled to my feet. My hurt leg would have let me down if I hadn't had the wall's support.

As I stood there, trying to steady myself against the rough, cold stones, the sound came again. Convinced now there was someone down there, I longed to feel that help was near. But nothing would persuade me to reveal myself.

The next sound I heard was a series of light taps. Scared and puzzled, I listened, trying to make sense of them. When the taps grew louder, I identified them as footfalls on the echoing stone steps. In that alarming moment I was able to collect my wits sufficiently to roll up the sleeping bag and tuck it swiftly, silently, back into the corner of the wardrobe.

The rising footsteps stopped, and in the blessed respite it occurred to me that I might try slipping down the winding stair to peek and see who the intruder was. If it was Herlihy, he might be so engrossed in whatever he was doing, I'd be able to flit past unnoticed and gain the open door.

Sticking close to the wall, I crept quietly across the room, praying that the activity below was loud enough to mask my mouselike shuffling. The busy sounds continued when I reached the stairwell, giving me nerve enough to start descending.

But just then I heard a sound to make my blood run cold. A terrifying squawk. My mind flashed on the crow shape that the Morrigan assumed as harbinger of death. What if the presence in the room below were less—or more—than human? The stiffening went right out of my bones.

Then events took another turn. The footsteps resumed tap, tap, tapping up the stairs. Panic put the use back in my limbs, but there was nowhere I could hide. Unless, unless I climbed the flight toward the closed door to the parapet. If the presence turned into the Stranger's Room, it might leave me free to whisk past down the stairs.

In a twinkling I had mounted six steps of the final flight and turned the bend heading toward the intimidating door. To be swift and quiet cost me considerable pain in my hurt knee, but it was nothing to the anguish of suspense I suffered cowering below the frightening door. What if whoever it was came past the Stranger's Room, straight on up the stairs, what would I do then?

I dared not wait to find out. I wouldn't have time to act if it headed on up. I had no choice but accept the lesser terror.

I turned the knob. It yielded readily. Quickly passing through, I deftly closed the door behind me, and leaned against it struggling to catch my breath.

Sandwiched between two equally menacing unknowns, I went weak with dread. Who knew what the creature was behind the door, a being with the tread of a man and a bird's squawk for a voice. But on this level where I now stood even greater perils might lie in wait. Already the frightening rustlings once more assailed my ears—louder and more unnerving than when I had listened on the stairs.

My eyes raked the darkness. Although I was in open air, I was not up on a parapet. Against some ghostly clouds I made out the outlined indentations of a section of the battlements many feet above. Obviously, part of the original roof had fallen in, leaving what once had been a floor of the final story to take its place. Corroborating this hypothesis, a pale oblong of a loop or slit pierced the wall above, and a makeshift roofing of galvanized corrugated iron sheets grated underfoot. In effect I was trapped at the bottom of a well of walls, unable to look out and try to signal, even if I dared.

In the dimly lit area of open sky, I could see nothing to account for the odd fidgeting which counterpointed the wind's soughing in and out the castellated cutouts. But in an area of dense blackness where part of the original roof apparently remained, heaven alone knew what might be going on. Remembering Sean's mention of a roost of bats, I became more and more apprehensive that that, indeed, was what swarmed above my head. I grew sick with fear they would swoop and tangle in my hair. Or, worse yet, vampirize me with rabid fangs as I had seen them do to Mexican cattle on TV. Gasping involuntarily, I jammed my fist into my mouth.

But better to know the worst than suffer the terrors of imagination. I felt around for my flashlight, intending to risk a brief flash on the darker masses. The flashlight wasn't where it should have been, in the pocket of my jacket. With a jolt, I remembered I had left it on the floor where I had laid the bedroll. More painful than its lack was the fear it would reveal my presence in the tower.

As though by some contagion of my panic, the restlessness above my head increased. To the rustlings were added strange mutterings almost human in their sound. Prickling, I thought of an old belief that the souls of the dead migrate into winged creatures. It was an absolute orgy of dread that I experienced—a hundred ways to be afraid.

I knew I must get out of there as fast as possible before something popped inside my brain. But with the door closed I had no idea where the intruder was. How could I tell what he was doing? How would I know when the coast was clear?

With utmost caution I cracked the door, but there was nothing to be heard above the rustlings and the wind. Was the visitant still on the premises?

As I strained to catch some telltale movement down below, a brush of air whipped past my face like a breeze of wings. Instinctively I put my hands up to protect my head. Caught in the same sudden draught, the door bounced against its latch, making such a clatter that I knew if whoever had been below was still about, he'd be bound to come and check. That put me in a frantic spot, with no place to go. My only hope was to stand behind the door where I'd be hidden from a casual glance inside.

That six-step journey across the pinging metal was like a nightmare trail across a volcanic-fissured waste. Another gust pulled open the door several more inches as I shrugged in place against the hinge side of the jamb. I was not a minute too soon. Steps were rising. A pale shaft of light flickered through the gap. I shrank deep inside myself, holding deathly still. At least my breathing would be obliterated by the background sounds.

As the door was flung wide, it bounced against me, and

sprang back again to right angles with the frame. But whoever was on the other side appeared not to notice that the door hadn't hit the wall. His attention had apparently been drawn above.

Like a stick stirring the debris in a murky pool, the flashlight beam probed the upper darkness. As it touched the unknown shadows, incredible towering structures of sticks and mud came into being. In another sickening moment, I recognized their nature. They were nightmare nests built in the ruins of the parapet.

The dipping, waving light obviously intensified the disturbance that my presence and free-floating terror had aroused. It incited a cloud of erratic whirring wings and a hideous cacophony of belligerent "tchacks" and "kiaws."

It was then I saw that the creatures of the dark weren't bats. They were a rampant colony of black-feathered birds.

The dream of hostile and marauding wings that had plagued me since I hit the shores of Ireland had finally broken through into the realm of sensory reality. That recurrent nightmare had been no other, I suddenly realized, than a precognition of my first night in the Tower of the Crow.

36

At the moment when the birds began to dive and swerve, whoever held the flashlight on the threshold switched it off. In another second he pulled the door behind him and closed it tight with a resounding click.

It should have been a moment of relief. But I had survived one ordeal only to be thrust into another.

The birds now knew that I was there, an alien presence, an interloper on a privacy that had endured perhaps over many generations. From the towering, rickety structures that the light revealed, I knew these corvine birds to be the same as the vindictive daw that had attacked me at Yeats's tower. I had learned from Michael that the building of such nests in ruins distinguished the daws from their tree-favoring, ledge-nesting cousins and continual companions, the rooks, the ravens, the hooded and the carrion crows.

From Michael, too, I had learned of the daws' cunning and brazenness. They were almost as notorious as magpies in their pilfering. It was their habit to dive boldly on the backs of sheep to pick ticks out of the wool. They also sadistically pulled hairs from cows and horses with which to line their nests. Was it possible that these roused plunderers would dive and raid my scalp, and even, awful thought, pluck the shining gewgaws of my eyes out of my head?

The raucous noise did not diminish. If anything, it increased, resembling the wild rattling chorus that had followed us down the lane at Thoor Ballylee. What if daws really did have some sort of system of telepathy or telegraphy enabling them to flash signals from afar? Even, since they could fly so well, a courier service to relay intelligence? What if this group above me had somehow been infected by the furious hostility of the daw who had punished me with his wounding beak for holding a black "hostage" in my hand? Were they massing even now in the shadows overhead to gain some kind of retribution?

If they were, what could I do to protect myself? Stay very, very still, and hope the moon would not come out again. So when the masking clouds began to sprinkle, I didn't dare try to shelter under the roof's remnants, but stoically endured the drenching.

My wrenched leg, however, could not support my weight indefinitely. I furtively slipped down the wall to sit with back propped and swollen limb stuck out in front of me. The cold, ridged metal was a wretched sort of bed, but better than the agony of standing up.

Although the clamor was subsiding, if I as much as raised my head, the fidgetings intensified, threatening a new outbreak. At the slightest shift, great scissoring shadows plummeted past the lighter areas, followed by a whoosh of frightening air.

Like prisoners in solitary confinement who hang on to sanity by building houses in imagination, or who, by use of reason in solving problems, stave off its crumbling, so I struggled to remember a passage in Yeats's poem "The Tower" that had always managed to elude me. There flashed across my memory a stanza marked with a huge question mark about chattering, screaming daws dropping layer upon layer of twigs inside a loophole of the tower. Well, now I knew its meaning. An allusion conquered by direct, frightening experience.

The mental exercise had such a steadying effect, I turned the thing into a game, trying to recall all the passages I could in the *Collected Poems* that dealt with birds. When my memory ran out of references, I tackled other themes and symbols—the gyre, the tower, the stone, the moon. It helped take my mind off my throbbing leg, the damp chill seeping through my clothes, and the torture of my self-imposed rigidity.

The rhythms of recalled quotations must have acted as a soporific, for I kept lapsing into semiconsciousness. At last I was sucked under, like a spinning feather into a swirling vortex, while all around flapped dreadful screaming creatures with the hooked beaks of harpies and the talons of furies . . .

When I came to, I had my head wrapped in my arms. My temples burned, my eyes ached and I guessed I was running a slight fever. My mouth was parched; I needed a drink in the worst way. Remembering the sprinkles of the night, I explored the corrugated iron both sides of me with cautious fingertips. Moisture had collected in the dips, but I was afraid to taste it in case it was contaminated by the droppings of the birds.

Terror, dampness, cold, pain, lack of sleep, had taken a wicked toll of me. My leg ached excruciatingly. My whole body was in rotten shape. Adding to my wretchedness was the fact the daws had begun intermittently to tchack and flap again—like humans coughing and stretching when they wake. My alarm accelerated, not only for the threat they posed directly but for the possibility they might alert the one below, if he was still around.

Fearing that my own agitation disturbed the birds I tried to control my shivering. But it was impossible to keep still for long. Never before had I experienced such an ordeal. I began to despair the night would never end.

But just as I approached my lowest ebb, I became aware that the gap over my head and the long slits in the wall had grown less black than the solid stone. A few minutes more, and there occurred the faintest lightening of an area in the adjacent wall. It became increasingly clear that it must be another aperture—one I hadn't noticed earlier from the angle where I sat. Its shape suggested a small jagged hole at shoulder height. My heart jerked hopefully. Here was a place through which to watch and call for help when daylight came.

The next thing I noticed was that the wind had died back leaving a hiatus of expectancy. A surge ran through me like a mild electric tingle. Maybe the night was almost over. Maybe dawn was just over the horizon.

I felt a great urge to get up and look out of the jagged hole. When I tried to rise, my head swam, but I steadied myself against the icy stones and painfully made my way around the wall, praying I would not incite the birds, but too desperate for a view of the outside world to think of stopping. My eyes punched bright holes in the darkness, and flashing zigzags crossed my sight.

When I reached the hole, fearful of losing consciousness, I leaned my arm against the wall, clear of the crumbling edge, and rested my head against it.

The dizziness passed. I raised my head, opened my eyes and stared into the charcoal velvet of predawn. The air was still, as though the whole world held its breath.

A faint streak scarred the blackness like a single fine strand in the delicate network of a bloodshot eye. By degrees it grew to be a pin scratch. As I watched, I became aware of stirrings on the lake, faint whisperings of air and delicate whistlings. And from up above me in the battlements came the increasing commotion of awakening birds.

At last the pinprick became a gash between threatening clouds. A fan of faintest pearl spread up from the horizon, and I knew that it was dawn.

A few minutes more and the whole land was created before my eyes. Out of the blackness came forth gray; out of the gray loomed shapes of hills, then skyline-silhouetted trees, and finally the lake itself. As light bloomed behind swirling mists, so did the breeze. The surface of the lake looked like silver seersucker or the scales of bream. Whitefronted geese fussed in the stiff, cold reeds at the margin of the water. A lone mallard set sail out of the weeds, and a small flock, perhaps of widgeon, whistled across the choppy lake. The distant ocean sprouted cotton bolls. The nearby trees burst into sound and movement as the rooks woke up.

The sight imbued me with new courage. I even felt physically better.

I turned back to the inside of the tower where the daws had now begun cawing up a storm. The dawn had conjured up their nests, incredible architectural tours de force, stacked stick upon twig many feet high. Birds peered from the broken battlements, but they were frank and cheeky, not at all coercive, looking quite willing to countenance joint occupation of the premises. Though bodily debilitated, my spirits climbed.

Now, if only the invader of my tower had gone away . . . and if only he had left the outside door ajar . . .

I had no choice but to try to find out how the land lay. My leg needed attention. I needed aspirin to bring down my fever. I needed warmth and sleep, or heaven knew what I'd catch—another cold, if not pneumonia.

With infinite caution I inched open the door and closed it carefully behind me. My knee protested at the slightest movement, but I bit my lip and started down the steps, grateful for my rubber soles.

A quick glance in the Stranger's Room revealed that there was no one in it. But what I saw baffled and astonished me.

The room had been swept and dusted. By the soft dove-gray light of that early misty morning, it looked positively beautiful. In the great stone hearth, logs were laid across the iron dogs, their brass terminals newly polished like the shining candelabra on the table. The mantelpiece and the stone sills of the windows were trimmed with green boughs as at Christmas time, except, instead of fir or holly, the leaves looked, from the doorway, more like oak.

But the most startling part of the whole scene was the refectory table, laid now as for a banquet with exquisite cut crystal goblets, perhaps antique Waterford, and two superb decanters, one sparkling with white wine, the other red. Beside each place setting of delicate opaline Belleek china and chased Georgian silver lay a strange yellowed twig that I could not identify from the distance of the door. I didn't dare traverse the room until I was assured there was nobody below.

Moving silently on soundless sneakers, I continued down the steps. The third- and second-story chambers were the same as previously, save for several items that had not been there before. One room held a vase of sweet, almost cloying wildflower blossoms, frothy, lacy clusters of the meadow-sweet. Another held a sight so bizarre, I wondered if my eyes deceived me. A glossy black bird, a huge crow or raven, almost filled a crude wicker cage. From the frantic way it beat against the bars, it was clear it had been wrested recently from its natural habitat of the wilderness into this intolerable captivity. Its presence explained the squawking that had so terrified me in the night. The bird so obviously shared my plight, I wanted to release it instantly. But I didn't dare until I found out how I stood myself.

On the floor of another room, what appeared to be folded

sheets were stacked neatly on brown paper. A primitive flail, like one I'd seen in a display of items recovered from a bog, lay nearby. Attached to the handstave by leather thongs, the heavy beater used for thrashing was rough and knobbed.

The strangest item was a curved blade like a scythe or sickle of pale gold metal like the moon. I intuited in my marrow that it was ancient beyond comprehension. This, the wild profusion of blossoms, and the beating bird were all so incongruous to each other, they seemed like random symbols in a dream. They smacked of the macabre rites about which Sean had hinted after Father Flanagan's sermon. The whole business was extraordinarily eerie and unsettling.

No one was on the lowest story, either. There, everything was much the same as when I'd entered, except for a wrung-out mop propped near the sink and some fresh water splashes on the floor. I treated myself to a drink in my cupped hands.

To my dismay the front door was as unopenable as the last time I had tried it. Now that the light was better, I searched harder for a key, but again without success. I was still a prisoner in our own property.

It was imperative now that I break out of there, and fast. If I didn't get rest and medical attention, I was in danger of ruining the remainder of my vacation at the very least. Beyond that I wouldn't let myself speculate—it was too disheartening.

Well, there was nothing to be done but try to pile the crates, endure the pain of climbing them, and keep my fingers crossed that the loops weren't barred outside. If that didn't work, I'd have no option but to resort to calling from the hole below the battlements until someone heard. But the ghoulish paraphernalia warned me it was more perilous than ever to alert Padraic Herlihy to my presence there.

If only the crates were not so heavy. I tested those that were accessible with negative results. Maybe I could empty some. Once outside, I could come back and refill them, and nobody need be the wiser. Red's jimmy would make it easy to pry off the tops.

I levered away at a crate of pine for several seconds. The nails soon popped out of the soft wood, and the top came free. I saw that the box was full of the same miniature "lipstick cases" as the one I had noticed in the cave. Perhaps Padraic Herlihy did a little light manufacturing on the side to eke out his spare farming operation—except, where was the machinery to bear out that hypothesis?

I had stopped puzzling over the identity and nature of the contents, and was wondering how temporarily to dump them pending my use of the box as stepping stool, when an abrupt click smacked my ear. Someone outside?

My heart leaped to my throat, beating like the bird upstairs against its bars. I hoped desperately that it was Red. But in the same ambiguous moment, dread told me that it had to be Padraic Herlihy.

In a panic, I looked around for somewhere safe to hide. The crates weren't high enough and too close together for me to crouch behind. I sped as fast as my hurt leg would carry me, back up the crooked stairs.

Remembering the murdering hole, I limped across the floor of the first-story chamber and knelt to peer below.

Breath bated, I watched the door yield and swing wide. Framed in the arch against the morning light, a perfect target for my spear if I had had one and could use it, was the figure of a man. Not, thank God, of the stature of Padraic Herlihy. Someone tall, athletic.

Another moment, and, to my very great amazement and relief, Jack Morton's face came into focus.

37

I shuffled down the stairs as fast as I could bear, calling "Jack, Jack," as I went. As I came around the bottom spiral, he stood, clearly bewildered, frowning in the direction of the steps.

Then his face broke into smiles as broad as mine.

"Am I glad to see *you*," I said enthusiastically, hobbling toward him. "You saw my camper, did you, and figured I must be around here someplace?" He had a gun tucked under his left arm. He had undoubtedly come this way for a spot of duck shooting. Perhaps he had seen Red, who, quite possibly, had hung around all night waiting for me to emerge.

He turned his gaze to stare down at the crate I had just opened. I said shamefacedly: "I wasn't being nosy. I couldn't drag it to the window. It's too heavy. I thought if I took out some of the stuff, I could manage it." I finished lamely: "I intended to replace it afterwards."

He said: "Why did you want to drag it to the window?"

"The door slammed shut, locking me in. I was going to try getting out through that." I pointed to the loop.

He returned his gaze to me, peering at my leg. "What have you done there?"

Shaking my head disgustedly, I said: "Like an oaf, I fell and twisted it on those stupid stairs. It's a bum knee anyway. I hurt it in a skiing accident last winter."

With a gentle nudge he seated me on an unopened crate and leaned down to take a look. Quite expertly he felt knee, ankle and shin. "It'll be okay," he said, straightening. "Nothing's broken. Just a sprain. I'll take you now and get it bound."

"I think I may also have a temperature," I said, my hand up to my forehead.

Making sympathetic sounds, he offered his hand to raise me. "Don't worry. We'll have you as right as rain in no time."

Without more ado, he put his arms around me and picked me up. He smelled of soap and shaving lotion, of tweed and leather, and I felt very conscious of my own messy, damp, slept-in appearance. Cradling me as tenderly as a kitten, he carried me to what he called his shooting brake. The station wagon was parked along the track that took us past the Herlihys. The ferocious dog, his ruff bristling, practically choked himself on his rattling chain. But there was no smoke coming from the chimney, and neither Padraic nor his mother came in sight.

Once clear of the Herlihys' cottage and onto the main road, I leaned back against the seat and closed my eyes. Safe at last, and in kind, competent hands, I relaxed with a deep sigh. All tension left me, and I floated on a comfortable cloud.

The next thing I knew, we were pulling to a stop. All around me stretched magnificent parkland dotted with giant oaks and beeches. Groves of clipped yews stood like sentinels on the flanks of a splendid house. We were parking in the side drive in such a way that it was possible to see a half-view of the front. The muted lavender of its dressed limestone blended breathtakingly with the weathered rose brick of the sides. Its plain, flat façade displayed above the basement three stories of many long, narrow windows with heavy glazing bars and numerous panes. Altogether the house had the solid foursquare eighteenth-century look of the restorations in Williamsburg.

I said: "Where are we?"

"I brought you home," he said. "I thought you'd be more comfortable here."

Morton House. I should have guessed. This was a gentleman's demesne.

Supported by his strong arms, I limped through massive doors into a spacious hall floored with polished black-and-white tile and priceless Persian runners. Through open double doors each side, I glimpsed the delicate elegance of Hepplewhite mahogany, Adam fireplaces and decorated plaster ceilings. The house breathed the same *Zeitgeist* as Mount Vernon.

He helped me up the graceful curving staircase, with its banister of turned and polished wood, to a sumptuous bathroom on the second floor. There I luxuriated in a perfumed tub drawn by a shy Irish girl—practically a mute, she talked so little—who brought me a snowy robe and slippers. Escorting me to a spacious bedroom, she bound my leg with an elastic bandage from knee to sole, fed me a tall glass of hot Ovaltine with aspirin, and tucked me into bed.

I awoke to an exotic scene in pale pink bas-relief of Aphrodite chasing Adonis above my head. It took me several seconds to remember where I was. Dragging my eyes away from the Elysian ceiling, the masterpiece of some eighteenth-century Italian stuccador, no doubt, I sweepingly took in the shell-pink beauty of the room. The ormolu clock on the marble mantelpiece said four o'clock.

Ashamed at having slept the whole day away, I began leaping out of bed until I rediscovered my sprained leg. It felt, however, a good deal better. My fever had subsided too. I lay back, stretching luxuriously, my eyes caressing a writing desk and chest that looked like genuine Regency.

I carefully got up and went over to the long, narrow windows overlooking terrace, lawns and woods. A well-tended fish pond with a fountain and a neatly clipped box maze spoke of lavish care.

The little maid had carted off my clothes and I couldn't find a bell to summon her. If I didn't let the household know I was awake they might leave me undisturbed all night. I belted myself into the robe, worked my toes into the fluffy slippers, and peeped into the upstairs hall.

There was nobody about. The house felt empty of occupants. I went hesitantly downstairs and glanced into the drawing room and dining room, my eyes absorbing such exquisite details as the Wedgewood medallions set in the mantelpiece and a Gaelic harp.

I found Jack in the library, a sombre room lined with heavy mahogany and glass bookcases. When I entered he looked up from a huge leather-bound tome over which he had been poring. The pages looked like vellum, the script like mediaeval lettering.

He got up and came toward me, taking my hand. "Feeling better?"

"Much," I said. "Thanks to the rest and care. I feel guilty at having slept so long."

"You obviously needed it."

"Well, I'd better be going. The Rorys will be worried."

"Oh, don't worry about them," he said soothingly. "I phoned to let them know that you were here with us, that you were resting a sprained leg."

"That was thoughtful of you. But I should be going now, in any case."

"At least eat something. You must be famished."

I was, indeed. The last meal I had had was the picnic on the island almost twenty-four hours before. So he didn't need to twist my arm to lead me to a pleasant glass-domed room decorated with dozens of potted ferns and flowers. A white-painted wrought iron table with a glass top displayed an eye-appealing meal of salads and cold cuts.

As I ate and sipped a delicious concoction as close as I'd ever come to the cowslip wine of fairy tales, he drew the story of my night's captivity out of me. I relived the ghastly experience down to my discovery of the curious items. I said: "The more I think about them, the less sense they seem to make. Those things don't hang together." They struck me now as random images that had surged out of Yeats's *Spiritus Mundi* into my overwrought imagination. "I feel as if I dreamed them up."

Pleasantly refreshed when I had finished the fine meal, I said I wished I could stay longer, but I ought to go. "Would you ask the maid to bring my clothes, please?"

"What clothes?"

"The clothes I came in."

He looked embarrassed. "She's already gone for the day." He added apologetically: "When the family's not in residence, she's here only in the mornings."

"Are you alone, then, in the house?"

"Except for you."

"Your family doesn't live here?"

"They spend a good deal of the summer here. But they're presently at Ascot."

"Well, my clothes shouldn't be too hard to find, I wouldn't think."

He scratched his cheek. "I have no idea where she might have put them. She may have sent them to the laundry."

He could have gone and looked, of course. But not to make an issue, I said: "It doesn't matter. I can go as I am if you wouldn't mind driving me home now. I'll return the robe and slippers in the morning."

But first, he insisted, I must see the gallery of famous thoroughbred racehorses his family had owned. Then, when that was done, it was the manuscript he had been reading. I laughed at such persistent hospitality. I didn't want to be rude, but I was beginning to feel uneasy. I said: "I'm supposed to have a date with Sean this evening. I wouldn't want to stand him up."

"The Rorys will tell him where you are," he said.

"Well, just a few minutes more." I felt like a helpless grownup trapped by a persuasive child.

In the library, he poured us a liqueur, green, but paler than the emerald of crème de menthe. It had the taste and fragrance of a forest of new leaves. Sipping it, I sat beside him as he turned the great vellum folio.

What began as forced politeness soon turned to interest as I viewed the marvelous illuminations. They were every bit as impressive as those in the famous Book of Kells, which I hoped to see in the original at Trinity College before returning home. A highly ornate initial colored in green, blue, yellow, red and gold took up the best part of the page to which he'd turned. Designs of intricate laced ribbons, mosaics, spirals and intertwined circles drew me, like mandalas, into their mystic centers, until I seemed to rise into another plane of consciousness.

My exclamations of delight and wonder obviously pleased him. I said: "It looks incredibly authentic. But, of course, it's got to be a copy, isn't it?"

He said evenly: "As a matter of fact, no. It's the original."

I couldn't believe it. "I thought all the early Irish manuscripts would be in libraries like Trinity College or the British Museum."

"Most of them are. This is an exception."

I shook my head with incredulity, but not because I doubted him. The faded text was penned in extraordinarily neat, but not quite perfectly formed, Irish majuscule, that gave the piece the stamp of authenticity. "How old is it?"

"Probably the oldest Irish manuscript extant," he said. "Dating from the Dark Ages. But it's undoubtedly a copy of a much, much older text."

"How did you get hold of it?"

"It's been in our family's library for centuries. According to family records we had it long before the present house was built. There's a lot of family mystique bound up in it. More than just a simple case of pride of ownership."

"Where did it come from originally?"

"Nobody knows. It may have been copied in the *scriptoria* of the monastery of St. Columcille. Though I rather doubt that theory. One report has it that it was found in a secret room in Tur Bran back in the seventeenth century. But it's bound to be much older than the tower."

It was a greedy thought, but I couldn't help wishing that the manuscript had remained there through the centuries for me to find and own when I came upon the secret room—a room that I was now convinced existed. I said: "I understand there was a castle on that site before the present tower was built, a castle dating perhaps from mediaeval times. It could have come from that."

"I like that idea better. It makes more sense than thinking it was written in a monastery."

"Why do you say that?" Weren't monasteries the sole centers of learning in mediaeval times, when the lay world had been totally illiterate?

"Because it's not a Christian document," he said. "Its weird spelling suggests the original was in Old Irish—an older version, now lost, recorded before the Christians came." He qualified: "Of course the scribe who copied this edition of the manuscript was probably taught to write by

Christian monks. But all the time he was acquiring his skills, he must have secretly remained of the old persuasion, copying the manuscript sub rosa."

"What old persuasion?"

"The lore of the fili—the seers, the bards, the ollaves of the Druidic priestly caste."

Michael had told me that the Druids had no written literature. Rituals, charms, occult secrets about the heavens and its movements, and about the seasons, were committed to memory by privileged initiates. Transmission of the sacred corpus was supposed to have been confined exclusively to an oral tradition. If this manuscript was a record of that pre-Christian lore, it was enormously significant.

Lightheaded with excitement, I said: "Can you read it?"

Taking "read" to mean, apparently, "to utter," he began reading from the text directly, intoning in what I figured must be some early Irish vernacular. The sound was hypnotic and compelling, sonorous like a chant. Its incantatory spell washed over me, diminishing my sensory awareness, floating me into an unaccustomed state of consciousness a little this side of dreaming, and I was psychically transported back to the time when the words were new.

When he stopped I slipped only part way back into the present. I said: "You sound like quite a scholar. I'm impressed." I was indeed.

"I've studied old, middle and modern Irish. And other Celtic languages. To make up for the neglect I suffered at my parents' knees."

"So you understand the text?"

He nodded.

"What does it say?"

"It concerns the death and rebirth of the God-King Bran."

Bran. Bran. My nerve ends tingled. My senses wound and wound around the winding staircase in my head. My tongue thick in my mouth, I took a sip of the cooling green liqueur to say: "Tell me about this Bran. Who was he? What did he do?"

"Bran is the Crow God. Our Irish manifestation of the universal Oak King. In the Irish mythologies he takes other forms and names: Lugh, Finn, Ogma, the Dagda and his son Oengus. Cormac, Cuchulain, and Diarmaid are all attenuations of his ancient power."

The last were all familiar from Yeats's poetry. The others also seemed well known to me. As Jack Morton's learning went into my head, it was as if I'd always known the things that he was speaking of as intimately as I had known my parents' names. I had the experience that had led Robert Graves to write *The White Goddess*—according to his own account—the experience both of what he called proleptic thought, that prodigious mental leap in the dark toward a truth that could not have been reached by inductive reasoning, and of analeptic thought through which the poet recovers lost events. Just as in Graves's description of those special states, Time felt suspended, the Past and Future bore upon the Present as occurs in dreams.

Out of my new knowledge, or my new adeptness at putting together what I knew subliminally, I said: "Bran is Dionysus, isn't he?"

"And Cronus. And Hercules. Adonis and Osiris, the Spirit of the Waxing Year. King Arthur, too. Even Christ is a theophany of the Sacred, Suffering King."

To moisten my dry mouth, I took another sip of the fern-cool liquid. "What does the script say?"

"It tells of the ritual murder and supercession of the Crow-God-Oak-King Bran. For half the year, as the sun grows stronger and the days grow longer, he reigns over his twelve henchmen. Then, at the mystical moment when the sun reaches its most northerly station and turns around to begin its journey back down the sky, he yields life and limb to his successor, his tanist, his sacred twin."

It all rushed together in my head, including the version I had heard over a week ago when Sean had interpreted the thrust and burden of Father Flanagan's reproof. I wasn't quite sure if I was awake or sleeping—perhaps on the edge of consciousness when the body grows gargantuan and buoyant. Perhaps at that moment that precipitates a nightmare. Perhaps at the threshold of Yeats's *Hodos Chameliontos*, the dread Path of the Chameleon, a thicket, a turbulence of uncontrolled images in which the poet had sometimes lost himself.

Jack Morton said: "The rites are all spelled out in detail here. First the Oak King is made drunk. It even gives the recipe: ivy, vine and toadstool in a honey mead. Next he is blinded, castrated, flayed and bound with five-fold willow thongs to the Tau of a lopped oak. His crucifixion is accomplished by impalement on a mistletoe stake. The Blessed Twelve then tear him limb from limb, hacking him on the altar and roasting him in the sacred fire. Finally, they partake eucharistically of their slain king, eating his flesh, drinking his blood, and sprinkling it upon themselves."

Swallowing hard, I said: "I really have to go now."

He put a strong detaining hand upon my arm, his other hand following the text assiduously. "After it's all over, the genitals and remains are floated westward in a boat to the sacred isle. There the King's orgiastic priestesses inter him and await his resurrection, his soul having risen to the stars. Perhaps you've heard the story in another manuscript which tells about Bran's sojourn in the Otherworld."

My dizzy mind flashed upon Arthur floating to the Isle of Avalon, blurring with Julius Steinberg's voice talking of the Isle of Women. My throat felt like Death Valley, and I took another sip from the gleaming verdant prisms of cut crystal. "Now I've *really* got to go," I said.

But he went on turning the crackling brown-edged pages, pausing at an elaborate illuminated S ending in a pair of demon animals. Their compelling spiral eyes seemed to draw me in like magnets. Taking my hand he crooned conversationally: "This tells about the crowning of the Oak King's twin, or tanist, who reigns until the winter solstice when the Oak King is reborn. It is the tanist who must light the Oak Fire, who lets drip the last dregs of the Oak King's life with the stake of sacred mistletoe. For the tanist is reserved the Oak King's heart when they tear apart his body, and the first drink of his blood. How beautiful to make that sacrifice. To be taken into the body of another in perfect union."

The room seemed suddenly to palpitate. The lines of walls, windows and bookcases began to bulge as though my eyes possessed wide-angle lenses. In the next lightning instant the lines began collapsing in upon themselves. The room pulsed like a beating heart, inflating and deflating to the loud throbbing rhythm in my head.

His voice droned on: "This page tells about the secret source and reservoir of life itself. As Frazer speculated, the mistletoe is indeed the Golden Bough containing the vital substance. It remains green even in the dead of winter when the oak on which it grows is dead. It does not, as other plants, touch desecrating earth, being born of thunder and lightning, belonging only to the sky and air. It is the emanation of celestial fire, of sun itself. The seminal, phallic properties of the sticky substance of its berries bespeaks its generative force. Its cutting is symbolic both of castration and of the cutting down of life. It is thus the proper weapon for the coup de grâce. This graceful letter G"—he traced the gilt illumination of the huge initial—"represents the Golden Sickle with which the priests cut down the ritual mistletoe."

In my mind's eye, I saw the golden sickle in the tower, and memory flashed instantly on the yellowed twigs flanking the Belleek and crystal place settings on the banquet table in the oak-decked Stranger's Room. I said: "My leg is hurting. Please drive me home."

He behaved as if he hadn't heard me, turning another piece of vellum to another dazzling riot of design and color. "Here it tells of how the continuity of royalty between the murdered Oak King and his tanist is achieved. It is not only by the new king's eucharistic ingestion of the flesh and blood of the suffering king but by their respective and consecutive union with the Queen of the Woods, the Moon Lady, the White Goddess. The Crow God lies with her before his agony; the tanist assumes conjugal rights as the first act of his new reign."

I jerked my hand out of his grasp and got abruptly to my feet. But I swayed dangerously and had no choice but to stop and grip the table. Rising to take my arm to steady me, he said courteously: "What do you want?"

"I want to go home," I said. "That's what I want." I heard my voice like muffled thunder in my ears.

"Come," he said, "it's time to dress."

Relieved that I was going to get my clothes at last, I tried to follow him. But my legs felt filled with lead, the sprained one hopelessly incapable of carrying my weight. The lines of all surrounding objects wavered as though refracted through a shimmering liquid.

All at once, with the clarity of revelation, I realized what had happened. The nectar I had drunk at dinner, the liqueur that tasted of a forest of green leaves I had been sipping . . . "My God," I said, appalled. "It's the recipe you read out of the manuscript, isn't it? What was it? Ivy, vine and toadstool?" But the words were sticking to my tongue like uncooked dough. I could hear their gooy mishmash in my

ears as I tried to utter them. It was quite clear to my brain
that I was incapable of speech or action, so clear, in fact, that
I felt a rush of dread like jackdaw's wings.

In the strong crook of his arm he shepherded me into a
neighboring room, a sort of study, and set me down on a
leather sofa. From a hanger on a hook behind the door hung
a white diaphanous dress. A pile of delicate snowy nylon
underthings lay on a chair. These beautiful garments, so
innocent in themselves, took on a horrifying meaning. I
said: "I'm not about to play your horrible charade."

His brow wrinkling, he cocked his head inquiringly.

"I'm no Queen of the Woods," I said. But the words
weren't set enough to turn out of their moulds. I heard their
runny garble in my ears. My thoughts, however, were as
sharp and lucid as a diamond. If he was trying to cast me as
Queen of the Woods, what did that make him? The
reigning Oak King? The Crow-God Bran?

Panicked and frustrated, I began violently to shake my
head. "No. No. No. No. No," I cried. I must try to reach
the door. My head spinning, I managed to make it to my
feet and lunged.

Grabbing me, he held me in a vise-like grip. I beat
frantically against him. But very calmly in his cultivated
accent, his well-bred tone of voice, he said: "Now, now.
Steady on. I wouldn't hurt you. Women aren't . . . don't
. . . I mean I'm not . . . I can't . . . You've no need
to fear anything from me. Do you hear me? I'll not touch
you. Our union will be one of minds alone . . ."

Muttering soothing nothings, he led me back toward the
couch. "Now get into your things, there's a good girl. Shall
I stay and help you, or can you manage on your own?"

I gave him a furious push, and he went out at once,
closing the door.

I sat on the sofa like a great spiral-eyed, owl-faced lump

of weathered stone of the ancient mother-goddess, going in and out of consciousness. In the fleeting moments when my mind was crystal clear, I realized my plight. Even if I could believe Jack Morton as the Oak King posed no immediate threat, there would be his tanist to contend with. With a horrifying click, the morsel of information Sean had imparted on our Sunday morning walk fell into place: that Padraic Herlihy stood next in succession to the Oak King's throne in the St. John's Eve ritual. As if to corroborate this information, my mind cast up a memory of the mistletoe pin in Herlihy's lapel the first time I had met him. I had no doubt of its significance, and what implications it must hold for me.

Disoriented by panic superimposed upon my intoxicated state, I went into a tailspin for the next few minutes. I had got to get out of there. I simply must. I was so frantic and irrational, I would have taken a dive through the closed window if my first few tottering steps hadn't landed me in a boneless heap on the thick tweed carpet. For a few moments I had the structural strength of wet sand. The tears sprang to my eyes and spilled over down my cheeks. It was a disembodied kind of grief as if the weeper was separate from the hurter. Nothing seemed to hang together.

Once more the mists dispersed and allowed me to think straighter. I pulled myself erect and leaned against the marble mantelpiece. Maybe if I could lull him into believing I would go along with what he had in mind, I could trick him into giving me an opening to get away. If I dressed up in this terrifying costume, for example, he would think that I intended to cooperate. In any event, fully dressed, even looking like a Vestal Virgin, I'd be in a better position to make a break than in robe and slippers.

My arms felt like those of a sand-stuffed doll. The way I lurched, it took me several long minutes to put on bra and briefs. I felt like an image—projected at drastically reduced speed on a screen—of some vaudeville clown doing an uncoordinated drunk routine.

Try as I would I couldn't manage to zip up the dress. But in the middle of my strange contortions, Jack Morton came back into the room and did it for me. Then he kneeled down and worked my feet into a pair of flat, thin-soled, stretchable kidskin slippers which moulded well enough to fit.

Shivering, I let him brush and comb my hair and bind it with a wreath of moonflowers, white morning glories. He encircled my neck with a lunula, a crescent of pure beaten gold, emblem of the Moon Goddess. I could believe the ornament to be exactly what he claimed it was: a genuine Bronze Age relic dug from a bog. On my left arm he clasped a gold bracelet shaped like a torque or gorget with zigzags, lozenges and spirals of intricate design, and on the other arm he placed a bracelet made from a coiled bronze strip ending with a triskele, emblem of the three-fold goddess.

More hair-raising by far than any of his previous actions, when he had finished my elaborate toilette, he bowed three times, calling me the Triple Crow Goddess, Badhbh, Nemhain and Macha—the Irish Furies, the dreaded Morrigan.

I endured it all with patience. Little by little my churning world began to sort and even itself out. Sensate perceptions became less distorted. He was occupied now at a silver salver on a carved buffet, pouring liquids from crystal bottles into a large silver chalice. Bowl, foot and handles were inset with bands of intricate gold filigree and studded with beads of red and blue glass, a chalice not unlike the one found in a potato field at Ardagh in the nineteenth century. He had brought the vellum folio and was apparently consulting it for the correct quantities and proportions of the libation he was brewing, perhaps for the relevant incantations to be uttered over it, for he murmured the whole while. So intent was he upon his work that he didn't see me work my way along the couch toward the door.

I already felt a great deal steadier. A more realistic sense of timing had returned to me. My motions felt less weighted, less retarded. Leaving the support of the sofa back, I forged toward the door. My legs held under me. I managed to stagger into the hall toward the outside door.

But the vertical lines began whipping in and out again, and the horizontals started buckling. There was the sound of running footsteps in my wake. The more the frenzy grew within my head, the more my movements slowed until I ground to a virtual standstill only inches from the door.

Then a miracle happened. As if I had said "open sesame," the double door gave in. There on the threshold, truly a friend in need, stood Sean Danaher.

38

The next thing I knew for certain, I was in Sean's Land Rover, babbling away nineteen to the dozen. I had to talk to work the fear out of my system. "Thank God you came," I said. "I was afraid the Rorys had forgotten to tell you where I was. The guy is mad. Stark staring crackers. He has this horrible obsession he's restoring Ireland to its ancient faith. He told me all about it in the pub the other night, but I didn't think too much about it then. But tonight," I rattled on, "he showed me what I figure is his Bible—this incredible manuscript as old as the ark, which is supposed to give the secrets of the Druids' rites. You know that hocus-pocus you described to me? The stuff that's supposed to take place up at the stone circle tonight, Midsummer's Eve? Well, he's probably the leader—at least he's current Crow God or the Oak King or whatever. I shudder to think what was in store for me if you hadn't shown up when you did. I mean, look at this weird dress I'm wearing! I'm supposed to have been his Queen of the Woods. No wonder Siobhan O'Brien plunged over the Leap last year. The whole thing's sick. He's ill. Hey, come to think of it, I bet it was he who wanted to buy back the tower for his rotten fun and games. He's emotionally unstable. It's really pretty gruesome, isn't it?"

But Sean appeared not to be following me. Maybe I was still talking so much nonsense. What was so clear in my head wasn't necessarily jelling into well-formed speech. Maybe I'd been blathering again.

I said: "If I don't make sense, it's because he's been feeding me these intoxicating drinks. He brewed them up from a formula in the manuscript. I'm pretty smashed, I guess. I don't feel very good. I'm so thirsty I could drink an ocean. I wish that there was something I could do to sober up. It'll upset the Rorys seeing me like this."

Something I said must have connected, for he pulled over to the side and started fishing in the glove compartment. He brought out a pill box and put a capsule in my palm. "This should fix you," he said, encouraging me to wash it down with a long drink from the canteen that he kept in back.

I screwed the top back on the canteen when I was through. Then, while he started off again, I replaced the pillbox in the glove compartment next to my flashlight and Kris's pocket compass.

The sight of the compass brought tears to my eyes. I remembered her wearing it the last time I had seen her. I took it out, holding it by the fob, glad it hadn't gone with all her other things back to her home in Holland. Had Sean kept it for me as a keepsake? How considerate of him. Mumbling my thanks, I slipped it in the pocket of my gauzy dress.

I lay back against the seat to try to stop the bumping in my head and sort things out. Something was bothering me. Something small and niggling, like a dormouse. It was gnawing at my newfound peace.

But my attention wouldn't focus. It began straying with

my eyes to the passing scenery. Unfamiliar hedgerows set me idly wondering if the road we traveled was not, as I'd expected, the road back to Dunderg.

Then, in that part of my brain where some sort of logic was still functioning, I registered—via what mechanism of perception I had no idea—that Sean was driving in second gear. That must mean that we were climbing. I looked outside. True. We were climbing steadily. I said: "Where are we going?" The words sounded jumbled in my ears.

But my mind was like a grasshopper, hopping in all directions. An absolutely disconnected thought flashed through my head. The inflamed, caked eyes of Tom, the milker—I knew them now. They were the styed eyes which had peeped out from between the floppy brim of the sou'wester hat. The milkman cyclist who had steered me across the bog and Tom were one.

The next thought went through my head like a red hot needle through a ball of wax. *My* flashlight? In Sean's glove compartment? *Was* it mine? In cumbersome slow motion, I pulled it out to look at it. Turning it over in my hands I forced my straying vision to focus on the letters: "Made in USA."

I looked at Sean. He was concentrating fiercely on what apparently was a hazardous route, a sand road crunching rowdily under the wheels, spitting up against the chassis, as we climbed into the hills. I said: "That's funny. Where did you get this?"

He didn't answer. Perhaps my words were still too viscous to be understood. But he didn't need to tell me. Even to my impaired, dulled brain, the answer was quite obvious. He could only have found it where I left it—in the tower—the previous evening.

Amazed, I said: "Don't tell me it was you last night? No kidding! Whatdoyouknow?! If I'd only known, I could have saved myself that lousy night out with the birds . . . And I wouldn't have been there to get into that crazy mess with Jack this morning."

He still said nothing, staring grimly at the road. My mind ticked over like a water meter when a faucet drips, click after long-winded click. Still fast enough, however, to make connections—for memory to fasten on the banquet table, the mistletoe, the golden sickle, all trappings of the cult which connected last night's preparations in the tower with the heathen liturgy in Jack Morton's manuscript.

And Kris's compass . . . Shouldn't it have smashed to smithereens when she crashed into the rocks? Didn't it mean that someone had unpinned it from her shirt before she fell? Someone who had coveted it and removed it from her senseless body before they pushed her from the cliff?

Had I . . . had I fled the bull only to stumble in the bog?

So sharp the realization of betrayal when it came, I felt like saying "And you, Brutus?" But in that instant my mind began to tumble over the edge of a deep brown hole. In another instant, the deep, dark waters of unconsciousness closed above my head.

39

Made doubly captive by my antagonists and my crippled leg, there wasn't much I could have done if I'd had all my faculties, so I suppose my loss of consciousness was more blessing than catastrophe. Indeed, it would have been a mercy if my blackout had been absolute, if I'd stayed completely out for the whole episode—though I was cushioned by the fact that when I did bob to the surface, I wasn't too aware. Those passages of semiconsciousness had the texture and the force of a bad dream. I saw everything with terrifying clarity, but I wanted to believe that it was really only happening inside my head.

When I came to the first time, I found myself slumped in a rough, rustic chair in the shelter of a rocky arch decked with boughs and garlands. In my lap, under my slack hands lay the bunch of sickly-sweet blossoms I had seen that morning in the tower. The air teemed with birdsong. The sky was flecked with crimson cloud, casting an opalescent sheen over grass and trees. There was nobody in sight, but straight ahead rose the Tau of the lopped oak and the circle of standing stones. I felt the rising waters again swamp my senses, and was content not to resist . . .

Now I was having a nightmare. I was washed up on an island, where, in a sacred grove under a pale moon, I saw twelve menhirs turn into Druidic priests. In their flowing white robes, they cut the sacred mistletoe with a golden sickle, catching it in a white sheet to save it from pollution of the sullied earth.

The nightmare thinned into a long tunnel of white mist. When the swirling vapors cleared, I saw before me an enormous wicker cage contrived of woven twigs of sally, behind whose bars flapped the huge black crow seen that morning in the tower. Drawn screeching from its cage, it was plucked alive to the rhythm of a beating flail, its eyes gouged out with a stake of mistletoe then used to crucify the dying bird on the T of the warped oak. This hideous charade, the immolation of the surrogate crow god, was enacted to the accompaniment of a shuddering chant in which the name of Bran recurred repeatedly as a refrain. The scene faded as revulsion drenched me like a tidal wave.

The next time I came awake it was to the leaping flames of a bonfire centered in the circle of dark stones. The evil stench of burning bone and feathers made me want to retch. At the round-stone altar beneath the lopped oak, the white-robed figures tore the murdered bird apart. In Dionysian frenzy they ate the flesh and drank the blood, splashing and smearing each other with the gory dregs. This time I *wanted* to pass out. I almost willed the drowning waters to rise over my head.

Later yet, I awoke into a dream of dancing, leaping forms circling the bonfire in rounds and figure eights. They moaned ecstatically, mumbling strange chants. I felt the inexorable pull of evil, a stretching of its tentacles to draw me in.

But behind me was no escape, only the cold, dark smell of death. I sensed that I was situated in the dolmen portal of an ancient tomb, a mound or barrow humping its gray stone and earth above me. The hole into the hidden hill, which I had read about in Mr. Rory's *Book of Ancient Monuments*, was no legend. This was it. Horror before me, horror behind me. My wits dissolved into a puddle of insensibility.

When I opened my eyes again, the blaze had died back to a steady fiery glow. The frenzied dance had ended. The mood had changed from one of cannibalistic orgy to high solemnity. The white-robed figures stood one for one against the megaliths. In the dancing light I could see some of the faces beneath their cowls, and fancied that I recognized the bachelor monks from Innis Ree. But the diabolic rapture of the men's expressions masked their identity. I could not be sure of anything. Not even if the scene I watched was no more than hallucination. I let myself be rocked back into the cradle of my stupor.

When clarity returned again, I opened my eyes on a naked man standing between the fire and the lopped oak, intoning in a strong resonant voice. The voice was frighteningly familiar in that unfamiliar context. It shocked me all the way back into my senses. But the chunky, naked celebrant was hooded and masked with the head of a carrion crow crowned with an oak-leaf wreath. I could only guess it was Padraic Herlihy.

Fascinated as by a snake, I listened to his recitation. He was apparently delivering an oath, composed of promises and pledges of action and abstention. Between each segment of the oath the white-robed twelvesome chanted an antiphony. This demonic litany was clearly the final phase of the long ceremony—the coronation of the tanist-twin.

His arms outstretched in imitation of the tree, he sang: "I shall not listen after sunset to the fluttering of a flock of birds."

"The king is dead. Long live the king," the henchmen of the Order of the Oak responded.

"I promise not to go uncovered in the open air."

"The king is dead. Long live the king."

"I solemnly pledge not to touch a corpse or go where there is death."

"The king is dead. Long live the king."

"I vow to perpetuate the continuous thread of kingship and divinity by assuming conjugal rights with the Divine Goddess, the Mother of Earth, the Moon-Queen of the Woods."

"The king is dead. Long live the king."

Despite the cool night air striking through the veil-thin fabric of my dress, I felt feverish. I was very close to danger now. They had timed it just right for me to emerge from my drugged daze for participation in the final rite of this depravity. Any minute now they would come to fetch me for the inevitable finale—the mock-marriage that would turn the sacrificial orgy into a fertility rite. I could be sure Padraic Herlihy would have no reservations about his rights in me. My hideous revulsion was deepened by the prospect of a public exhibition in which all the oakmen would participate.

The fear which until then had held me paralyzed, spurred me now to flight. Somehow I must get away while the Order was still occupied in the crowning segment of the ritual. But where could I go? If I left the shelter of the dolmen, I could only move out into the area floodlit by the fire and the pale silver of the moon. There was not much hope that I could slip away unnoticed, especially hindered by my twisted leg.

Well, whatever the consequences, I couldn't remain here and accept the horror of Herlihy's advances, followed by banishment to some isolated prison called the Isle of Women, or, worse yet, to a fate similar to Siobhan O'Brien's the year before. However forlorn the hope, I must leave that chair and make a run for it.

Just then, as though to lend me cover and support,

thunder clouds obscured the moon. Except for the small circle of light from the bonfire's dying glow, the area was cast into comforting darkness.

My heart took strength. I had a chance.

But when I tried to rise, I couldn't move an inch. Not that my legs were numb and leaden—though they might well be that. I was securely bound about the waist and thighs by silken cords to the heavy chair.

As helpless, as captive, as doomed as the wretched crow who had helplessly beaten frenzied wings against its wicker cage until its final agony, I touched the flash point of despair.

40

But I had not yet reached the apogee of fright. There was further yet to go. A movement in the cold dank dark behind me stirred the mouldy air and raised the hair along my nape. Dear God. Through the midnight crack between day and night, through the crevice of the solstice between the waxing and the waning year, the white ghosts were said to trickle. A sepulchral whisper and a spectral touch on my shoulder convinced me that the dead walked even then out of their ancient graves.

A shriek gathered in my nerve ends and rushed into my throat. But the greater terror of the naked tanist stretching his arms to make obeisance to the retreating moon choked it back to a squeaky moan.

Now the supernatural force was hovering about me, whispering my name. Then I heard another name.

"It's me, Red."

No words could tell the turnabout in my emotions. Gratitude was too pale a word for the feeling that suffused me as I recognized the boy through his mask of dirt and grime. He had come, like a celestial messenger, to aid me at the fifty-ninth minute of the eleventh hour.

The beneficient lightness of his touch as he cut my bonds filled me with fresh courage. As I rose, the silk ropes fell away and the flowers cascaded around my feet. Small arms encircled me as I tottered weakly. I steeled myself to walk, clutching his small hand and letting him lead me into the shadows. Limping on drugged, uncertain feet, my gait further distorted by my stiffened knee, I managed to follow him into the turgid gloom.

Through a death-cold passage in total darkness, we penetrated deeply into the funeral mound. The boy's eyes must have had their own light source; no hesitation marred his movement as he guided me through what seemed to my bruised wits to be a tortuous labyrinth. My trailing fingers felt walls of corbeled stones disappear into niches where the bristling dead must crouch. My inflamed imagination fancied it could hear the creak of bone, the chink of bronze.

So disordered were my senses, I had no idea how far, how long, we walked. I only knew that I must keep on putting one dogged foot before the other through interminable blackness, despite the rapid diminution of my strength.

At last Red stopped, pulling me abreast of him. "Here is a little tunnel. Get down on your hands and knees and follow me."

But my sprained knee would not bear my weight. I had to propel myself along on my right hip, dragging my left leg behind me. The rough rock floor of the narrow tunnel tore at my flimsy dress, then at my skin. Tension was increased by a continual shower of loose earth and pebbles.

Now Red whispered with great urgency: "We've got to hurry."

Though the cost in pain was high, I obeyed like an automaton, and was repaid at once by my narrowly escaping a fall of dirt into the space I'd just vacated. My dragging leg was momentarily buried, and I had to extract it warily to avoid dislodging another load of earth.

Forced to lie flat on our stomachs, we had to wriggle now like worms along a burrow. It did my confidence no good to realize that this constriction of the passage was caused by the caving of the roof.

The dread of being interred alive now rose to plague me. It would be better to yield life voluntarily at once than suffer such a fate. Veils of semiconsciousness descended. But like a brainless eel through bottom mud, I continued to squirm through soil and rubble.

It couldn't be long before I finally went under. My strength depleted to its final drops, I was slowing to a halt. My center had become a vacuum. I collapsed in upon myself.

The old recurring nightmare sucked me back into its snare. The black bird with Gorgon head and stinking body like the host of Zeus tried to snatch me by the arms and carry me off. I struck out, struggling to break free of its clutches.

A voice said: "For heaven's sake, girl, relax."

The pulling ceased. I was enfolded in a pair of arms, much too large and strong for a small child's. Strong enough, in fact, to pick me up and carry me through a roaring maelstrom.

My senses snapped awake. The arms could belong only to Padraic Herlihy. I twisted violently to free myself from their vise-like grip, trying to hit the ground and make a dash for it.

But the voice said irritably: "For goodness' sake, be still, Jan. You're safe, now. Look, it's me."

Instantly stilled, I turned my head and looked up through a turgid brew of pelting rain and darkness into the shadowy face of Michael Cunningham.

41

The gladness which rolled over me left little room for chagrin at my impossible appearance—the flimsy dress now hanging in filthy tatters around my grazed and dirty body, my face and hair undoubtedly a sight to beat a chimney sweep.

Asking explanation of the miracle, I gathered that Red had waited all night for my return, growing more and more disturbed. At dawn, fearing for my safety, he had ridden his donkey all the long way to Lough Arrow, where, thanks to Michael's having asked directions, Red knew him to be camped. When they had driven back that evening, Red had intuited my role in the Midsummer festival at the ring of stones—where their scouting then located me. Michael's detailed knowledge of the relationships of shapes of mounds to the internal structuring of megalithic tombs had enabled him to figure there must be another entrance besides the one where I was trapped. But when they discovered the second portal, the tunnel was so reduced in size by fall-in that only Red could negotiate it safely to bring me through. What it had cost the child to swallow back his superstitious dread I could only guess.

There was no time to learn more. While Michael wrapped me in his jacket, a tousled, dirt-encrusted Red said breathlessly: "They're already after us."

Michael muttered: "Is that them up the hill?"

"It is."

"Then we're cut off from the car, by the look of it."

"Aye. That we are. We better head for cover yonder."

With me in his arms, Michael set off at a jog over the rough terrain. But the mere sight of him had been enough to set new energy coursing through my veins. I told him: "Put me down. I can make it on my own."

"Hush," he said, continuing to carry me across the incredible obstacle course of furze, heather and bilberry. Red took the lead, picking out the surest path through an area treacherous with potholes. The storm, which had threatened moments before Red's rescue, was now blowing up in earnest. But it was worth a beating by rain and lashing wind to have them form a shield from our pursuers.

Feeling Michael flag under my weight, hearing his labored breathing, I begged him to release me just short of the wood. But the minute he set me down, I tripped over my useless feet and went flying headlong into a patch of scratchy bracken and needled gorse. An involuntary cry escaped me.

In a second, Michael and Red were at my side, raising me to my feet. But the noise had alerted our pursuers. Above us, on the hill, loud shouts rang out. Michael grabbed one arm, Red the other, and together they practically swung me into the sweet cover of the hazel bushes bordering the wood.

But the sounds of running men were all around the wood's perimeter. We resumed our flight, penetrating deeper among the trees, stumbling over vines, ploughing through wet vegetation to the stream.

"The cave," I said. "We could hide down there."

"What cave?"

"The Cave of the Demons." And I swiftly briefed him on the route of the expeditions to the tower.

"Where is it?"

"About a mile downstream."

"Can you make it?"

"I can try."

"Try" was too inadequate a word for the effort I put out, floundering in and out of the icy stream with Red or Michael as my crutch. I relapsed into a daze again, numb enough to tolerate the misery, aware enough to navigate, with fear my constant goad. We heard voices all around us, but we made it to the yawning hole without their picking up our trail.

Nothing would induce Red to penetrate the cave. He preferred to take his chances with the natural hazards of vindictive men than risk the perils of the supernatural. Having protected us with signs, and seen us safely off, he darted like a squirrel into the underbrush. I took comfort in the fact that since the oakmen had never seen him with me, he could hardly be their quarry. He was safer on his own.

The next steps of the ordeal, from the tricky walk along the diaclase to the chimney's ticklish descent, were made especially hazardous by my injured leg. The sudden downpour had swelled the subterranean stream into a torrent, almost turning the funnel-section into a dreaded syphon. There was just space enough between the level of the water and the roof for Michael to hold his "torch" aloft and keep it dry. With the aid of his strong stroke, I made it into the giant cavern with its honeycomb of anterooms.

But above the wash of water spreading from the sump into an underground lake already knee-deep, we heard the echoes of strenuous activity. Not a second too soon, Michael shoved me into a side cubicle, pressing me against the clammy wall.

Through a ragged peephole of dissolved limestone, we saw, in a circle of lamplight, two men splash from the outlet of the stream. They wheeled a barrow piled high with pine crates from the tower. The distance was too great, the light too dim, to recognize the men. But they both looked large and husky, like Sean's cousin and Jimeen. They took the fork that had attracted Kris.

"Where do we go from here?" Michael whispered to me in the dark.

"Certainly not to the tower," I said. "They're probably all congregating there right now."

"That branch the men took, where does it lead?"

"I don't know. Kris figured it might be an old bed of the stream, perhaps leading to the sea."

"Game to follow?"

"Do we dare?"

He flicked on the flashlight long enough to show me a scum mark on the wall at shoulder height. "I'm afraid we could get flooded out here. If we follow those chappies, the rumpus they're making should drown out any of our sounds."

We waded through the pool, trying to keep our splashing to a minimum, using the flashlight only in brief bursts. On the high ground near the entrance to the passage, a swift flick of the beam picked out the tiny canister. It was no time to ask Michael what he made of it. I bent and snatched it up.

We tried to keep the men in sight to profit by the beacon of their lamp. The rumbling of the barrow over planks bridging the potholes informed us of their progress when we couldn't see.

Soon the passage began sloping more perceptibly, and the light faded beyond a bend. Then the trundling noises stopped, to be replaced by a puzzling, eerie sound that echoed back along the vaulted roof. Feeling our way carefully, we crept toward the faint glow up ahead, and found ourselves at the entrance to another cavern. But this one had a sandy floor.

There in the faint light of the lantern at the far end of the cave a group of men stowed boxes into a couple of rowing boats. In a second, I realized the nature and source of the loud boom and shush. It was the crash of breakers merged with a gale-force wind now gusting through the cave. In all probability this was one of the black holes in the cove where Kris was killed.

My mind played jigsaws with a few stored scraps of information: Red steering me to the cove when I was looking for a boat. Sean warning me not to enter the dangerous holes. So Red's information had been correct. Sean's solicitude had been no more than a ruse to prevent me from discovering the boats—whose purpose was now amply clear.

It was easy now to guess how Kris had met her death. Inquisitively entering this very cave, perhaps, she might have surprised some members of the oak gang at their game, whatever that might prove to be. They had had to kill her to avoid exposure. Perhaps they had knocked her out here, then thrown her from the cliff to make it look like an accident. But before doing so, some stupid, greedy fellow had removed the pocket compass for himself. Perhaps realizing how incriminating such a piece of evidence would be, Sean had taken it away from him. It might be possible to identify the actual murderer from the prints on it . . . if I still had it in my pocket. I ran my hand over my hip. Despite all my gyrations and exertions, it was, thankfully, still there.

There was no chance to share my thoughts with Michael. The two men started to return across the cave with the unloaded handcart. The wheels encumbered by the sand, their pace, fortunately, was slow. Michael caught my hand

and yanked me back along the passage, our noises muffled by the ocean's roll.

Around the bend, Michael briefly pressed his flashlight button. He pushed me into the nearest crevice, cramming in after me. The space was barely large enough for two. Despite the danger, our sopping clothes, my exhaustion and my rocky head, apart from the pain of knowing he belonged to someone else, I found a kind of pleasure standing close against him, enfolded in his arms.

Jammed against the freezing rock, terrified my teeth would chatter, I waited, barely breathing, for the men to pass. An eon later, the trundlers drew even . . . and went on, oblivious to our presence in the rock.

When they were well past, Michael whispered: "Did you see who it was?"

I had been too petrified to look.

Michael said: "One of them was the man on the cliff when you discovered Kris's body. I *knew* he was running *from* the cliff when I drove up that day!"

"That jibes," I said. "He's the one who lent me the leaky curragh."

"What do you suppose they're loading on the boats down there?"

"Boxes from the tower." The canister I had picked up was still gripped in my fist. I transferred it to his hand.

"What is it?"

"I don't know. The box I opened was full of them."

Under cover of the jacket he switched on the flashlight. "It's some kind of cartridge or explosive device, perhaps. I'm not sure what exactly. It's not something standard."

"My God," I said. "I nearly tried to open one."

He said abstractedly: "It looks familiar." Then he gasped. "The mixer tube had a piece that looked like that. I wondered fleetingly what it was for."

"What mixer tube?"

"On the camper stove."

"My God," I said again. "My life really must be charmed. I only wish poor Kris—"

He said: Can you imagine all the places they could plant a lethal little thing like that? I wonder what their game is—if they're Protestant extremists or the IRA. It's so close to the border . . . The Provisionals are rumored to have training grounds down here. They can ship stuff round the coast and nobody's the wiser. Come to think of it, a shipment of foreign arms was seized not long ago. Aboard an Irish boat somewhere off this coast. Highly sophisticated experimental stuff. Maybe part of the shipment managed to get through."

Then the pieces fell together in my head. I whispered excitedly: "I bet it's all in aid of a Pan-Celtic movement that's supposed to restore Ireland to her ancient heritage—*pre*-Catholic, *pre*-Protestant. It's tied up with that cult stuff you just saved me from." And I swiftly filled him in on everything that had happened since I'd seen him last.

"We've got to get out of here," he said urgently, "to call the police before they get away."

I turned reflexively toward the passage.

"Steady on, old girl," he said. "Not that way. It's too risky."

He cast the flashlight beam along the crevice into which we'd crowded. It was not much more than a crack between solid planes of rock, but our thoughts meshed gears. We began to move along this snug, straight alley.

Shortly, however, the passage began to lose itself in a giant warren. We pressed anxiously forward for another hundred feet or so.

But at last Michael called a halt. "I don't like this one bit. We could get lost."

We already were. When we attempted to retrace our steps, though everything looked frighteningly the same, nothing looked familiar. One could very quickly become confused, disoriented—like white rats in an experimental maze. One could end up like the expert speleologists Kris had spoken of, trapped in interminable labyrinths, never to be found again.

My tolerance for fear was almost gone. My nerves had lost their elasticity. Utterly exhausted, all my rope played out, I began to cry.

Michael said: "Oh, darling. Please don't. I can't bear to see you so unhappy." He caught my arms and pulled me to him, clasping me close, cradling my head against his shoulder. "It's all going to be all right, truly it is. We'll get out of here, don't doubt it for a minute."

But my tears wouldn't stop. They poured into his already saturated shirt. Far from staunching them, his tenderness, his compassionate protectiveness, released my pent-up feelings.

He said soothingly: "It's been a long, hard ordeal, darling. But it's almost over now. We'll make it out of here when we've had a little rest. We've got to, haven't we? We've got all our lives before us, all our marvelous lives."

But ever since I'd met him he had said consoling things to cushion me against shock or disappointment, always treating me like a sensitive child who needed shielding from an all-too-harsh reality. "You're just saying that to shut me up," I said between sobs, freeing myself angrily. "It's a big con like there's a Santa Claus and I'm an infant."

He laughed. "I love you," he said. "You're such a scrapper and a skeptic. But that's a lie too. Don't believe a word I say. I'm just pulling your leg."

Utterly tangled in his involuted irony, incapable of unraveling it, I just stood there sniveling, aware of what I looked like in the dim light of the flashlight propped in a limestone niche, with no Kleenex, no handkerchief, just a damp tatter of the filthy dress with which to dab my eyes and nose. That I was a feisty skeptic he might very well believe, but the "I love you" could only be the amused patronage of a fond adult for a comic child.

The next minute he had drawn me back into his arms, and before I realized what was happening, he was kissing me, dirt, tears and all, and telling me he loved me, and saying how marvelously brave I was.

My sobs increased. That was the unkindest lie of all. I tore furiously away from him.

He said tersely: "I'm sorry. I was stupid enough again to think you might feel the same way about me as I feel about you."

"How can I?" I sobbed, "when you belong to someone else."

He stood there, looking slightly stunned. "Someone else?"

"I almost feel sorry for Cathy," I said bitterly.

He stared at me, ridges of puzzlement between his brows. I said hesitantly: "Isn't Cathy . . . ?"

"Cathy?" His eyes widened. "Cathy?! You mean you think, you thought she was my girl? Oh, Lord, you are a chump. What an incredibly silly goose you are."

I stuttered: "You mean she isn't?"

He laughed softly for several seconds. Then his mood turned sober. "Cathy was engaged to my best friend. He was flying to a dig in the Middle East a couple of years ago when the plane went down. I have a sort of familial responsibility to see that she's all right. We're like cousins. Nothing else."

42

What is there to say about that moment? Only that that hideous freezing subterranean tomb suffered an incredible transformation. It became the place where I wanted most in all the world to be.

I couldn't say anything. I wouldn't have been able to in any case. My lips had better things to do.

As a token of the magic that was to permeate our lives: though the flashlight beam was growing dim, I could still see Michael's face.

Suddenly he half-turned me in the direction he was facing: "Do you see what I see?"

A chink of light filtered to us through an intricacy of cavities resembling, on a giant scale, the lacy pores of sinter.

We zeroed in on it like moths to flame.

As we approached, we saw that a crystal stream had worn an opening in a cleft large enough for us to edge through, and we emerged to our amazement into a bell-shaped structure of corbeled stone. I recognized it instantly. It was the half-beehive, the oval clochán with an open front, built where the water from the Cave of the Demons issued purified and purged.

It was Tober Tullaghan. St. Patrick's Holy Well.

As we waded out from its spring waters, we saw that the rain had stopped and the wind had died down. The cruiser Lugh was standing off the headland. Now the sea was calmer, it was obviously waiting to receive the loaded rowboats. A group of men in fishermen's clothes like the cultists of Innis Ree were on the point of launching them.

Simultaneously, a troop of Gardai came swarming over the rocks into the yellow cove. It was no mystery how they got there. Beyond the shield of the crescent's horn, Red waited with his donkey.

At that moment, the sun rose over the enchanted hills of Ireland, and touched his head with gold.